WHERE THE VALLEY MEETS THE SKY

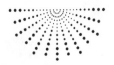

BEN MERRICK

HAPPY HOUND PUBLISHING

ISBN 978-1-7371226-1-6 (paperback)

ISBN 978-1-7371226-0-9 (e-book)

benmwrites.com

PRAISE FOR WHERE THE VALLEY MEETS THE SKY

"A rollercoaster of a story...this reminded me of Guy Gavriel Kay's *The Sarantine Mosaic*." -Anniina Moilanen

"I am so grateful for the experience of having felt the soles of my feet in another world. *Where the Valley Meets the Sky* is a wonderfully told story." -Eric DiCarlo

"...a fusion between literary and commercial fiction...[Merrick] managed to capture the elegance and sophistication of literary fiction." -Nicole Boccelli-Saltsman

To my family, who spoiled me with books.

To Heidi, Andrew, Andrew, Mick, Jesse, Angel, Clark, Hunter, Forrest, Briar, Kristin, Lee, Amelia...forever my favorite characters.

And to my incredible wife, with whom I share all adventures.

Thank you.

Lightning flash–
  What I thought were faces
  are plumes of pampas grass.

— MATSUO BASHŌ

1

LIKE THUNDER

"Our dive into the spring will bring
  the heat to make us move.
  The sleeping bugs begin to tug
  at restless soils, too!
  The hawk above, the salmon below,
  the bison and the wolf will show,
  that spring will bring a love for lands
  a clan must roam to know!"

— *CHILDREN'S SONG OF SPRING*

I signaled for my brother to take the shot. It was only after a few moments passed that I knew he was hesitating.

Turning to look at him more directly, it became obvious that he was taking all the time in the world to study the creature's movements, to watch the direction of the wind on the tops of the towering grasses, and to press the bowstring against his fingertips.

The oryx had wandered from its herd to graze alone, and

with its tall, curved horns it stuck out against the moving grasses. My brother and I crouched among the stalks downwind of the animal. I was too far away to say anything to him without spooking the oryx, so I simply waited. Being no stranger to the hunt, I could wait for hours in a single spot if it meant getting the right shot, but now I grew frustrated with my brother's inaction.

A good hunter knows to take the shot when it's right.

With a loud *"Hyaa!"* I stood and startled the oryx away. It leapt into the air, springing high above the cover of the grasses. The seed clusters at the tops of the grass stalks flew into the air as they were pushed aside by the fleeing animal. Avid, my little brother of only eleven years old, deflated as he walked over to me.

"Why would you do that? I almost had a good shot!" He threw his hands skyward. The grasses grazed his chin even when he stood up straight, pale amber streaks against his skin.

"You *had* a good shot. I wanted you to know the consequence of doubting yourself," I responded, watching the oryx disappear westward in the leaping momentum of its panic.

"But I had time!"

"You won't always. You need to react much, much more quickly. Part of that is knowing your intent. You came out here to kill an oryx, so as soon as you get the chance, you do it. You think too much," I finished, pushing him playfully backward. The deep cut in my arm, an injury I had foolishly earned that morning, stung when I pushed him, but I ignored the pain as best I could.

"I still could have had it..." he mumbled under his breath.

I let my eyes wander as I took in the crisp spring air.

"That's enough for today," I told him. "Let's go ahead and walk back home. We'll prove that old badger wrong someday." I smiled down at him.

"Why is he always so terrible to us?"

I shrugged. "Some people feel strong when they put others down."

"At least I *have* a chance. I don't think the old folk will ever give you one."

"No," I said, "probably not. But that doesn't mean I can't help you." Much of the clan, or at least the important older ones, had indeed decided my fate long ago. The superstitious don't trust children of immense luck like me.

Some luck, I thought, shivering at a memory kept at bay.

"You don't need to help me walk back," he piped up. "I can do that on my own."

"Avid, you're shorter than the grasses in some spots. You know mother would kill me if you didn't show up for a week."

"We've made the walk a thousand times, Rennik. I *know* how to get back. Can't you let me make my own mistakes?"

"Not when they can get you killed."

"I walk to the river all the time. I'm not a little child! I can make it back just fine."

True, he was familiar with the area. I swallowed my protective instinct.

"Alright," I conceded. "Go ahead. I'll stick around here for a while."

Avid shouldered his bow and turned north, pushing into the grasses like a swimmer through water, one hand clutching the arrows at his hip.

At least he's headed in the right direction.

He was right to want to strike off on his own. The path

from boy to man can be long, and Avid seemed at all times to walk it back and forth, teetering from one side to the other. That said, I'd been much younger when I was forced to live by my own abilities. My mentor, Gatsi, told me long ago that pressure is the best teacher.

I decided that I could keep an eye on him without making it obvious. Leaving my brother to his own path, I turned northwest toward my plateau.

The plateau was an abrupt pillar of earth that rose impossibly above the surrounding plains about two miles south of my village. Its walls were spotted with the occasional small tree sprouting solitarily from the rocky soil. These trees, along with dense collections of large shrubs, veiled the only trail leading up to the plateau's height. Pushing aside the foliage, I began the steep climb.

As I made the lengthy journey upward, the herd of oryx below was laid out plainly in my vision. They grazed slowly and bedded down about a half-mile away. I'd heard it said they were strange to this land, but they'd been here as long as I could remember. For some reason, with the entirety of the expansive Kalanosi plains to explore, that herd of oryx, as well as a sizable herd of bison, had kept somewhat near to our village long before we arrived here. It's said the oryx traveled a great distance just to rest in this spot.

I suppose their complacency isn't too strange, as we too were once a wandering people. I remember settling down at our current location about ten years ago, and though I was raised for the life of a nomad, we'd all been sedentary since then.

Perhaps it was the great river that flowed powerfully from the south, about a mile east of our village. Its fresh water and food were good reasons to stay, but then again, the herds could travel great distances without needing a large source of water. Perhaps there was no mystery to it. Maybe the grasses simply tasted better here.

If they don't kill you first, I thought, noting again the burning wound on my arm.

The rocky handholds made for an easy climb when climbing was necessary, but most of the trail was a simple slope. My fingers found their familiar positions in the stone of the final lip, and I pulled myself up and over.

Reaching the top of my plateau, I quelled my heavy breathing and slipped out of my hide shoes. This perfectly flat top was a quarter mile stretch of peaceful earth, and the animals endemic to the plateau's peak gamboled playfully as I settled in. My arms stretched outward and up, and on days like this, I felt as vast and ceaseless as the plains. I approached the cliffside, looked for Avid's snaking trail, and thought of the strange few days I'd had.

I hung my toes over the edge. Hundreds of feet below, rolling hills and pastures billowed out like a sea of amber grass and dirt. The sheer edge atop which I stood lay in high contrast against the soft slopes that rose and dove for miles around. Normally, the wind at this height makes the trip up difficult to accomplish, but today there was a warm and gentle breeze coming from the west.

It was this same soft wind that gave motion to the fires in my village. Tongues of flame would be licking tonight's dinner of lean prairie fowl, and if we were lucky, salmon from the river. This breeze would carry with it the laughter of my family as they cooked and conversed outside of our hut. It would carry the artful words of Gatsi's storytelling, as children leaned in close and their parents lingered nearby, secretly fearful of missing a single syllable. This wind would course through the tall grasses like the waves I saw once as a child, along the beaches to the east. It would provide the hunter with cover and the child with wanderlust. It would give the bird its journey and the bison its warning, as scent was carried on its wake.

Similarly, this wind would give *us* warning of coming danger. It would act as a harbinger of storms as the changing air rolled overhead. It would lift wisps of smoke that promised wildfire on the horizon. It would announce the coming of winter as biting cold crept through, and consequently portend the small, circular movements of the bison.

If we were vastly unlucky, the wind would bring with it the signs of our violent neighbors. The warning would sometimes come in the form of a massive cloud of dust, big enough to eclipse sunlight and thick enough to make its rays dance with panic if one were inside to see. It would come like thunder, and we would count the days after the dust swept through like the seconds after lightning struck in the distance. If no other signs came to be, we might be safe.

If evidence of a warring clan was found close to our village, it meant we would pack up and leave. If we didn't, we'd easily be caught up in the wake of another people's warpath. The threat would be too great to ignore, even if the other clans mostly warred among themselves. Everything we had learned to love would have to be packed tightly on sleds and carriages. Animal-skin homes would be folded up to a fraction of their size. Nothing makes a child feel smaller than their whole world being pulled behind them on a drag-sled made from two branches of oak and a piece of leather. This was a familiar act in my clan's history, though I'd only experienced such a migration once before when I was very young.

In our language, Kalanos means "people of the horse," and from what I'd learned, the warring clans had perfected their breed. Their quick and powerful hooves would beat into the earth and tear the tall grasses, like people, out from their place. With no roots by which to anchor itself, miles of dirt and dust would be taken by the wind and carried across the plains, obscuring everything in their path.

Like these clouds, the warring clans wouldn't care who stood in their way.

And as I stood atop my plateau, hanging my toes over the edge, I saw this tell-tale cloud of dust. Though some may view the dust as a natural child of the winds and wilds, an Achare must know this omen well. Seeing it here, I felt as if the warm, playful breeze had shifted suddenly into a bone-chilling cold. It came over the hills to the west. It was unnervingly silent. Somewhere in my mind, I knew something so big shouldn't be so quiet; a herd of bison shakes the earth when it arrives, and a surge in a river is foreshadowed by its roar, but here, staring at the amber grasses that had been my home for most of my life, I saw first-hand this noiseless threat sweeping across the plains toward my village.

I looked back to Avid's trail. The dust did not signal immediate danger, but logic is rarely the first occupant of a panicked mind.

Then the calculations came quickly. How long would it take me to get back home? How long before we knew if we were safe here?

Worry locked my feet in place. What else could I do but picture my family run down by a charging, heartless horde? The thin lattice structure of our huts burned like dry grass in my mind's eye.

Straight south. I would collect my mother and Avid, and that's where we'd go. We'd be faster on our own. Surely the clan wouldn't miss just the three of us...

And then there was the unwanted sort of ache tugging

dutifully at my chest. Leaving home, even one so unwelcoming as this, would not be an easy thing to do.

No, I thought. *Tonight we leave.*

I looked away. I picked up my bow, slung it over my shoulders, and started the trek back to my home, knowing full well it may never feel like one again.

2

BEFORE THE DUST

"Journey leads to wonder, and wonder to journey."

— GATSI

I had come to understand that everything moved in well-worn circles. Even before the dust came through, there was a restlessness in my village that echoed a long history of travel. We were old wanderers who'd found their promised land; whether I went out to hunt, went east to visit the river, or went to walk the grasses north, the gravity of our home always pulled me back in.

The few days leading up to the dust cloud were far from typical, and for many reasons — the first of which was a villager named Tella, whose hut had been nearly destroyed by the previous day's wind.

The weather on the plains of Kalanos was usually fair, although the winds were known to be unforgiving at times. It was, however, rarely an issue — especially if one knew how to live in it. This was Tella's problem. She seemed to lack knowledge in many things, and if not for the effort of those around her, I was convinced she wouldn't survive a single night in the grasses.

I can't say everyone in my village would help my family, but most of them kept an eye on Tella. We were known as the Achare clan, though we rarely had use for our name. I had scarcely spoken it in conversation, and usually just when traders from Rucost came to our village.

Avid and I had just come in from riding horses down the riverside that morning. The goal was to show him how to spot tracks from a mounted position. Though we had no horses of our own, it was part of the Kalanosi lifestyle to be on horseback often. Ikoda had been more than happy to let us borrow two of hers that day. As we passed Tella's hut, we saw that it had abandoned its normal round shape for a more crooked one, like an angry wind had punched the roof inward. I shook my head.

"They told her not to prop it so high," I reminded Avid, pointing to the windblown hut. "They told her the winds would take it if it rose above the crest of the ridge."

It was ordinary in terms of our village. The walls were canvas made from hide, and it was framed using timber found along the river or the sparse arboreal patches more immediate to us. It initially doesn't look like much. First, one must make a latticed, circular frame that spans the width of the hut-to-be — typically fifteen to twenty-five feet. Then, once the roof poles are put in place to shape the pointed ceiling, several layers of cloth covering are attached. This was a process that, once the pieces were secured, took about two hours to complete. It was designed to be quick to put up and even quicker to tear down, in case another clan necessitated our immediate migration. Some homes had, since we settled here, adopted a more permanent construction. My mother always insisted we kept ours the way it *should* be.

Tella was younger than she appeared. Worried eyes and light wrinkles veiled the fact that she was probably only twenty-six or so, about eight years older than me. She had long brown hair that she refused to cut until she tripped on it, and she dressed in eccentric jewelry of wood and bone.

The mistake Tella made was threefold. Firstly, she wanted her ceiling to be higher, claiming that lingering smoke can bring about demons. Secondly, she moved the hut closer to the hill that surrounded our village in a kind of ridge, which of course brought the construct up even more in elevation. And lastly, Tella was out of her mind. Even at that moment, she just stood staring at her crumpled home, babbling incoherently about wind spirits. When she spoke, she just repeated things she'd already heard, but sometimes she'd come up with strange, original ramblings. Luckily, we passed by without earning her attention. Even for her, this was a rough situation.

After weaving past a few huts, we came to our home. Our hut was not blown over. In fact, it was larger and in much better shape than that of our less-than-sane acquaintance. I threw off my shoes and stepped inside. Avid and my mother were already arguing.

"You're going to help put it back up," my mother was saying.

"But we told her not to change anything, and she had it moved anyway! She won't listen to advice!" Avid was young and had yet to learn when it is right to argue, and when it is right to do as you're told. He was still a child, but already he had a keen mind for building, so of course he'd be asked to help. I'm not sure many adults would bother to do so in this case.

My mother's intense eyes bored into him as she raised an eyebrow. "You and Rennik are going to help that poor woman. Either she gets to sleep in her own home tonight, or she stays with one of her neighbors." I smirked and looked for Avid's reaction.

He shrunk a little at the implication. "Fine," he replied, and he stormed out of the hut. Behind him my mother traced a circle over her heart and went back to her work.

Avid's corner of the hut, his coordinated domain, was an organized collection of childhood miscellanea accompanied by the markings of a soon-to-be man. There were two bowls, stacked together, each stained purple from berry-picking; these stood on the ground next to his bow, which lay parallel with his wooden chest. His moccasins were stepped side-by-side, stained green from his attempts at hunting for the family; next to them were a few flowers plucked from the earth simply because he liked the way they looked.

My mother had a raised bed, a selection of hide-working tools, and a cozy pile of blankets that had found much use this winter past. In the evenings, she would take her tools outside and work. One couldn't help but hear the soft *pluck* of each stab into the hide as she made shirts, pants, and shoes for whomever brought her materials. Her days of hunting were long past, as she had inherited her father's predilection for weakening bones.

My section of our home was not so much organized as it was sparsely piled. I tended to keep very little, and the things I did have were easy to keep track of in their modest heap.

I placed my bow and quiver against the wall next to my adze and reminded myself to make more arrows later. As I turned, I noticed that my mother had put out the mirror I had given her a year ago. A few skins and a bison horn were all the traders had wanted for it the last time they came through. It was only about a foot wide, but as I looked I caught a glimpse of my face. I was reminded of how much I looked like my brother: tawny skin, green eyes, and dark, braided hair, though his hair hung much longer. Even though I would never tell him, I had a suspicion that he would grow to be taller than me.

"Nothing this morning?" my mother asked, smiling as she looked to me.

"Your voice sounds strong today."

"I feel better than I have in...well, I'm not sure how long."

"You must be — you even seem like you're standing taller," I told her.

"Don't think I've forgotten the question."

"We didn't see a single thing. He's not exactly subtle on the approach."

She kept her face pointed at the hide she was cutting but cast a knowing look in my direction.

"He'll get there," I told her. "He's still got some growing to do, and spotting from a horse isn't easy."

"More hands make less work, Rennik. Especially out in the grasses."

"He doesn't have to be a hunter, you know."

"Right," she said. "He can make a living fixing Tella's hut every week."

I laughed with my mother and left.

I caught up with Avid. By the time we made it back to Tella's hut, we had been joined by a few of his friends, all of whom were just as young. They clearly sought to prove their maturity by aiding in the construction of something. This, however, didn't stop them from speaking like children.

"I heard she doesn't sleep, and she just stares at the moon all night."

"I heard she tames falcons to hunt children."

"I heard she eats her venison raw."

I walked behind them, shaking my head. Tella was certainly not normal, but the rumors these children spoke of were outlandish. At least, I told myself they were.

Eating raw meat would explain being out of her mind...

I was never overly embarrassed to be with my brother. True, I was older, and no longer considered a child, but I wanted to be sure that Avid was sent in the right direction. There were other children who were growing up without fathers in our village, and after seeing what they tended to become, I wanted to keep Avid on the right path. Someone had to teach him the way of things. Gatsi, the village story-teller, had done something similar for me. I had been told that as the oldest hunter of the family, I was in charge, though I wasn't sure my mother was aware of such an arrangement.

We approached Tella's hut, and the boys got to work cleaning everything up.

"You can't raise it higher," Avid lectured her. It was interesting to see an eleven-year-old speak to an adult with his hands on his hips. As he continued to talk, he lifted a hand to point out the things to which he referred, mimicking the authority of the village's other builders.

"You have to keep it under the crest of the surrounding ridge, otherwise the winds will eventually ruin it. It may not be tomorrow or the next day, but...eventually. Because it won't stay one way, and it might be sort of...soft winds one day, and then the next, it might be..."

His speech was losing steam, and Tella had long since decided to stare out at the horizon instead of at him. Avid gave up and went to work.

The latticed walls of the hut were only damaged on one side, so the boys repairing it didn't have too hard a job to do.

Avid and two others were plotting out the exact fifteen-foot section of ground to which the hut should be moved to be both level and protected. I stayed on the edge of the affair, helping only when they asked me to lift something heavy or bind some of the taller pieces of the lattice together with twine. I felt this was more a project of theirs than mine.

It was after twenty minutes had passed when Chaska, a stern older man, strode by with his dog close at his side. I thought he might be grimacing at the boys, but then he turned his attention to me, and I was reminded of what his grimace could really be.

"Spoiled. The whole lot of them. That's what they'll be if they don't do things on their own," he growled over at me.

I simply nodded once to acknowledge his presence, then kept working, knowing that if it weren't for my help, the boys would be here all of two days trying to close the top of the lattice frame. Chaska stepped closer to me.

"You're spending time with children. What's the matter, can't decide if you're a man yet?" I did my best to ignore him. He twisted his mouth to generate another insult. "No wonder you haven't found a woman. Cold should've taken you."

Now he was grasping at whatever he could. "Cold should have taken you" had been one of the more popular forms of verbal bludgeoning to beat against me. The old man wasn't original. Resisting the urge to turn and engage him, I kept busy with the rope.

"A true disappointment your mother has to depend on two children for her food. Can't hardly believe you do enough for her."

I clenched my jaw but knew I had shown too much. He could see he was getting to me. I channeled my anger into tightening the knot I made, using all of my strength.

He gestured to my brother.

"Or maybe boys without a father can't help but depend on charity."

I wanted to break his nose. Instead, I inhaled deeply through my own and turned to face him. Chaska was a full four inches shorter than me and older than the earth, but I figured the old warrior still had fight in him. His old age had afforded him a sour disposition, an ugly countenance, and a lonely personal life, no doubt. All of these things and my fists were tools I could employ to strike back at him, but my mother would be furious if I fell into a fight, especially with an old man.

His dog let out a low growl as I looked down at his master. Would it attack me if I hurt him? That seemed to be likely, and I wondered if his dog was the reason the old man could afford to be so mean-spirited. No one would hurt him with his guardian at his feet.

I decided in the midst of my intimidation to let it go to the grasses. I turned back to the lattice and finished the binding as if nothing had happened. Chaska was about to speak further, obviously interested in getting me into trouble, when a hand clasped down on his shoulder.

"Enough, grandfather. I think you've embarrassed him thoroughly." The new voice belonged to a man named Ciqala, just a little older than me. He had broad shoulders, strong arms, and a voice filled with confidence. Chaska had always bragged about his family being somehow related to the chieftain. It never made much sense to bring it up. Our leaders are chosen by the villagers, not by blood.

Chaska grinned at his grandson, chuckled at what he perceived to be his victory against me, and walked away. Grateful as I was to be done with the exchange, the wary feeling that sank into my stomach at Ciqala's presence lingered. I simply never liked to be around him.

As they left, I glanced over my shoulder at Chaska's dog. It looked tame enough, although I'm sure it could turn fierce in a heartbeat. Such dogs were the color of their surroundings — ambers, browns, and gold with black markings. The larger ones stood with their backs at my waist, and though they weren't as wide, their thick fur made it look so. They had an exceptional mane around the head and neck, and in the springtime, their hair shed and occupied every bit of space in the village. It seemed wrong, somehow, for an intelligent animal to be following such a terrible master, but such is the price of loyalty.

I listened to Avid and his friends talk among themselves.

"You think we could get some timber and clay? It'd make for stronger walls," said Avid.

"But how would she move it if she needed to?"

"Well, she wouldn't. Why would she?"

"My father says we should always be ready to leave."

"That's old people talk, Dalon," said Avid. "Mud brick like Gatsi's might be nice."

"Sounds like too much work. We're done, anyways."

We finished the hut and stood back to admire the job well done.

Unsurprisingly, the lower parts of the hut repaired by the boys looked like new. The sections I covered with my height reminded me that building wasn't my calling. The boys watched Tella flit in and out of her hut hurriedly, moving the things she had previously placed outside back into her home. Glass objects, bought from traders, no doubt; a large, white, collapsible fan; thick furs that wouldn't be worn until winter, almost a year away; and several bags and small boxes that gave no indication of their contents.

"Maybe that's where she keeps the raw meat," whispered one of the boys.

A falcon cried overhead, and they all flinched.

Suppressing a laugh, I thought of what Chaska had said and leaned over to Avid.

"We're going hunting, day after tomorrow," I told him. "I want to see how much better you've gotten. We'll try south this time."

Avid nodded, unexcited. "We're going to the river," he informed me. "I'll be back later."

"Mulberries again?"

"They're the sweetest ones on the bank! If you had some, you'd understand," he said over his shoulder. They turned and made their way east.

I shook my head for what was hopefully the last time that day and walked in the direction of Gatsi's. Wading through the village reminded me of a forest to the west I was told of, where thick trees stood high overhead and grasped beams of sunlight in their living clutches. The sun here was tracing its way past the tops of huts, tanning racks, and people, as they moved in slow, independent paths, each to their own destination.

I passed the chieftain's home, the village's largest hut at thirty feet, and wondered how long it would take my brother and his friends to construct something of that size. The chieftain was a terse but fair man who generally left everyone to their devices, lest they cause harm to one another. I once saw him break up a tussle between two scouts simply by shouting, like a man commanding well-trained animals. We made eye contact as he stepped out of his hut, and I gave him a respectful nod.

Gatsi's hut was a cloth covering stretched over a wood and mud brick foundation that sat in the middle of the village, near the chieftain's home. I had been in that structure nearly as often as my own. Gatsi was the man responsible for much of my upbringing. Learning the basics of medicine, the history of the clans, and plants and animals were all part of his curriculum. Above all, however, he insisted on learning to speak well. I always felt that the lessons were wasted on me, as I had learned long ago that I wasn't the village's favorite conversationalist.

As I approached, he was kneeling with his back to me, hanging herbs on a small rack. I had seen him do this before, and I knew he was drying them for either medical use or for tea. Sometimes it was hard to tell which he valued more.

"Morning, Gatsi."

"I see you've returned from the ride," he said, still turned away from me.

"I have. It was mostly to give Avid some practice, but getting some time away from the village is nice now and then."

"You were supervising the rebuilding of Tella's hut."

"Avid's the mastermind. I just did as I was told."

"I hear tell she spends her nights barking at the moon."

I was shocked to hear an adult say something of the sort. "Gatsi, that can't be true!"

He laughed his signature, good-natured snicker as he turned to me. "My work is in our stories, Rennik. Fact and fiction both!"

Gatsi stood a full three inches higher than me, and I was considered to be much on the taller side of our people. In either case, the taller a Kalanosi is, the better they can see over the grasses. It was a comfort knowing that some things were made clear to me that weren't clear to others. Gatsi's height also granted him long, slender arms that were perfect for the gestures he made while telling tales to children. Though some in the village would use their height to intimidate, Gatsi's peak held no scowl. Instead it bore a warm smile and playful brown eyes that held up his short and messy gray hair.

"The stories surrounding Tella are rumors, mostly," he said, "although I do take a personal interest in her worshipping the Wahkeen."

This was interesting. Most people I knew recognized Dremma, the force of life, and were wary of Drakka, the force of extinction. That duality seemed simple. I hadn't heard of anyone who worshipped the Wahkeen. They were the legendary creatures who birthed storms from their throats and punished the living harshly.

"Why would someone worship the Wahkeen?" I asked.

"Fear, I suppose. The same reason one takes cover from a storm. Or perhaps she feels some sort of debt to them, after her childhood accident." Gatsi walked into his hut without so much as a glance in my direction. It was a tacit invitation, and a common tactic of his. I followed him into his hut, and he continued. "She and her family had gone into the grasses for whatever reason, but only she returned, and almost a week later. The days she'd been gone were riddled with heavy storms and winds. Some of the worst weather I'd ever seen. Even the herds near the village were scared into a panic. Our people were in a different place then, of course.

"We had given up waiting for them, and any lookouts we placed on the hills couldn't see their own hands in front of their faces until lightning crashed overhead. Those who could see with the flashes of lightning said that the storms had made new rivers that were tearing through the plains, and one would look out to see the lightning reflected among the tall grasses. The rainwater in our village wasn't draining fast enough, so we were forced to turn our attention to moving to higher ground. We were so preoccupied with the work, we nearly forgot about Tella's family...

"Until the last of the storm was finally past. There were shouts from the lookouts. We ran to the outskirts to see young Tella, alone, silhouetted by the first sunlight in days. I took her in until she regained her strength. She hadn't eaten in a week and was delusional. When she recovered, she spoke only of tormenting demons, and the death of her family. She said a bird, whose wings stretched for dozens of feet, threw lightning down to protect her. She claimed the Wahkeen themselves delivered her." He sipped from his cup. "Neither her parents nor her brothers were ever found."

I found that in that short time I had unknowingly sat down on a bench and was drinking tea. Gatsi's resonating voice was hypnotizing as he told stories, and I often became lost in them. I had been learning from him the ways of story and legend, and I found myself dissecting the story of Tella's childhood. Where was the embellishment? Was it truth, or a was it a new legend Gatsi was spinning for me? He often liked to make a point with fiction. I decided he would be disappointed if I inquired directly.

"There was once a time," Gatsi continued, "when Tella would have been revered upon her return, instead of untrusted like she is now. Kalanosi once believed that children who survived impossible things were a source of wisdom." His eyes met mine for a second too long. "Now it's shifted. The older generation seems to harbor some amount of distrust for those individuals."

"Believe me, I'm aware. But why don't the younger people act that way?"

"You'll find that not every bit of lore is passed down the same way. Certain stories aren't often told anymore."

"You mean *you* don't tell those stories."

He raised an eyebrow and nodded. When you speak as often as Gatsi, a silent gesture can be heavy.

"I don't understand," I continued. "What about that kind of survival makes someone wise? Tella's hardly all there."

The old man shrugged. "Some believed that close encounters with death granted insight."

"That explains my unending knowledge."

Gatsi grinned and shook his head.

"People believe strange things."

"Indeed they do, Rennik."

Gatsi and I sat and discussed such things for a few hours. He moved eventually to the topic of Shivers — creatures that walk through the night and seek to create fear in the hearts of man, though I couldn't keep Tella's story off of my mind.

On the way home, I made several stops at the few friendly faces around. First, I found Kinran to trade her a badger pelt for several pounds of dried meat; she'd been badgering me herself to bring her a good pelt for a while now. Apparently she valued my services too much to join the other older folk in shunning me. Then I came by Graff's hut, next to which sat a tall clay forge, and found myself in possession of a higher-quality drawknife than the one I had; he owed me a favor from months ago. I spoke briefly with Ikoda about her many animals, answered a child's question about bee-eaters, and finally turned toward my home. I had planned on giving myself an easy evening after doing some chores, but things rarely go as I plan.

When I was nearing my family's hut, I saw that Tella's had resumed its routine. A steady stream of smoke billowed from its roof, denser and darker than the usual smoke from huts. Tella stood outside, hands at her sides, staring up toward the pillar of smoke in the sky. I found myself wondering.

What was she burning?

MY CHILDHOOD WAS DEFINED BY THE ENMITY OF ELDERLY people.

I remember walking through the village, several fish on a line in my hands. Twelve years old was an age at which I wanted little to do with my mother, nothing to do with my young brother, and as I was fatherless, I was very much free to wander the world as I pleased.

"Boy," the old woman had called after me.

I hadn't known her name at the time. In fact, I could have named maybe two of the elderly people within my village. They treated me with such disdain that I had learned to avoid them.

"Who taught you to fish so well?" she demanded. To anyone else, it would seem an innocuous question, but I knew better.

I grumbled my answer and turned to continue walking.

"Speak up, boy! An old woman can't hear you."

"My father taught me."

She spat on the ground. "You feel no shame, do you?"

I should have known to evade her lure, but curiosity had always been my weakness.

"Everyone fishes," I answered nervously. "I don't think there's any shame in fishing."

"You know what the Wahto do, don't you? They cast their children into the grasses in groups — don't let 'em back for weeks. Only half return, and they're fools to take 'em. No child could live like that unless somethin' *helped* 'em."

"I don't see what this has to do with fish."

"They're fools," she repeated, "to ask for cursed children. They think it weeds out the weak ones, only lets the strong ones grow up, and when they grow up they just have more babies to cast out into the wilds. Half come back because they traded the other half for their own lives."

I stared at the catfish's dead eyes on my line. He returned my gaze, unblinking, and I wondered which of us looked more like he didn't want to be there.

"Shameful to be practicin' something your father taught you when you're the reason he's dead."

I snapped from the silent conversation with the catfish and looked instead at the woman's eyes. "What did you say?" In my chest I felt the first fracture before breaking down.

"No child can live out there unless they trade their life away. It's not any coincidence that—"

"*Crone!*" the voice of my mother cracked the village like stone to an egg. She stormed toward us, placed Avid into the arms of an unprepared neighbor, came straight over to the old woman, and slapped her hard across the face. There were various gasps from the villagers.

The old woman twisted across, then down, and caught herself with a surprising dexterity. She looked up at my mother to speak. I like to remember my mother as strong and well-spoken as this.

"Raisha!" she began. But my mother was faster.

"Listen to me! My son is a fatherless boy and that is nobody's fault but Drakka, and if you think you can sit here and insult the son of the man who saved you from that deadly horse of yours—" here some of the villagers began to laugh "—then you've made an enemy in me."

"Your boy is the reason—"

"My *son* is the reason his family will eat tonight! My son is the only one in our home not raising a small child! The last thing he needs is to mistakenly adhere to your dusty beliefs about children!"

"You're a fool to place your faith in this boy, Raisha," the woman finally got out. "He's been marked by Drakka. He'll be the death of your family."

"Then let's hope that day is far from now, so my *other* son can live in a world without your bitter words and horrid breath, you ancient...*ancient*..." my mother had lost the wind to her words. She pushed me into walking and guided me straight toward our home, plucking a placid Avid back into her arms.

"Thank you for the fish, Rennik. I'm sure they'll be delicious."

"But..." I muttered. "I actually caught them for Liril's family."

My mother stopped, hung her head, and took a moment to deflate. She leaned down to me and spoke softly.

"I know it seems important to do things for her, Rennik. Really, I do. In a way, it's normal to be thinking of girls before your family. But your family needs to eat. The venison has run out, and you know Teneran one hut over is just as old and dusty as the rest of them."

"He can't spare one bit?"

"I think we just need to take care of ourselves. Okay?"

"Okay."

3
SIMPLE TRUTHS

"A person is learned through conversation. A people are learned through their stories."

— GATSI

It was never a formally announced event. Sometimes a group of children or parents would suggest hearing Gatsi speak, and suddenly there would be a skein of tangled listeners waiting outside his home for the night's entertainment. Most people, myself included, would shrink at the thought of the spontaneous attention of dozens of people, but Gatsi was simply cut from a different cloth.

I was standing back, near the adults but not with them, looking in toward Avid. I imagined the older folk told themselves they were here to watch the children, when in truth they were present to remember what it was like to be one. If their feelings were like my own, that is.

Gatsi liked to vary the kinds of stories he told, and it was a pattern I was beginning to pick up on. By my reckoning, we were due for something dramatic.

He emerged from his hut with a steaming cup of tea, and the crowd grew quiet. Without acknowledging the back row of adults, he peered mysteriously around at the eager eyes of the children. Then, on his own cue, his booming baritone shook its listeners.

"The Wahkeen had called for an ominous sky, and each sweeping cloud on the horizon seemed heavier than the last."

He dropped his voice to no more than a mutter, and everyone simultaneously leaned forward, ears turned to catch his words.

"Now, Kivik knew better than to question the portents of nature, but with a storm at her back and her husband Talmar separated from her days before, the mother had little choice to make. It was a simple truth that the child in her womb held the future of her clan. It was a simple truth that propelled her deep into Kibara — land of the shifting faces. Sometimes," Gatsi counseled, "the simplest truths are those to which we must cling most desperately."

By the time he had spoken the latter phrase, I caught myself mouthing the words along with him. I had heard the story so much growing up that I knew every syllable, pause, and shift in tempo. The rhythms were as familiar as hoof-beats, as expected as an echo to a shout.

Any speaker of Kalanosi knows that the first syllable of "Kibara" meant "people", but in the sense of something passed. "Ara" was simply a word for "land". The story was, however, not usually told to the village as a whole. I was interested to see their reaction.

The next section of the tale took up a quicker rhythm to usher the audience into the adventure proper:

. . .

"WITH GRASSES BRAIDED 'ROUND HER WRIST FOR MANY WHO HAD gone,

our Kivik sought to find the faces of those long passed on.
If sister found a sister walking in those windblown lands,
her face would come familiar; her soul would be but sand.
Though the lands were damning and its creatures' souls were pitch,
another simple truth required Kivik's iron wits.
To find the thief of voice and visage, motives grown in guile,
the mother must look close to see the darkness in its smile."

A PAUSE, AND THE STORY TOOK TO PROSE AGAIN.

"The sun had set, its final streams of desperate gold dragged into the horizon, leaving night to take hold over the strange land. The only light came from Kivik's undying torch, her other hand white-knuckle around the shaft of the steel axe given to her by the wise trees of the Inkwood.

"The axe had been given as a symbol of faith, a symbol that the trees trusted her with their greatest fear." Various children nodded with emphatic understanding. They all knew the story of Kivik in the Inkwood. "But now Kivik struggled to come to terms with what she must do. The axe had served her well and protected her when she most needed it, but to claim the lands of Kibara for her people, she must break the axe upon the evil that resided there. She knew the grasses were filled with vile creatures, and as she looked over the wilds of Kibara, she spoke to herself:"

"*It's us or them,*" I mouthed along with Gatsi.

"It had long been known that evil comes in threes, and armed with blade and knowledge, Kivik thought herself prepared. It was her heart, however, that would be tested in the lands of the dead.

"As she walked," Gatsi continued, hands reaching out to push away phantom grasses, "a voice called out, 'Kivik! You have come to help! I have been lost for the passing of three suns, and there is no water among these hills!'

"Then came the speaker, emerging head-first through the stalks. It was a young man she recognized from her own clan...a man she had seen *killed* at the hands of their enemies. The shadows of his face danced as the torchlight flickered, and in her chest was the deeply-rooted guilt we all would feel at harming another of our kind. But in her mind she wrestled that feeling with the knowledge that this man — he who she had known before — was *not* of her kind. Not anymore.

"She thrust her torch into his chest with all her might, and erupting from the creature's lungs was a scream that tore the illusion of the boy from its face. The nameless evil before her fell to dust, scattering to the wind."

Here Gatsi stood and pantomimed the death of the creature, the eyes of our clan leashed to his movements. A few children laughed. It was a tactical moment of levity.

"Another hour passed," he continued, his voice low. "The darkness of night had deepened further when a second voice greeted her. 'Kivik!' said the woman, stepping from shadow to torchlight. 'Mother wants us home!'

"Kivik looked into the face of her sister, who had been taken by sickness years before. Her eyes filled with tears as she remembered her mother's voice calling them in for dinner, and her father teaching them both to sing. She remembered the long death, painful for her sister and perhaps more painful to witness..."

Gatsi paused, my own people's tears beginning to trace their faces.

"Kivik knew she could not bear it again. A pit of sorrow she had been trying to fill for years was made larger, her small successes over grief now brought to no avail. But still the wrestling of truth and heartbreak tumbled through her chest, and the fiendish creature before her took its first step.

"Then came the black ichor from her sister's mouth, like a tree of the Inkwood cut and crying. The blackened soul of the creature leaked slowly, granting fault to the illusion, and like its predecessor it fell to the touch of fire from Kivik's undying torch, screaming with a scream that was not her sister's."

The silence that followed was laden with the weight of second-hand grief, though I wondered how many of the people around me needed the space to push away their own experiences with death, trying not to relate too much to Gatsi's tale.

"Kivik knelt and cradled the child in her womb, promising again and within herself to make the land safe before it came into the world. This she did until her legs found the strength to stand, and when they had it, she started to walk again.

"Finally, as if to lift the darkness from her heart, the sun's gentle hand pushed the smothering blanket of night away. Kivik looked joyfully at the soft horizon. She breathed deeply of a land made free from evil, a land ready for her people.

"Then came the rustling of the grasses behind her. Never to be taken by surprise, Kivik spun quickly to ready herself for the unexpected.

"And unexpected it was! A cry of joy and relief flew from Kivik like birds on a warm spring morning as her husband

Talmar stepped into the clearing, made rough from his days alone in the grasses."

The young and forgetful in the crowd let out audible sighs of relief, shoulders dropping, finally weightless and free of tension.

"She stepped forward, catching her husband's embrace, and dropped her torch and axe to the ground.

" 'Talmar,' she spoke into his ear, 'we've done it. We've defeated the...'

"And here Kivik stopped. Not because she was overjoyed with the rediscovery of her husband, nor was it because she could not find the words. Here, Kivik stopped because a single drop of black ichor spilled from her husband's mouth and ran slowly down her arm.

"It was a paralysis of emotional shock, or perhaps the quickly crushing embrace of the imposter's heavy arms that kept her still. Her eyes moved downward, seeing that her torch had rolled too far away to reach. To her right, however, the axe had landed safely upon her foot.

"The air in her lungs began to leave her as the beast tightened his grip, and she was not sure it would return. With a voice strained by weakened breath, she asked aloud when her husband had died and tried in turn to push the truth away from her, knowing more deeply that she would get no answer from this malicious being. It was a simple truth that led her to action, though a reluctant action it was. It was a simple truth that her child must not be harmed, and that her husband was now gone away from her.

"Looking into eyes turned black with hate, she spoke again, more for herself than anyone."

I'm sorry, I narrated with him, this time internally.

"Kivik pushed against the creature and made enough room to dip down. Lifting the axe with her foot, she caught it in her hand and swung swiftly, burying its blade into the fiend's back, never breaking from its gaze. The creature screamed once as the axe shattered against its spine, breaking apart as her husband now did before her."

~

"INTERESTING THING ABOUT THAT STORY," GATSI SAID TO ME once we were inside his hut. I was snacking on a bit of bread, and he was cooking some salmon over the fire.

"What, is it meant to be even more sad?" I asked. Gatsi gave me a look that was probably meant to be reproachful, but I think he understood.

"No," he answered, annoyed. "Well, actually, knowing the medium, it probably *is* meant to be a little less...lighthearted."

"You're joking."

"I'm afraid not. But that isn't what I was going to say. Most stories we tell include the same cast of individuals, personalities that embody a necessary role of the tale."

I listed off a few. "The Hero, the Child, the Challengers..." Growing up with Gatsi, this was all rote by now.

"But," he continued, glancing at the cooking fire and punctuating his point with a raised finger, "someone was absent from Kivik's tale."

I thought for a moment. "The Wise Elder."

"The Wise Elder," he repeated. "The hero sacrifices health for what is right, the child's innocence is kept safe from the challengers, and the wise elder must make plain the truth of the hero's course."

"But Kivik had the legends of her people to tell her that 'evil comes in threes', and the trees of the Inkwood gave her the axe...well, the trees would be the Patron, I guess.

But their lore itself could take the shape of the Wise Elder, no?"

"An astute point, Rennik, but there's an unfortunate facet to the elder's role that you may not have noticed yet."

I waited for him to tell me exactly what that was, but in typical Gatsi fashion, he simply turned back to his cooking.

"You said 'medium' a moment ago," I said. "What did you mean?"

"I mean the story has been filtered. It isn't actually an Achare legend to begin with."

"Really? What is it then?"

"It's not even Kalanosi. It comes from the Inkwood. The Yohri were the first Kalanosi to hear it since they're the closest to the Inkwood, and the story found its way through other clans as they met with each other. The Yohri tend to strip the mirth out of everything they touch, so any degree of Inkwood happiness would've been lost in translation. Funny how things change over time, eh?"

"So Kivik is just an Achare addition?"

"A substitution, really. Everyone has their own heroes. It's always a pregnant woman, though. I suppose the mention of the Inkwood trees has simply stayed put as it gets passed along."

Gatsi poked at his dinner over the fire.

"You think the black ichor means something more to them, then?" I asked.

"How do you mean?" I sensed his question had more to do with quizzing me than carrying a conversation.

"Well, the trees are sacred in the Inkwood, and using the axe seemed like it broke some sort of — I don't know, an oath, maybe — so the creatures of the dead seem more connected to the trees than anything, don't they? Like the axe was used on its makers?"

He smiled and nodded. "The Inkwood trees often punish living things in their stories."

"I don't understand. How can a tree *do* anything?"

"I worry, sometimes. You beset upon yourself the curse of reason. Must you dissect everything, or can't you let a story breathe?"

"Isn't there a truth to the tale?"

"Fact and fiction both, Rennik," Gatsi reminded me.

I rolled my eyes. "Is Kivik meant to be fighting against the actual land she's from, then?"

Gatsi nodded. "Somewhat, yes. It's meant to symbolize finding danger in the familiar and sacrificing that which we hold close for the greater good."

I took a bite of bread. "Interesting that the theme of the story didn't change when it was handed off to another culture," I noted.

"There are many universal pains in the world," he said without looking up. He scraped the fish from the pan and eyed it with a grin before speaking again.

"Fighting the people you've grown to love is one of them."

DREAMS OF DISTANT THINGS

"Riding in wagons all this way? How soft their soles must be!"

— ACHARE CRITICISM OF RUCOSTI
MERCHANTS

I've heard foreigners say that the plains of Kalanos are featureless. This I find to be a misperception; Kalanos is not only the earth, but the skies and the people, too.

Looking up from the grasslands would reveal mountain-sized clouds towering in the distance, filling the horizon with the threat of rain and shadow. Long, streaking clouds can pattern the skies like a woven blanket from end to end, enough to conjure wanderlust in the stoniest of hearts.

The people are smaller, but move our world as much as the skies do. It was in the morning that I watched a group of scouts, some of whom were designated clan fighters if the need arose, arguing among themselves. Avid and I were sitting on the ground, and as we spoke, their group blundered through the village with the grace of a bull who'd sustained a head injury. We watched with a detached sort of interest, as one tends to watch people with whom they avoid association.

"You scared the entire herd away!" a tall woman shouted at an expressionless man. His round head was shaved to stubble, and his forehead wrinkled as she continued. "You're an idiot, Banar."

At the mention of his name, I remembered Banar. He was as dumb as a hunter could be, if my memory served.

"No," he replied, "I'm not. Those bison have been on this piece of land for as long as we have. Anytime someone scares them into moving, they just run out a couple miles and run right back."

"Why the hell were you even following me?"

"I was practicing," he replied, a dumb grin slowly forming across his face. "You know, praying." He drew a circle over his heart but ended the motion by cupping his chest in a crude gesture.

The group chuckled at his remark.

"You could've gotten us both hurt," the woman replied. "Not even *your* skull is thick enough to survive a stampede."

Just as I was about to suggest moving on, Avid spoke up.

"Rennik," he said, "it's wrong to follow people without them knowing, right?"

"Well, those two are normally pretty close friends, so I'm not sure. And I doubt the entire herd started moving. We'd have felt that."

"I'm not talking about them."

I looked at Avid and waited for him to continue.

"I was just thinking. It's not right to lie to people because it's dishonest, so watching someone when they don't know you're there is a kind of dishonesty, right?"

"I guess it depends on the situation," I answered vaguely.

"I think I might have spied on Gatsi," he confessed. "On accident!" he added upon seeing my reaction.

"I'm not sure you can *accidentally* spy on someone...but what did you see?" I frowned at him, trying to be disappointed, but I couldn't deny that I was curious. It wasn't hard to overhear things in the village, but Gatsi was mysterious even to me sometimes.

"Well, I was out near the river to look for mussels — and because it's just nice to be alone sometimes — when I saw someone walking along the bank. I don't think they saw me since I was still in the grass a bit, but I wanted to know who it was, so I followed them for a second — just a for a second—"

"It sounds like you were spying on purpose."

"It was different!"

"How so?"

"You know how in a dream, you sort of have a sense of what to do or where to go, even though you don't know why?"

I nodded. Avid's stories were typically dramatized, and this seemed no different.

"It was like that. Like sleepwalking, except I *knew* I was walking. I followed him and didn't question why, and I didn't think about why until afterward."

"Okay, so what did you see?"

"Well, I was following Gatsi through the grasses, and every time he turned to look around — he looked like he was making sure no one was following him — every time he turned around I ducked just in time. And one time, when I was in the shorter grasses, he should have seen me, but a bird — I think it was a longspur — swooped at him and got his attention. He just kept walking after that. It was like I was *supposed* to be hidd—"

"Avid," I interrupted. I felt bad cutting him off, but he was clearly exaggerating, and he had a tendency to expand the unnecessary parts of his stories. "What was Gatsi doing?"

"He just sat there for over an hour!"

"Back up. Where?"

"Under this big oak tree. He was burning something — it smelled kind of like lavender, or maybe laurel — and he just sat there!"

"I thought you said you only followed him for a second."

"Well, I didn't have to *follow* him once he stopped. That's more like..."

"Spying?" I asked with a critical tone. "Avid, you said yourself that you were by the river because it's nice to be alone sometimes. Can't you let other people sit alone when they want to?"

Avid looked down guiltily. "I just thought it was weird, is all."

"Gatsi is...a little strange," I conceded, "but I'm not sure spying on him is the right thing to do."

"It was just..." Avid trailed off. "I don't know. It was just strange, is all."

I don't know what Avid was so worked up about, but I suppose it wasn't so difficult to imagine Gatsi taking time away from the village to sit in silence. I sometimes stayed in the grasses for hours longer than I needed to, just to get away. As much as Gatsi was one of the more interesting people in my village, I decided Avid was making it into something it wasn't. It was like him to be bored.

But it was not always my own people in whom I took interest.

Later that evening, merchants from Rucost arrived at the village. Their fifteen-foot wagons came pushing through the grasses in a tight line, opening up the wilds with a temporary trail that would refill itself in a few days. The oxen at their lead would press the grasses down for the wheels to run cleanly over, lest the many stalks tangle themselves up in rotating parts. As always, there was the initial buzz of exchange as my people traded things like animal hides and furs, dried meats, horns, fine bows, jewelry and similar crafts for the products the merchants brought, like sophisticated metal tools for the artisans, cheap loads of charcoal for Graff's forge, fine clothes, cooking supplies, and other things that were generally difficult for us to produce.

One of the more notable commodities, however, were saddles and bridles. The Rucosti had long ago tried to trade saddles for our valuables, as we tended not to use them — many still prefer bareback riding — but their saddles were wide and cumbersome, meant for their much larger laboring horses. Our horses were slimmer, and once they made saddles to fit our needs, they became an expensive and high-demand item for those of us with enough to trade. I saw Ikoda within the crowd, trading one of her actual horses for one such saddle. They often tried to sell us metal horseshoes, but those were never of interest to us.

After about an hour the crowd around the merchants dispersed, and the circle their wagons formed was entirely empty of villagers. Avid and I approached their camp, laid an armful of furs on a table they'd set out, and sat at their fire without invitation. A pot hung over the blaze, producing some delicious aromas.

Potatoes, leeks, carrots, and...chicken?

A pale woman with some sort of stringed instrument plucked a quiet and happy melody next to me.

"Yer a little late," a squeaky voice mentioned from across the fire, marked with the expected Rucosti accent. A slight, pinkish boy with red hair stood and walked around the fire toward me with what looked like an undeserved confidence. He wore a well-crafted shirt with buttons, and boots that looked like he tried a little too hard to keep them clean. He couldn't have been any older than me. "Yer *Atch-air* friends have already loaded us up with animal parts," he continued, pronouncing "parts" like "paerts". He looked pitifully down at my pile of furs as if having any more animal to deal with would make him vomit. "If we do take any more, we wouldn't pay much, seeing as how we're overstocked and all."

I nodded thoughtfully at the fire. His was an age-old effort to devalue my furs, but luckily I knew enough not to deal with him at all.

"This must be your first time here," I began.

"How's that?"

"Well, for one, it's pronounced *Ack-ar-ay*, and two, it's usually Tenal who comes to talk to me."

"What's that? You nervous about trading with someone new, grass-eater?"

"I'm skeptical about someone who doesn't know flawless furs when he sees them."

Before he could respond, a booming, thickly-accented voice filled the air. "And if ye call 'em grass-eaters one more time, they'll add yer pelt to the pile!"

A large, balding, red-bearded man, built as broad as his wagons were, stepped toward us. Two clay bowls sat in his palms, dwarfed by the sheer size of his hands. The hulking man shouted something in Rucosti and pointed to a wagon, palming a bowl upside-down. The shout sounded to be part scolding, part command.

The young boy did what he was told and cast me a dour look on his way to the wagon.

I considered Tenal to be one of my only good friends, even though I only saw him once every year or so. Hearing him talk about things that were distant to me was a true joy of mine.

As he approached, I stood and smiled, holding out my hand. He reciprocated the sentiment and squeezed my palm a little too hard — a Rucosti tradition, or maybe just one of Tenal's.

"Rennik!" he boomed again. "Sorry about the nephew. He's an idiot. I was starting to worry we wouldn't see you!" Now that he was talking to me, his accent more or less disappeared. Tenal was a talented linguist, and I'd been told Kalanosi was a tough language to master.

"I think you were worried you'd leave without any good furs," I quipped. I normally wouldn't be so forward and confident with anyone, but I knew Tenal well enough, and the merchants had always been much more interesting than the people in my village.

Tenal chuckled, his big, stiff beard raising up as he threw his head back. The man was always quick to laughter.

"You might be right," he responded. "And don't think I forgot about your request from last time. I brought just what you asked for. But first, let's have a look."

Tenal sat, reached over, and examined one of my furs by the light of the fire. He turned it over, made a few approving grunts, and turned it back again, his eyes speeding over its surface all the while, looking for imperfections. There were none, of course.

"It's been over a year," I mentioned while he studied the furs. "I thought you might be lost."

"Your people aren't hard to find when you haven't moved in ten years," he mumbled from the other side of an outstretched fur. "I don't know how you do it," he finally said, admiring its quality.

"I wouldn't mind telling you how. It's not like you'd give me any real competition."

Tenal chuckled again at that. "No, I don't suppose I would. These are a good collection, boy. They'll fetch a fine price as coats for more noble men than you and I! They like to enjoy nature once it's nice and dead."

"And for me?"

"Right!" he thundered, slapping his thighs as he stood. He gathered the pelts gently in his arms and took several long steps over to his wagon.

Glancing to my left, I saw that Avid was running his hand along the bottom of one of the wagons, listening to a woman explain how the whole thing was caulked for the river. I wondered how long it'd be before he'd try to build something like that for himself.

"I've gotta say, Rennik, I'm a bit surprised you'd ask for this," said Tenal, coming back from his wagon with a leather-wrapped parcel.

"You're surprised that a horse-born savage wanted a book."

Tenal's face grew sober and his voice dropped low as he looked down at me. "Now you know that's not what I was saying, boy. You're as much a person as I am. I'm not my nephew. You're not a savage. Let's just be the only two people in the world with some sense, hm?"

I had meant the comment to be taken lightly, but now I just felt guilty. As quiet as I kept in my village, I didn't often get to practice the intricacies of conversation, especially with foreign merchants.

"I'm sorry," I said. "I didn't mean it." I reached out for the leather-wrapped book and placed it on the ground next to my feet.

"I was only saying," he continued, his hands defensive in

front of him, "that I've never met one of you that can read. Kalanosi isn't a written language. Not condesending. Just stating a fact."

"You sure this book is a fair trade for the furs?" I asked, pushing my luck with a smirk.

Tenal grinned. "That book isn't easy to find, Rennik. It's still pretty new. Scribes haven't made too many copies — They don't see much value in keeping records of Kalanos, I suppose. But since we go back..." His thick fingers fished around in a pouch and brought out a few silver coins. He flicked one to me with a metallic ring, then poured the others into my palm. I raised one up to observe it.

"What am I supposed to do with these? I'm in the middle of the plains!"

"Save it for next time we come," he said, chuckling again.

I shook my head, but smiled and accepted the exchange. I wasn't even sure what they were worth. Tenal reached toward a pot over the fire and filled a bowl of soup for me. He gestured toward my brother.

"I don't think he'll eat," I said. "He seems distracted." Avid was now giving close consideration to the joints on the tongue of the wagon, ignoring the wary oxen nearby.

I slipped the cold silver coin around in my fingers and studied its sides. On one was the face of some important man in profile, and some words I could almost make out. On the other side was an artistic rendering of the sun — some sort of spiritual reference.

"Are you religious, Tenal?" I asked. He sat down next to me.

"I wasn't aware there was much else to be. Why?"

"Gatsi has been talking a bit about the religions of your people, the idiosyncrasies and such."

"Idiosyncrasies," he echoed, shaking his head. "You think you know everything, do you?"

I nodded and smiled.

"How many candles burned on a full moon?"

"Three. Something about taking light for times that are lacking. One candle for yourself, one for your home, one for your neighbor."

"Four."

"Four?"

"Four. One for the king."

"That must be new," I said.

He shrugged. "Been done as long as I can remember. My parents did it too. Your information is outdated, Rennik."

I looked confusedly toward the fire.

"Personally," he continued, "I like to wear one of these." He reached into his shirt and produced a silver symbol on a chain, shaking it for emphasis. It was a cut-out of the sun, their central symbol. "But I have to say, I've never been told straight what you all worship. And I'm tired of always telling you things — why don't you tell me something of *your* people this year."

"Well," I explained between mouthfuls of soup, taking the moment to think, "as far as big ideas go, there's Dremma and Drakka. Dremma is the force of all of life, and Drakka is the life-eater. Some people worship some...stranger things, like spirits, but mostly we just consider the big two."

"You speak of belief strangely, as if it were an option. What other truth is there besides the truth you've been taught?"

"Truth is a matter of how far you can see, and what you're taught parts the mist in the way," I said. It was something Gatsi had told me once, and though I said it confidently now, I'd often contemplated what he'd meant.

Tenal grumbled and thought. "So Dremma is sort of the good one, and Drakka's something to avoid?"

"No," I responded, slightly annoyed at the presumption. "It's not that simple. That's how your belief works, not ours. They're not *going* to do much of anything."

"Explain it, then."

"Well, at the core of everything, there's life, and life isn't supposed to disappear. We made that mistake once already."

"Once? What are you talking about?" asked Tenal. "You kill all the time. You just sold me furs."

"Right, sorry. I don't usually have to explain this. By life, I mean the bigger picture. Think an entire species rather than the individual animal."

He nodded, but I wasn't convinced he understood.

"Okay. What colors do you see in the woods where you're from?" I asked.

"Oh, you know, browns, grays, greens."

"Right. So Dremma and Drakka made a lot of deals with each other, one of which is the construction of a creature. The species, not the individual, necessarily."

"Hmm," he responded as he sipped from his bowl.

"So these woods of yours," I continued. "Imagine there are four kinds of birds making their home there. Red birds, green birds, brown birds, and orange birds. When the birds were originally forged, Dremma instilled them with helpful things, like excellent eyesight and quick movement. Drakka added the unfortunate aspects."

"Like what?"

"Well, which of those birds are going to die first?"

"Orange and red."

"Why's that?"

"They don't blend in," he answered.

"Right. That's Drakka. If something is keeping a creature

from surviving, it's because the life-eater is hungry. He helped design them that way. He aims for failure."

"So Drakka eats birds," said Tenal, half-joking.

"No. Drakka eats everyone."

It came out a little more dramatic than I intended, and Tenal's smile dropped. "How do you mean?"

"Well, you've got these four birds. In fifty years or so, will you see any red or orange birds in the woods?"

"Probably not, if they've all been hunted."

"When all of the orange birds have died out, it's because Drakka has taken them. *All* of them. There will never be orange birds there again unless they come from somewhere else. Drakka is like all of the little weights added to a raft until it sinks. He doesn't want a part of the raft — he wants the whole thing."

"Sounds more like he's the flaws that were in the boat from the get-go, not the added weight."

"Fair point. Sloppy metaphor."

"Okay," he responded, gesturing with a concise hand, "but something is eating those birds too. Something is bene-fiting from the death of the birds, so isn't this whole weak-ness thing just another species' benefit?"

"The whole point," I responded, "is that both of them work for equilibrium. Give and take."

"The good one and the bad one work together?" He looked confused. I gathered my thoughts and continued.

"I mentioned earlier that my people made a mistake once. Many generations ago, there were massive mammoths in Kalanos — big hairy creatures with tusks and a trunk, like the elephants in the Inkwood. My people were the ones migrating with them. We were the clan who killed them all off. Sometimes it seems like predators benefit from weakness in prey, but the older Achare tell me that the plains have changed dramatically since the mammoths have disappeared. There's an imbalance, and in the same way a bowl of water will make small waves until it calms itself, we've been seeing what might be the repercussions. Animals acting unpredictably, herds making strange migrations, predators killing to excess. There is an imbalance, and as of now it doesn't seem clear whether it will end with calm waters or an empty bowl. Taking advantage of that creature's weakness might have been a mistake, but from where we are now, it's hard to tell."

He looked at me thoughtfully. "You sound like you belong in the university back home. But you seem uncertain, and that means you've got some thinking to do. Best a man makes peace with the world early."

I chewed a chunk of potato slowly as I considered what he said.

"So how in the hell do you pray to this Dremma figure?"

Some of the people in my village would have been offended by the way he talked about our belief, but I knew he meant well. "Hell" was a Rucosti word, after all.

"I'm not sure what you mean," I said.

"When we pray to Ityx, our goddess, we ask for things. You know, a safe trip, and good harvest, that and the like. But you said yours aren't going to do anything. You recognize give and take...Ityx just gives."

"You really think Ityx would change the world for you?"

"Sure. What else is there to think?"

"I think our take is a little different than yours."

"You might be right. For you, it seems like Dremma already dealt you all the cards with your—" he lifted up my arm— "brown feathers."

I rolled my eyes. "We don't really pray or expect change. It's more of a recognition of the things we have. Strength, quiet, good hearing, you know. We don't pray to Dremma so much as we *recognize* Dremma."

"Your worship is just thankfulness?"

"It's knowing that we're built to survive."

"So what happens when one of you is weak, or blind? Dremma just didn't like that one?"

"Achare don't do much about that. Now, the bigger, more intimidating clans take it much more seriously. They'll leave crippled or otherwise unfit children out in the grasses. It's their way of making sure their people stay strong. Isolating Dremma in their clan."

"And you don't?"

I shrugged. "We take care of each other best we can. Sometimes things are just the way they are. It's not like Dremma is going to intervene after something's already been born."

"But *our* worship," he started, "is much more... optimistic."

"Is it?" I smiled. His comment seemed to be more cheeky than anything.

"Yes. Ityx is an active figure. She is an entity that *does* intervene. Sounds like your Dremma and Drakka are just what you call the things you see rather than what you think is...you know, *beyond*." He finished the statement with a flippant gesture upward, but he kept his eyes on the food in his bowl.

"What we call the things we see..." I echoed. "What else would we worry ourselves with? You really think something 'beyond' is going to change the world for you?"

Tenal furrowed his brows. "Of course we do. Making a hard sell, cooking a good soup. Ityx is the good in life."

I told him it sounded like skills from Dremma.

"Well, yes, it's similar," he clarified, "but not just those things. The nonliving things, too. Good wind in your sails, a warm day."

"I'm not sure I can control the weather."

"Maybe all you need to do is ask," he responded, looking into his soup with a grin.

"Maybe you're afraid to admit you don't have control," I responded, pausing for his playful scoff. "See, the world would be full of the good and bad without us. Telling myself I can pray to change the world doesn't make it so. Doesn't change come from the actions of living things? You know, the things we can *see*?"

After a quick "Hmph" from the man, I could tell the idea made him think, but soon enough an amicable silence set in as we finished off our soup.

"So," he finally spoke, "how'd you learn to read?"

"I've got a good teacher," I smiled. "I'm pretty sure he knows everything. It's terrifying, really."

Tenal chuckled. "Sounds like it." His eyes wandered to the book at my feet. "Brallic Severin's study of Kalanos...now why exactly did you want a book about the things you already know?"

"Well, I'm still in the learning process with reading, and I won't find much material here," I said as I gestured to the plains with my spoon. "I figured it'd be easier to learn the language if the subject was familiar."

"Hmm," Tenal grumbled in agreement, bowl tipped toward his mouth. "How's your spoken Rucosti coming along?"

I responded in Tenal's language by saying something like, "I can speak it well enough," but judging by the humorous look on his face, I think I made a few mistakes.

"But really," Tenal continued, "where'd your *teacher* learn all of this? Haven't you all been walking around the grasses since the dawn of time or something?"

After a moment of consideration, I realized I'd never thought to ask. "Well, knowledge doesn't come from just one place He's old, so...I always assumed he traded for books and spoke with foreigners. But honestly, I don't know for certain."

"Be sure to ask him for me."

I made a mental note of it, and deciding that our conversation had run its course, I refilled my soup bowl.

I stayed at their camp for a few hours more, quietly listening to stories and jokes, laughing along with them, doing my best to glean the nuances of their language. By the time I realized Avid had already left, I figured it was time for me to head back to my hut and call it a night. I thanked Tenal for the food, wished him safe travels, and left, already looking forward to the next time we'd meet.

The village was settling in as I combed through the huts. The stars shone, free from clouds, and the soft hiss of the grasses ebbed and flowed with the wind. It was that liminal stage of night, the transition from a lively village to a sleeping one, when the only sounds are the thrumming of nocturnal birds, the dirt-scratching of small rodents, and the occasional muted laughter of someone in a distant hut.

My home was quiet with the soft breathing of my sleeping family, and I made to join them.

I DREAMT OF MY FATHER. IT WAS WINTER, AND THE WORST ONE I'd ever seen. I couldn't have been more than seven years old.

He had taken me to the river to fish through the ice. The surface was thick, and I remember his laugh as I slid on my tiny legs from bank to bank before he reminded me that ice wasn't something to play with. I loved making him laugh.

He let me help him pierce the ice with an awl before he carefully used those points to break a hole through the surface. The water underneath was clear and crystalline. I remember handing him the decoy, a wood carving in the shape of the prey that a bigger fish would try to attack. My father laid a blanket on the ice and lay on his belly with a small tent-like structure over his back to keep the wind off of him. He held his short spear at the ready and peered down into the moving current. It was a waiting game, and I quickly grew bored.

I struck out to find something to do. The world had been coated in a perfect white, and I was bewildered. I remember the tree branches that arched over the ice, like a bark skin rooftop that held the snow, perfect and undisturbed, over my head.

I remember a loud cracking, like a forest being felled all at once, and the brief sensation of falling.

The cold hit so fast that I didn't feel myself swept away by the current. It hurt my eyes and my ears, fingers, and toes were promptly lost to my senses. There was only the stomach-churning of uncontrolled motion as I was taken under the ice and down the river.

I had remembered that I was supposed to recognize Dremma when I felt scared, but in that moment, I only thought of my father.

Then, there was a blinding light.

My lungs inhaled painful breaths that were like my first as the winter air met with my icy throat.

There was a new sensation of movement. It felt like I was being carried.

There was fire. With it returned the clarity to my vision

and the feeling to my body. I could see the blackness in my fingers. My father's face was lit by the firelight, and he looked worried. He worked feverishly to feed the flames. The trees were dark behind him — I had no idea how much time had passed.

After a while I could stand again, even under the heavy weight of the blankets and my father's thick coat. He had given it up to keep me warm, and I thought he might be cold. The wind was biting as it threaded through the trees.

The feeling that came back to me revealed the many painful bruises I had earned while being thrown against the rocks under the current.

As I stood, I smiled at my father. I remember feeling confused that his laughter came from a face with tears frozen fast to its cheeks.

I loved making him laugh.

I woke up and shivered against a cold that wasn't there. I reached for the animal hides that had fallen away from my sleeping body and pulled them over me. The heat they kept came quickly.

Sleep did not.

5

THE GRASSES

"...and still to this day, the Kalanosi peoples roam their grassy plains ceaselessly, as wayward ships in the sea searching for their homes to no avail. All clans, from the imposing Wahto to the small and softly-spoken Hetanos, practice this lifestyle, reaching ever toward the impassible horizon.

There is one clan, however, that seem to be the only exception, and only recently so. Of all the Iket in Kalanos, the Achare are the sole clan to have stopped their wandering and rooted themselves in one place. This is why, for the last few years, one may have seen Kalanosi goods appearing in our Rucosti markets. The more daring merchants from the cities of Dellimair and Periloe have been traveling to this newly static clan for expedient wares and novel artifacts.

Rucost's scholars — myself included — have sought the grand reason for this relatively sudden pause in movement, but have unfortunately found nothing to note.

Of the region's fauna, however, it does seem noteworthy that the non-indigenous oryx who had, without apparent cause, migrated to the plains of Kalanos over a generation ago, have since settled in the Achare region. Some among us have argued *that the correlation is simply circumstantial, and with the grasslands as violent as they are, we may never find potent evidence to the contrary."*

— EXCERPT FROM BRALLIC SEVERIN'S
*KALANOS: A STUDY OF PLACE AND
PEOPLE.*

By sunrise I had crafted twenty good arrows. For the heads I used bone from a deer we had killed earlier that week, and the shafts were made from birches near the river. For the fletching, I attached the suitable wing feathers taken from a grouse. Grouse feathers aren't ideal, but it's what I had to work with. All of this I did by firelight until the sun rose, the book from Tenal open next to me on the ground.

I didn't like to think about that winter, the one I had dreamt of the night before. It was a sharp memory for me, but the people in my village made it worse. The older folk had never looked at me the same since then, and except for Gatsi, all of them had made the village a sour sort of place. I shook the thoughts from my head and focused on the task at hand.

Avid and I had been taking turns hunting, and I planned on taking him into the grasses tonight, but to be honest I wasn't counting on him to get anything. I was the better hunter, as I had the benefit of receiving my father's instruction before he died. My brother had done well under my coaching, but he still had a lot to learn. Then again, he hadn't been forced into the role. I had been hunting alone since I was younger than Avid, and if I didn't bring home something to eat, and my mother had no luck foraging or fishing, we'd have gone hungry for the night. Things got better after we settled here, about the time I was eight or nine years old. Someday, Avid would be ready, but for now his only hunting trophies were the red mulberry stains on his hands. Perhaps Chaska was right. Maybe I was spoiling him.

I stood and walked up the ridge that rose next to my hut. Looking out at the night-bedewed fields of wild grasses, I breathed deeply of the morning air. It was crisp. The air outside my village always tasted clean.

I descended into the wild.

The fields adjacent to my home were mostly feather grass. Their tips were a slowly waving plane of mountain lion gold; such a creature, often called nagithanka, finds the grasses easy to maneuver, as its furs are a palette of the grasses themselves. Feather grass was often gathered to craft baskets, jewelry, or other products. It was also of interest to the traders from Rucost, who claimed it made excellent paper for books. Lucky for them, it grew everywhere.

Often, one would find feather grass growing at much greater heights, but near our village, the shorter variety was more common.

Further out into the plains stood scattered fields of ripgut. Traders from the south often wondered at such grasses, informing us that in their homeland, its kind was weaker and much shorter. They said that theirs was only as threatening as stinging nettle, but ours were more like swords sticking out of the ground. I thought that might be an exaggeration. That being said, there were numerous cautionary tales of children running through the plains without paying attention, only to find themselves bleeding everywhere, on every limb, panicked, lost, and in need of help. If one were careful, traveling through such fields was easy enough, though I had no intention of sprinting through the plains to find the truth in those stories.

The entire landscape before me was its current spectrum of ambers and browns because winter had just ended. Soon, the hibernating colors would emerge, and I would be hunting through a world of vibrant green grasses with plumes and flowers of every color. It would be nothing short of breathtaking. A private piece of endless, living art, tossed by the wind and admired by few.

I couldn't wait for spring. I hated the cold.

The wild animals had learned by now to keep a safe distance from our village, though the large herd of bison and the slightly smaller herd of oryx never strayed too far from the river. Thirty minutes had passed before I saw my first promising sign.

I glanced down and saw a trail shooting off of my usual path.

That's new.

This new trail cut through the main walking path I typically use. The grass had been pushed to point northwest, so the animal had obviously traveled in that direction. Leaning forward as I walked, I began stepping one foot over the other, trying not to widen the trail. Judging by the width of the disturbed grass, I predicted this creature to be a deer. Hopefully a stag. My family can usually use the entire deer before the meat spoils. If not, we could always share our extra. It would also provide antlers for trading.

I caught the first sight of intact hoofprints. It was large enough to be an adult, and the length of the stride reinforced my prediction. Though the morning dew can wet the prints and make tracking more difficult, these seemed fresh enough for my confidence. I continued on my path.

My hunter's ears were well-attuned to my environment.

Cutting through the rustling of the grass came the chirping of insects, waking up after a winter's rest; birds flying overhead, now that their prey had emerged at the precipice of spring; and, most startlingly, the snort of a bison, just a few feet to my left.

I froze.

Bison were a fine thing at a distance, but they were deadly up close. I crouched down and waited. The wind shifted just enough for me to catch the creature's hefty scent for the first time.

Seconds passed.

A massive patch of grass moved all at once. I imagined the creature, over half a ton, almost ten feet long. Soon, though, I had no use for imagination. A deep and guttural grunt rumbled from within the animal, followed by an irritated snort. The beast of a bison rose high above my crouched position. A deadly shadow fell over me as it blocked the morning sun from my face. I moved my head slowly to look and found myself staring the threat in the eye. Its coat glistened with the morning dew, and the horns pointed skyward. I only hoped I had not somehow angered it.

It pawed the ground.

My hope left me.

I took one side-step to my right, then a hesitant follow-up.

It began to follow.

Then it happened quickly. With incremental speed I stepped away, walked faster, and found myself sprinting hard on the thin deer trail, a massive beast of crushing weight close behind me. The trail turned hard left, and I ran with it. I could hear the bull tearing through the grasses, and my imagination came back to me as I pictured his horns lowered to strike. I could almost feel his hot breath against my back.

Knowing I could not outrun the creature, I leapt right, rolled, and saw the bull hurdle past at bone-breaking velocity. The dew on the tips of the grass sprayed into the air, catching the sun's rays, followed by mud flinging upward as the bison halted abruptly and turned. With little faith in my hiding place, I jumped to action.

I stayed low to keep my head under the cover of the surrounding grass. I carved through the stalks like the wind itself, a mountain of a creature surely not far behind. I only once nearly lost my footing as I ran blind to the shape of the earth below me, but regained composure and turned swiftly left. I knew enough not to run a straight line, but bison are much more agile than one would assume.

I had nearly forgotten how fast I could run.

As the large creature pounded toward me, I looked further ahead.

A huge patch of ripgut stood just seconds before me. It had grown in a crescent around my trajectory, shaped like the bull's horns, or like the sickle whose blade it would imitate if I continued forward. It was the mouth of death looking to swallow me whole unless I could slow my pace.

I cursed my own idiocy and weighed my options, my mind racing faster than my feet. The last maneuver I had pulled granted me some distance, though the creature could doubtlessly close it quickly. I had just a few moments to think.

I could jump to the side, as I had been, and try to get behind the bull. This may earn me a few seconds to run east before he can turn around.

No. He was still a distance away and could alter his path if need be.

I could attempt to run through the ripgut and hope the bull had better sense than I not to come through it.

No. The cuts may be brutal, and if he followed me anyway, I'd be held tight by slashing stalks as the massive beast came crashing in.

I couldn't go through the ripgut like this. That was the truth of it. I had to stop and hide. If I could make my way slowly into the ripgut, I might have a chance.

I turned my foot and dug it into the dirt. My hands grasped the feather grass around me for balance and a quicker stop, steadying my feet as I looked toward the charging animal.

I could see the bull's horns above the amber wall ahead of me. The ripgut was to my right, to my left, and behind me. I positioned my feet and waited.

It barreled closer.

Every instinct in my body screamed at me to run, but I knew I must wait.

Then, as its breathing became audible over its thundering charge, and I saw the grass part before the raw force of its power, I leapt to the side with all of my strength, hoping to have the creature between me and the ripgut rather than the other way around.

I landed face-down, my hands to the dirt. My body bounced slightly from the impact of its hooves only a few feet away.

Then, it stopped.

Silence.

I heard its angry breathing as I tried to quell my own. My hands were shaking. I waited as the seconds went by.

The bull began to pace.

Is this thing actually hunting for me?

This was not normal. I thought back to the deer trail. What could I have done to offend the bull so greatly?

Just then, a soft and infantine cry sounded from where the chase had begun. It was muted by the distance, but it was unmistakably the sound of a newborn calf.

This isn't a bull. It's a mother.

I must have ventured too close to its calf. It had likely claimed that spot as its home for the night. The bison in this region normally wander through a large territory, but when they lie down for the night, they get defensive — especially if calves are present. It may have been simply defending its home. I decided that I was lucky not to have agitated the entire herd.

Still, something about its behavior was strange to me.

But I had no quarrel with this creature. Standing up halfway, I took stock of my surroundings. The bison was a good twenty feet away, and it was nearer to the cutting grasses, searching the ground with its hindquarters to me. While I considered my next move, a moment of stillness passed.

The bison's muscles were powerful. Her shoulders were bustling, and her veins were thrust to the surface and accented by the sweat in her coat. Her eyes were wide, dark, and above all...

She's terrified.

It was not only anger that drove this beast to action, but fear. The blood that pumped heavily through her body was moving for the cause of preservation. Every breath of air filling her great lungs pushed her massive frame outward in an ode to her home and to her child.

Somewhere inside myself I felt a pang of sympathy. It is good practice for a hunter to respect the beasts that are his prey, but here I actually felt bad for the creature. This newfound feeling worked to calm me, but I knew the urgency of the situation was far from over.

I laid back down and began to crawl as quietly as possible. I inched closer toward the ripgut to the east, at one of the points of the patch's sickle shape. Several times I heard the mother move or snort in frustration, and I wondered if she felt as trapped as I did. Eventually, my fingertips grazed the base of a blade of ripgut grass, and I waited.

I became suddenly aware of my body. My fingertips, calloused from the weight of my bowstring, could still sense even the softest touch against the dirt. My arms, strong from labor and from pulling arrows to my cheek, could have been crushed like baked clay under the bison's hooves. My legs, taught to endure the running of great distances, throbbed with torpor from the sudden chase. My chest heaved from breaths that were difficult to keep quiet.

My fingers found an arrow from my quiver, and I rested it across my bow. My last plan of avoidance — although I knew I truly had no intention of killing the beast. It'd likely take more than one arrow, and I could never haul all of the meat back before scavengers took the rest. Her hide was too thick to cut quickly. It would simply be a waste.

As my breathing lessened and my body calmed, the bison strode away and back to its child. At a distance, it seemed small, removed, and hardly dangerous.

I sat with my back to the blades and breathed freely.

ONCE THE SOUND OF THE BEATING IN MY THROAT HAD FADED, A wave of calm washed over me, and my acute senses returned. I couldn't quell the wonder pulsing through my mind, still reeling over the near combativeness of the bison, and how I had never seen that behavior before.

Above me, something fluttered clumsily over the ripgut and to the other side. The tops of ripgut were much lighter than the lower parts of the stalk, which prompted them to move quite a bit in the wind. If there had been any wind at that time, I would have dismissed what I saw as a trick of the eye; it was a fairly still day, however, and the only thing that flew like that was a plump grouse.

I was a bit shaken from my previous encounter, but my stomach reminded me that I still needed food.

I stood and turned toward the patch of ripgut, taking careful stock of its shape. If I were patient, I could weave through it slowly and emerge at its opposite edge. From there I could see where the bird had gone.

The tall grass was flat, the cutting edges relegated its sides. One could press against the grass on its flat side and keep the cutting edge of the blade away. I raised a finger, and with its pressure, the ten-foot stalk of grass pushed to the side, making my first step possible. The grass pressed back with an uncomfortable weight, but I knew that if I were slow, I would make it through unharmed.

It was here at the edge of the patch that I heard a muffled noise ahead of me, on the opposite side of the ripgut. From my position, I couldn't make it out.

I pressed forward, leading with the flats of my hands, pushing the living blades to the side of my path. Surprisingly, once I was fully inside the patch, sounds from both sides became muted. I had never had cause to realize this before, but ripgut must be a natural absorber of sound, like snow in the winter. The lightweight tops wavered back and forth above me as their base shook back into position behind me. At almost halfway through the patch, the sounds on the other side were becoming a little clearer.

Voices.

I stopped moving and listened more closely. Though the timbre of those speaking was clear, what they were saying was scattered and made no sense to me. I tried to rationalize the situation and considered my choices. I could make myself known, although I was in the middle of something most would deem unwise. I didn't want the whole village to know I'd combed through ripgut for a lousy grouse. Going back out the way I came seemed like a waste of energy at that point. I decided it best to stand still and wait.

The speakers were difficult to make out, but one voice was distinct. It was a man with a high voice that sounded more like the hiss of an angry hognose snake. I gave in to my urge to pry, and I cursed my position for keeping me in the dark. It would at least give some indication as to the length of the conversation if I could only hear them clearly.

Just as I wondered how long I'd be stuck there, the voices stopped. The unmistakable sound of a horse's trot struck up and just as soon faded away. I pushed further into the ripgut and soon found myself at the edge of the patch. A long breath escaped my lungs as tension left me.

Stepping out slowly, I searched for signs of people. A set of boot prints sat in the mud, and the unmistakable stride of a horse was trapped in its surface as well. The prints were of an unshod horse, which is typical of the people of Kalanos. But who had been all the way out here?

Suddenly, movement to my left caught my eye. I crouched quickly, but as I did, my right arm struck back instinctively to grab for an arrow in the quiver at my hip.

A burning sensation tore up my arm.

I'm sure I shouted, but the pain deafened me for a

moment. It felt like I was nine again, falling on the steel arrowheads the Rucosti traders had brought in. Glancing down, I saw blood pouring off of my elbow in an arch.

I carefully felt my arm with my left hand. The pain seared again, and I stifled another shout. Bracing myself, I did it a second time. The ripgut had torn my arm almost from shoulder to elbow. I reached down, grasped some soft soil from between the stalks of ripgut, and packed it into the cut on my arm. Gatsi had told me never to do that unless the threat of blood loss was greater than the potential infection from the dirt. I hadn't given it much thought at the time. Though the stream of blood was slowing already, the wound seemed severe. I turned to observe the stalk that had cut me, and on its edge hung thick droplets of my blood. I hoped it was satisfied.

I can't go home empty-handed.

Surely what I had seen had since been scared off by my shouting. I brought my bow over my head and gave the string a test pull. I managed only an inch before the pain was too much. After settling my bow back across my torso, my left hand closed into a frustrated fist.

Wounded, alone, and without dinner, I walked the fields back home.

6

UNTOLD STORIES

"Much like their use of takar, the northern towns in our own kingdom have adopted Kalanosi holidays to add spice to their lives. Our Autumn Eye is followed closely by the Kalanosi Week of Kanta. The pine, sun, and moon that are strung up for Autumn Eye are now accompanied by a bison's head. How long until one culture becomes another?"

— EXCERPT FROM BRALLIC SEVERIN'S
*KALANOS: A STUDY OF PLACE AND
PEOPLE.*

"I didn't come here for your fiction. You've made it obvious that you've seen something of my past."

"It was not my intent—"

"My question is how."

It was the chieftain's voice that questioned Gatsi in his hut. I stood in the shadowless noonday sun, just near enough to his closed entryway to hear the conversation. If it had been anyone else's home, I would have earned a few curious glances, but my presence at Gatsi's hut was the equivalent of seeing a fish in water.

I knew it was none of my business, but I couldn't remember a time before when I'd ever heard Gatsi speak defensively. Mostly, though, it was my need for medical attention that kept me leashed to the doorway. Blood still trickled down my arm, though a bit less than it had when I'd received the wound. Try as I might to tell myself not to listen, fascination turned my ear their way, but common sense kept me from barging in. I told myself it wasn't my fault they were speaking loud enough to be heard.

"When you asked for my guidance all those years ago," Gatsi responded, "I explained why we were to settle here."

There was a brief pause as the chieftain waited.

"And?" he asked. I could almost hear Gatsi shake his head.

"When you've spent your life studying story, they tend to find their way to you."

"Enough with the cryptic answers." His voice swelled. "Tell me what I want to know!"

There was the sudden sound of breaking clay.

"Perhaps," replied Gatsi — and I heard the slightest bit of fear in his voice — "since this story has been made clear to me, it won't need to find its way to the ears of others."

"I would hope that is the case," the chieftain said resignedly.

The sounds of the chieftain's movements were quick and careless, and I had only a moment to back away from the entrance before he stormed angrily from its opening, stopping for a second to eye me suspiciously. His face was swollen with anger, red like one big fresh bruise. He seemed ready to hit someone. The beastly man padded off toward his home.

I walked in to find Gatsi carefully picking up small pieces of a clay jar, its herbal contents spilled across the floor.

"How much did you hear?" he asked without looking up.

"Enough to know you never answered his question."

"And do *you* know the answer to the question?"

"No, but—"

"And do you know what it was he came to speak of?"

"No, Gatsi."

"Good. Have you come back empty-handed? Didn't you kill anything?"

I raised my left hand to show him the spoils of my hunting trip. "They put up a fight, but they were no match for my aim." I dropped the wild onions on his table and reached into a clay pot of fresh water.

He watched me wash the soil from my lacerated arm. A deep breath escaped him as he quelled whatever strong emotion he held, and he stood to face his shelves. "Honey or charcoal?" he asked.

His hands held my options before me. I took the crushed charcoal with my left hand, assuming the honey was more difficult to obtain. After lifting the cloth from my right arm, I pressed the black dust against the wound. My journey back to the village had kept the bleeding from truly stopping. The charcoal would slow the bleeding a little, but it was mostly to prevent infection. With a lifestyle such as mine, one takes every precaution to stay healthy.

I noticed that instead of putting the honey back, Gatsi turned from me and brought up his sleeve, revealing a series of deep scratches on the skin, and rubbed it in.

Did the chieftain do that?

After a brief study, I decided they must have come from something else. It looked fresh, but not the type of mark one would get from fighting. It was a strange wound — like something rough had gripped him hard and for a very long time, though not unlike bedsores. I had seen some similar marks on him before, and always assumed they were a consequence of his alchemy. Or, knowing him, some sort of tea-related disaster. I had asked him before, but he always gave me answers I never fully believed. I thought it simpler not to ask this time.

Instead, I filled him in on the details of my morning in the grasses.

"Ripgut," he started in, "is just trying to survive, you know. It's not unlike that deadly bison of yours. That creature attacked you to protect its child, but more deeply, it attacked you to protect its species. Even prey animals can be moved to violence. Ripgut is sharp so that the seeds at its summit will spread before they are eaten. Birds have trouble landing on it, and nothing bigger than an insect would succeed at climbing it." He cast his eyes up at me from the teapot above the fire. "Apparently, it also works against unobservant hunters." He bent down and started to wrap my arm in white cloth.

"Something startled me, though. I was—"

Gatsi waved my reply away and continued. "Nothing that is natural hurts unless it has a right to. The world is full of the motion of survival — everything moves to the rhythm of avoidance."

"So you won't tell me what the chieftain wanted?"

"No," he responded, "I won't."

Speaking of avoidance.

This was much less than the verbose old man usually said. Surprised and searching to find something else to mention, I stayed silent for a moment. I seemed to remember having something to ask him, but I couldn't remember what.

"You traded for a book," Gatsi finally stated, "with the merchants. What is it?" His tone was flat, and it was difficult to tell whether he disapproved of the action, or if he was failing to be conversational.

"A Rucosti study on Kalanos. I've skimmed through most of it and read a few sections more deeply already."

"Remarkably quick for someone who's only been reading for a few years," he said. He looked interested, the first shred of emotion he'd shown since I came in. "What have you read so far?" he asked.

"Well, besides the author regarding the people of Kalanos as "Iket", which I'm pretty sure is some sort of insult, she starts off talking about our legends and beliefs."

"'Iket', hmm? It's definitely condescending. Consider, though, that they don't see Kalanosi like you and I — we are two of a kind, in a way. They tend to run into more..." he glanced at the door, "...barbaric individuals. Nothing new you've learned, then?"

"Well, I'm still a little rough on Rucosti, so I could be missing a few things. The Wahkeen strove for power in the sky after the Dalkhur shook the earth to shape, Dremma and Drakka made pacts to quell the violence of the nonliving and allow for life to spring forward, so long as the transaction of death occurred."

"Hmph."

"What bothers me — and I may be misreading some of it — is that she seems to be defining all of Kalanos by a single strain of legends."

"A people are often defined by their stories. Sometimes it's all we see of them."

"But when we spoke after the story of Kivik in Kibara,

you said that story is told by other Kalanosi clans and originated in the Inkwood. With so many stories in common, how could they possibly know the difference?"

"Well, they don't define *us*. At least not often. I doubt most people in Rucost or the Inkwood could tell you the difference between Achare and Sree, in the same way a stranger couldn't tell you the difference between you and your brother. Except a few feet of height and some muscle, of course."

"And a predilection to stack rocks." I mulled his words over for a few moments. "She moves on to talk about the animals."

"Why did you select for a book containing information you already know?" Gatsi asked.

"Well, I guess I didn't actually know if I knew everything. As it turns out, I didn't."

Gatsi raised an eyebrow.

"The author discusses the presence of oryx in Kalanos and says they didn't originate here."

"You knew that."

"Yes, but I didn't realize how far they'd traveled. Over a thousand miles...that's far beyond the distance any Kalanosi clan wanders."

"It can be difficult to imagine such a distance."

"Why would they do that?" I asked.

"You tell me."

"Well," I conjectured, "I suppose some kind of predator could have driven them away. Something new might have come to the region."

"A sound thought."

"But the bison we used to follow...they've stopped here too."

"Yes. They have."

"Why would two competing herds tolerate each other in the same spot?"

"You know the routine. Attempt the answer first."

I searched for answers in my tea. "It could be that they value the river, but...that doesn't seem like the answer."

"Hmph."

Gatsi rose from his seat and led me outside. Sometimes I suspected he didn't know as much as he pretended, and just left me wondering when he could. We sat on the ground, enjoying the sunlight and watching people around us. Just as the handle of my bow is worn from the thousand grips of my hand, the padded dirt outside his hut made for surprisingly comfortable seating. He was convinced of the therapy in drinking a slow cup of tea while the rest of the world busied itself around you.

"The sections detailing the clans of Kalanos were mostly just obvious or filled with arrogance. I did enjoy the talk of Sree lineage, though," I mentioned.

"How so?"

"The author listed their leaders, who succeeded whom, and how. I knew they were violent, but I never realized they cull their leader solely based on who killed the last one. I can't imagine living in a clan so reliant on violence."

"Yes," Gatsi replied flatly, kicking a piece of broken clay with his foot. The chieftain's steps must have brought it out with him. "Can't imagine."

"Interesting that the Sree and Wahto have different reasons for staying in one small region of Kalanos," I continued. "The Sree have access to a nearby river — like us — and there are more distinct plants that they come across in their territory. More useful plants, anyway. The Wahto, though, they treat their region as a sacred land."

"Indeed they do." It almost seemed like Gatsi had a bad

taste in his mouth. He kept glancing around to his left, where my plateau, the chieftain's hut, and a group of playing children were all in view.

Looking around for something to say that might interest him, I finally gave in to my curiosity.

"Gatsi," I started, "what are those marks on your ar—"

Before I could finish the question, we heard shouts from the villagers.

7

ON THE HORIZON

*"Idiot nephew tipped a candle over, burned up half the wagon.
Glad we were in the water and not the tinder!"*

— TENAL

Whenever I break into motion in my village, my eyes travel to
find my plateau in the distance. It is a habit of the hunter to
navigate with landmarks when possible. But when I left
Gatsi's hut, my vision had been drawn to something new on
the skyline — a horizon that rarely changes.

A hulking mass of black plumes poured from the top of a
hut just on the edge of the village.

Fire.

My legs struck earth, propelled by instinct, and I began
sprinting to the source. I skirted around pockets of people
and ignored the fearful comments flying over my head.

"What's happening?"

"It might spread!"

"Whose is it?"

Their words traveled, yet there they stood, their muscles

bound by the ropes of fear. I dashed forward, estimating the fire to be just north of my own hut.

I leapt over the baskets of vegetables Makawee had been collecting. Their colors were bright against the sludgy black smoke on the ground. Looking up, I had just a moment to duck around Tashi's tanning racks, which were flanked by a tangle of children running from the commotion. Weaving through the small crowd, I found myself dodging a moving horse — one of Ikoda's, I think — and stepping to the left of a quickly approaching Avid. Once I passed him, he dug his heels into the ground and turned to follow.

"Mother is at the river!" he shouted behind me, nearly tripping. "Is it ours?"

"No!" *But it's close.*

"What are we doing?"

"I don't know!"

The chase in the grasses came back to me as the black smoke that slithered along the dirt rendered me blind to the earth under my feet. But this was different. I knew the dirt below me.

This dirt and dry grass was my home.

This fire could end it.

I passed another hut, and the thick smoke was now to my knees, pumping past like a surging river if it were slowed in time. It was then that I came to its source.

Traders from the south often spoke of distant mountains that spew fire and smoke into the sky. Before, such things were only seen in my mind's eye. Now, I saw a hut that could not be far from reality.

Tella stood outside her home — now a pillar of fire — her face paled with the fear of abandoned hope. Her skin, the color of the Shivers in our legends, stood in stark contrast to the blackness that swirled around her. She looked like a corpse.

I could not hear her voice over the roar of the fire, but the shape of her words seemed to say, "no, no, no..." over and over.

"Rennik!" Avid yelled from beside me. His eyes met mine and matched the fearful tremble in his voice. I pushed him toward the center of the village.

"Find water!"

He ran. I turned back to the scene.

The path of the smoke was strange to me, though I only had a moment to consider it. The stream rose straight up from the fire, but sank suddenly down to the ground, creating the rolling black tides at my feet. When I think back to that moment, I can still see the smoke rising from the cooking fires in other homes in the village — straight up into the sky.

That was not my focus at the time.

I lunged through the smoke and wrapped my arms around Tella's waist. A wall of heat hit me as I reached her. How she was able to stand so close to the flames is still a mystery to me. She did not resist when I picked her up.

I didn't have to step into the blaze to feel the burning in my arm. The diminutive weight of Tella's body was enough to rip open what little healing the laceration in my arm had undergone. I shouted as blood saturated the bandage, and I pushed myself forward, away from the fire.

She was limp, like the venison I was accustomed to hauling in. I would have thought her to be dead if she weren't whispering softly.

"It's okay, Tella. It's over," I said to her.

"It's over," she replied.

I made my way to the edge of the smoke and sat her

against a wooden box near my home. I started to turn away from her, but her hands suddenly grasped my head and pulled it close. She held my face and looked deep into my eyes.

Hers were an amber brown and focused like a bird of prey. They contained a depth greater than that which I knew in my own, and I felt for a moment as if I were pulled toward them. I wondered if she saw the same depth in mine.

"Over," she repeated, then added, "...all of us."

After a moment of surprised stillness, I wrenched myself away from her and dashed back toward the disaster. Avid stood, a resin-treated basket of water in hand, shouting commands at his friends.

"Not just on the fire, around it, too! Forget saving the hut, it's going to spread!"

Voices were nearly indiscernible this close to the crackling inferno. A quick scan of the huts revealed to me the presence of Gatsi.

He stood wide-eyed, his jaw clenched, sweat beading on his face. As a few people from the village ran past him to help, he turned and walked purposefully toward his hut.

The boys began wetting the ground and grasses around the fire, and several other people began throwing large handfuls of dirt at the flames.

I stood back, confident there would be a swift end to the fuel among Tella's possessions. The fire, the smoke, her gaze upon the flames. It all seemed so intentional and yet completely without reason. I watched the few things I could still see inside blacken slowly, turn from wood and hide and rope to an indiscriminate mass of lifeless charcoal.

All things back to the dust, I found myself thinking. *And she was almost part of it.*

When the fire had run out of things to eat and failed to

leap the wet cage the boys had made of the surrounding grass, it died with diminishing breath, small flames twitching and popping within the black. I noted her collapsible fan sitting just outside the range of the flames. It was no longer white, but a deep charcoal gray, stained by the disaster it had witnessed. As I studied the rubble, something caught my eye where her cooking fire would have been.

A few animal bones, difficult to notice as they were charred against the ashes, lay in the middle of the scene. I had no idea what to make of it.

Out of breath and coughing heavily, I turned to walk back to Gatsi's. Crowding before me were the villagers who had watched the fire burn. Few who stood in that line had lent their courage. They spoke quietly to each other, leering at the charred remains of Tella's home.

"Think he's warm enough now?" It was an aged, croaking, and spiteful voice that said it.

I pushed past them with a bit more force than was necessary.

The leather flaps that covered Gatsi's entrance fell heavily upon my back. I was angry, and I wasn't sure what else to do but find him again. I began to speak but cut myself short as I realized I didn't know what I wanted to say. Gatsi stood facing his table, muttering something to himself. I paced around him to see what he was doing. It was quiet, save for the muted voices of the passing villagers outside.

The contents of his shelves were scattered on the floor as if he had burst into his hut in a hurry to find something.

His voice was kept low, and I could not hear him. Almost all of the words he spoke made an "o" shape with his mouth. The muttering poured out of him with a slow, single-syllable persistence.

A copper plate sat on the table, and on its edge was

angled a small sort of dowel that burned at the tip. From it rose a continuous wisp of white smoke. Gatsi's eyes were fixed on its red-hot point like a hawk scanning the grasses. It smelled vaguely of laurel. He was trembling slightly. I thought to speak but decided against it. I remember my father once telling me that patience earns a truer view.

Then, as I waited, the thin trail of smoke caught my eye.

It was changing.

The white stream, snaking toward the ceiling, turned suddenly into a steady column of black smoke. In the next instant, the column collapsed, and the black smoke rolled across the base of the copper plate.

Gatsi's mouth opened, and the first, nearly inaudible sound of a word escaped its precipice before it halted. His eyes seemed to search the smoke for answers that I couldn't see.

Finally, he filled his lungs with the air of purpose, and as he looked away from the table, the smoke returned to normal. His eyes were distant.

"Go to Tella. She is to stay with your family. I will retrieve her in the morning."

I began to speak, but he cut me off with a sharp look. I eyed the white stream of smoke. My questions would have to wait.

"BUT SHE STILL SMELLS LIKE SMOKE!" AVID CRIED OUT TO MY mother, beleaguered by the insistence of neighborly duty.

They had been arguing for the better part of an hour. Well, more accurately, Avid had been slinging unanswered complaints for the better part of an hour. It was almost impressive how my brother could swing from young man to child with a simple change of scenery. The topic of Tella's temporary stay in our home did not resonate well with him. My mother coughed. The smoke couldn't have been good for her.

Tella sat just inside of our doorway, and her eyes had been locked on me for far too long. It was unnerving, but I thought it might be her silent way of thanking me. Regardless, I decided I didn't need to be present for Avid's poor attempts to dissuade my mother from opening our home. It had been a stressful day. I wanted to breathe free. I wanted to be in the wilds.

Gesturing for Avid to get his hunting gear, I told him to meet me after a few moments in the grasses for an evening of hunting, needing still to prove Chaska wrong.

I struck out toward my plateau.

At the top of the ridge, I turned to look at the scorched mark where Tella's hut had been. Surprisingly, I saw her outside my home. She must have followed me out of the hut, and she stood at its entrance now, looking toward me with her unwavering stare.

I turned and continued walking. Dropping down the ridge and well into the feather grass, I took a deep breath of air, hoping it could clear some of the smoke on my tongue. I spread my arms wide and stretched, spinning slowly to see my surroundings.

Tella stood not fifteen feet away.

I'm sure I looked ridiculous as I froze mid-spin, my arms still outstretched.

I took a step back in the direction of my plateau, and she took an equal one.

"Tella," I said slowly, "I've really had enough of being chased through the grasses today. Do you need me to help you with something?"

She stared.

My discomfort encouraged me to turn and walk away, but I didn't move. Her feet combed through the grass. I let her approach.

"I'm sorry if my family is a little hard to deal with right now."

She stood much too close and looked at me in the same way she had earlier, after I had taken her from the fire. Her arms were dreadfully thin, and as she wrung her hands, I noticed how broken and dirty her fingernails were. Her fingers twitched and played among themselves. I made a mental note to tell Avid that, oddly enough, her breath smelled of raw meat.

For a few moments, she was silent. Then I heard her speak above a whisper for the first time in my life.

"Took family." Her voice was melodic and high, but eerie, like a nightjar whose percussive call was smoothed out. I felt the hair on my arms rise a little. I hesitated, then spoke carefully.

"Took your family?" I asked.

She nodded.

"In that storm? Who took your fam—"

"Storms," she spoke before I could finish my thought, "wings, Wahkeen, mother and father, clouds." She struggled as she spoke without repeating my words.

I had stared more deadly animals in the eye than most people my age; I'd seen many strange things, but the tone in Tella's voice uprooted my comfort like nothing else.

"Clouds? Or...birds took your family?" I asked.

"Took. Showed signs. Showed clouds. Wind words."

"Words in the wind? They spoke?"

She shook her head. "Words in clouds. Words in...fire."

I couldn't find a response.

She clenched her jaw, like a frustrated child recognizing a missing word in their vocabulary.

Like lightning, her hands reached out and grabbed my face. She pointed it violently toward the top of the ridge.

"See," she commanded. She let go and walked toward the ridge. Soon, Tella had disappeared from my sight. Her fingers still skittered like centipedes in my memory, like she had plucked and crawled over something inside me. I collected myself and was about to turn away when I finally saw what she wanted me to.

A trail of smoke, coming from a normal cooking fire, was visible rising above the ridge.

Not wind words, I thought. *Smoke words.*

Within the gray smoke rose a short mass of black. It fell while the rest of the smoke rose.

Just like Gatsi's. Just like Tella's hut.

I ran to the top of the ridge. Tella was nowhere to be seen, but the hut's occupant stood confusedly at his doorway.

But what do they say?

I shook my head and left to meet Avid in the grasses.

8
BIRD'S EYE

"You have trouble thinking against the noise of the village? Imagine living in a Rucosti city. They must not think at all!"

— RAISHA

They say a domesticated dog has difficulty returning to its ancestral state in the wild. Its time with man renders within it a dependency that cannot be met elsewhere; they say, however, that it also gains a certain intelligence from its observations and taming. A domesticated dog has the ability to sense human emotions and communicate simple ideas to its master, while its wild brethren, having never met with man, could never grasp at such foreign, invisible things. It was vital for domesticated creatures to develop these talents.

I thought tentatively of Tella's childhood story — the one Gatsi had told me — and wondered if her supposed time with the Wahkeen could have led to something similar. If this really happened to her, had the Wahkeen shown her something invisible? Were there things in this world above the understanding of normal men, something only *tamed* men can see?

Creatures often hear things men do not. Dogs bark and take shelter when storms approach, even before their owners see it coming on the horizon.

What did Tella see in that smoke?

This was all nonsense. Tella was crazy. I refused to let myself believe in her delusions. But then again, I had just seen smoke behave like it never had before...

The day had certainly taken its toll. I had been chased by a creature that is known only to pursue short distances. Gatsi had refused me information when I thought he would always tell me all he had to say. I had saved an insane woman from a fire. I came close to believing in something that could not be.

A long breath escaped me. This plateau was my place of solitude, and it always delivered a sense of calm to me. The animals on its crown, where I currently stood, were naive and complacent. I had noticed years ago, upon discovering the trail to the top, that no predators hunted here. The normal prey animals — grouse and rabbits, among others — were fattened and reluctant to leave. This was a fortunate home for them. A place of peace. I had decided then never to hunt here, as it seemed somehow wrong to violate their sanctuary.

Looking out at the plains, I saw the wind running circles through the bright tips of the feather grass for miles — not the motion of survival, perhaps, but the motion of the world. Something greater than life and death. The stalks bent to the will of the wind, just as the thick forests far to the west ripple with its passing. I couldn't decide if the living grasses seemed bright and careless, or simply helpless to that which passes.

I placed my bow beside me and removed my leather shoes to free my feet.

I hung my toes over the edge. Hundreds of feet below, rolling hills and pastures billowed out like a sea of amber grass and dirt. Normally, the wind at this height makes the trip up difficult to accomplish, but today there was a warm and gentle breeze coming from the west...

9

AFTER THE DUST

"...though even when considering the fairly peaceful clans of the region, one cannot help but define Kalanos by its more notorious groups. Spend a little time in either of the bordering cities in Rucost, and you'll hear Dellimairan or Periloean citizens speaking of Kalanosi as the bogeymen of their nights. Few discuss the brilliantly made boats of the Rask or the complex philosophies of the distant Kazel.

Wander too far from the city, and it's said you'll be run down by a savage Sree Charger. Stay in the grasses a little too long after sunset, and you'll be kidnapped by a Wahto Shaman, according to urban legend. The merchants who brave the grasses to visit the more amicable clans have shared that some Kalanosi are just as terrified of the larger clans as we are, and go to great lengths to avoid crossing their paths."

> — EXCERPT FROM BRALLIC SEVERIN'S
> *KALANOS: A STUDY OF PLACE AND*
> *PEOPLE.*

I once saw a bison flip a man over his head. He'd been gored under the shoulder and broke his ankle on the fall — lucky, since any animal that big could've killed him. For the man, it was a sudden horror, but to anyone watching it was a fairly simple cause and effect. The man had put himself in the bull's path and had unintentionally aggravated him. Larger beasts are a force of nature. It's expected of them to make a show of it.

The chieftain flipped the flaps of our tent over his head as he pushed his way in.

I stood away from the hut. He clearly hadn't seen me, and after something like this, like the dust that covered the village now, his visit only meant one thing.

Walking back from the plateau, I had planned our escape. I'd take one of Ikoda's horses but leave her the Rucosti silver and some tools to compensate. My mother would ride the horse while Avid and I walked in its trail, limiting the amount of grass we set down. We could cover almost twenty miles by morning.

The chieftain wasn't part of the plan.

Reluctant to join the man I was to abandon, I looked around. I saw a side of my people that hadn't truly shown itself in years. The fighters among us, like the creatures who only come out at night, were combing around the huts.

The voices of my mother and the chieftain rose from within. Even from outside, I feared this was one bull I couldn't avoid. Then they emerged together, walking with purpose toward the center of the village, past my brother who sat silent and still in the short grass.

"Avid," said my mother as she passed him, "if you see Rennik, tell him to meet us at the chieftain's hut." But Avid did not seem to hear. My brother's face was covered with the dust that had passed, and he peered out from a hand-shaped spot over his eyes. He must have covered his face when the cloud came through. It gave him the seeming of a warrior's paint — a colored handprint across the face — though his was reversed. Between his fingers seeped something pulpy and red. He opened them to reveal what was once a cradled collection of mulberries, now crushed by nervous and shaking hands.

I approached shortly afterward and placed a hand on his shoulder. "Clean your face," I told him, "and go collect your things — quietly. I'm going to get you and mother out of here. Tonight." I stepped away, then back again. "Only the essentials. Don't bring anything you don't need."

Avid nodded slowly.

"It's been years since I've had to ask for something of this magnitude," said the chieftain, continuing the conversation with a collection of almost twenty people. I was nestled secretly against his hut, watching one-eyed through a sliver of the back entrance. "But the omen has found us and cannot be ignored."

"It isn't dust we fear," said a middle-aged woman named Satra. She was a close friend of the chieftain and a highly-regarded thinker. "Just because the wind blew our way doesn't mean the warring clans are coming."

"Dust clouds like that find a stopping place eventually. If it came through us, they aren't far off." The comment came from Ciqala as he stood up, and I was surprised to hear such a level-headed response from him. A few older villagers, Chaska included, nodded their heads as he spoke. "But we're all wondering the same thing. Is one omen going to frighten us away from our home? Do we cower and run any time the thunder rolls?"

"Sit down. Let rational people speak," said my mother.

"Yes, let's set emotions to the side for a moment." The voice belonged to Malik, an impressive huntress a little older than me. She was one of the few I considered to be better with a bow than I was, and she'd been one of the best hunters in our village for years. There was a sullenness in her that I found familiar; her sister and father had left to hunt far to the west when she was younger, and they'd never come back. "We know it takes a movement of hundreds of horses or bison to cause something like that. The elders have already determined bison an unlikely cause since there are no herds within a few days we know of besides our own. What remains undetermined are if it's the Sree or the Wahto on the move, if they have any interest in us, or if they even know where we are."

"It's been ten years," interjected the chieftain. "It may be wise to assume they know. Gatsi, you've been quiet. I hope you trust us with your thoughts."

It took a little shifting of my position, but I could just make out Gatsi's face among the other older villagers. He stared at the fire in the center of the hut for a moment before speaking. "There is danger in this omen. It is a simple truth, though no less difficult, that there is no reason to remain here. We are a moving people."

"No reason?" asked Ciqala indignantly. "The ridge protects us from violent winds. You can stand on that same ridge and see countless reasons to stay in the faces of the oryx and the bison. You can ask the salmon and mussels in the river for reasons to stay—"

"The Achare did not sprout from this soil," replied Gatsi calmly. "This is a wondrous place, but we must be wary of its spoiling effect. There are bison and mussels elsewhere. We are not a people with anchors, but, if you would let me finish, I think it wise to stay — *if* it is possible."

"Send Ciqala to the grasses," demanded Chaska, sour-faced as always. "Let my grandson lead a scouting party to find signs of danger. Let him prove that our home is a place to stay, not to leave."

"I must admit that I share Chaska's want of eyes in the horizon," said Satra. "We need more information."

My mother chimed in. "Why waste time? We should leave now. And even if we send scouting parties into the grasses, let us be wary of Chaska's intent. The purpose to send our strongest people into danger isn't to justify a want to stay but to determine the weights of each option. You will bias our people into thinking our home should be kept at all costs."

"Bias?" Chaska snorted. "Yes, Raisha, I am *convincing* them that this ten-year sanctuary is the best place to be."

"Raisha is right," Malik cut in. "We cannot assume staying is the right choice, but we cannot assume that leaving immediately is in our best interest either."

"You'll leave in the morning, then." The chieftain's voice was stoney, his decision immovable.

"And my grandson will be happy to lead," interjected Chaska.

Satra shook her head. "You should take notice when people ignore your comments," she told him. "Malik should go. She's one of our best."

A few people walked by my hiding spot behind the hut. I slouched slowly downward, making myself small, and rose back up to my sliver of sight a moment later. I felt absurd, but I hadn't seen my mother in this sort of situation before.

"Of course," Malik was saying. There was a convincing

layer of confidence wrapped around an appropriately apprehensive core. "I'd be interested to see what's out there."

"And you, Ko?" the chieftain asked. I hadn't seen the man at all, which was baffling considering his size. I suppose one can overlook a mountain when they see only an inch. Ko was a mammoth man with python arms and a boulder's disposition. It seemed that all of the strength in Dremma's world could be found in him. He did not speak in response, but in a short span of time the chieftain nodded responsively to an unseen corner of the hut.

"And why is Raisha here? Don't tell me you'll be coming along," Chaska said mockingly to my mother. He turned to the chieftain, speaking critically. "She has her family's weakness. Drakka's bad bones."

"I could not expect her to do something so dangerous," the chieftain replied softly. His voice was laden with something new to the conversation, something like shame, or embarrassment, or grief. "But I do ask something great of her."

Guilt, I thought. *He can't even look her in the eye.*

My mother stared at his face, eyes wet and shaking with a hopeless anger.

Finally, he returned her gaze. "Rennik is a talented navigator."

The mention of my name crashed against my plan to flee, and my own guilt was all that remained of the wreckage. There was a soft tug at the leash around my neck, attached on the other end to my home.

"He's hardly left the village," she replied.

"I can see it in him. He has his father's predilections. You know that as well as I do."

"You can't be serious," Chaska interrupted. "The boy's not

safe. No one could've come back from that river. *He's not safe!*"

"Quit your cowering, you old fool," growled my mother.

"If we can set our superstitions aside," said Satra, speaking to herself as well as Chaska. "What we see of Rennik is impressive. We shouldn't ignore him."

"He navigates the grasses without hesitation," said the chieftain. "He puts weight on his shoulders to take care of his family. These are the qualities not just of a great hunter, but a great leader."

"*Leader?*" shouted Chaska as he stood up. I could just make out the corner of a grin on the chieftain's face. "You'd tell me he'd make a great leader when his mother is here to speak for him? Where is the boy? Busy sulking in the grasses? Scowling at his elders?"

"Sit, Chaska," the chieftain responded. "Ciqala may be my nephew and your grandson, but there are no leaders in a scouting party, neither Rennik nor Ciqala. Rennik sees what needs to be done and does it. He does not operate under pretense. A mind like that is vital in keeping a group of people level-headed. He'd be good for them. Last I saw he was out hunting, but this meeting couldn't wait."

I didn't expect such praise from the chieftain and Satra. My guilt had become less a leash, more accurately a hole I couldn't climb out of.

There was a silence, made angry by Chaska and apprehensive by my mother.

"Raisha isn't just here for her council," the chieftain continued. "She's here that we may ask her for her son."

"No one asked for my grandson," said Chaska.

"No, you've been trying to throw him into the grasses yourself," said Satra.

"Any good Achare should be ready to do so."

"Raisha lost a husband to the grasses," said the chieftain. "I couldn't ask Rennik to go without speaking to her first." He stood and turned fully to Chaska with flinty eyes. "I am finished with your council. Leave us."

The old man stood from his position, cast a knowing look to his grandson, and spoke with a quiet fire.

"He's won over the young people in the clan. Quietly so, but I've noticed. They've forgotten what it means for a child to survive like that, the omen such a person becomes. You can't deny your worry of him. The Wahto leave their children in the grasses just for that reason. The ones who come back aren't just lucky. They're *powerful*. You put that boy in the scouting party, and I guarantee he'll be the only one coming back."

With that, he stormed through the front of the hut. I was suddenly concerned that some of the people inside might exit the hut my way, that they might see me for the fool I was admittedly being. But I remained where I was, momentarily entertained by the fact that Chaska considered me "powerful". Everyone in the hut seemed to ruminate on what he had said, eyes downward, old worries revisited.

The fire in the hut shifted slightly as Chaska left, its flames pointed momentarily toward me. Gatsi's eyes flicked up toward the back entrance and back to the floor.

The chieftain turned to my mother, dismissing Chaska's outburst. "Your husband was courageous in these trips."

"He told me he was terrified," she readily responded. "Every moment of the trip, he expected an arrow in the neck, because out in the grasses you don't know what's behind the next screen of stalks."

"Then why did he go? — And don't say it was because I made him, Raisha."

"No, it wasn't just that," she admitted. "He said that terror, that fear of the unknown...he said it stays in the grasses because we keep it there. He didn't want his sons to grow up in a place where that feeling came into their home, too."

"There are many children here now. Many who need to be kept safe. We cannot treat Rennik as a child much longer, Raisha."

"I have not kept him a child," she said, adding a bit of venom to her voice. "I've kept him *alive.*"

"As we all must do for each other. I am not here to take your son from you. I simply ask you—"

"You can't," she said flatly. "You *can't* ask me. He's old enough now. I hate that it is so, but it's unwise to deny the facts in front of me."

"And what are the facts, Raisha?"

"That he's old enough. That he can decide for himself." She hesitated. Her voice shrank from restrained anger to something resigned. "My son has been fetching food for his neighbors since he could pull a bowstring. He's loyal to the Achare whether or not they're loyal to him. The fact in front of me is that he has far too much of his father in him to say no to helping our people."

A stone. That's what my guilt was. A massive, crushing, immovable stone the size of the Dalkhur's hooves, pushing me slowly into the mud, sucked into the earthen bowels of the world with neither rope nor light.

Malik looked at the fire, clearly feeling, like several others, that she no longer belonged in the conversation.

"Your thoughts, Gatsi?" asked the chieftain.

"You were chosen for your powers of reason. Your decision is sound, as always." I knew a deflection from Gatsi when I heard it, and I felt as though the chieftain could sense it as well, but he said nothing to address it.

"Satra. Gather your party and head west in the morning

with a northward bias. Ciqala. Malik. Ko," the chieftain continued. "Make sure the others in your scouting party are approached and briefed. I'm sure Banar will join without hesitation. Speak to Macha, too. Ikoda will take a little convincing. As for Rennik...I suppose we'll see."

A few statements more and the meeting was over. Three scouting parties would be sent at sunrise. All were dismissed from the hut.

The reality of the journey at hand fell over me. A trip with Ciqala was sure to be dreadful, but with Malik there, things couldn't be so bad. Even Ko, who hardly spoke to anyone besides those his age, would be trustworthy. He was a friend of my father's when he was alive. That being said, company was one thing: surviving the journey...

"For someone who so loves to listen at a distance, you hid yourself quite terribly." Gatsi craned over my hiding place, head and shoulders eclipsing the stars in the sky.

"Did anyone else notice?" Gatsi had seen enough of me as I grew up. I didn't feel entirely embarrassed that he'd found me here.

"No, I don't think so."

I stood cautiously and joined him in a walk toward his home.

"You can expect danger," he continued, "both in the grasses and in the people you're with, which is exactly why you must distance yourself from them. Remember that you are an individual. You happen to be very important, although I don't think you know it quite yet. If it looks at all like death is coming, you must know to leave them. You are not responsible for them. Your life is your own."

"Then I should leave now," I whispered, if not to convince myself. I glanced around for prying ears. "*We* should leave."

"No." His response was terse. "There is safety in the herd,

at least for now. The chieftain thinks we may be threatened. You must run and find out for us. Just remember that you're no good to me dead." With that, he left me and continued his walk.

MY MOTHER WAS WAITING OUTSIDE OF OUR HOME. SHE MOVED forward and studied me carefully as I approached.

"You're the cleanest one in the village," she managed to say.

"I was out when it came through."

I searched her face for some indication as to what she was really thinking, but as I looked, her hard eyes softened, and her jaw clenched and trembled, quaking the foundation of her sharp cheekbones. Her brows furrowed like a gathering of clouds.

"You'll need some sleep," she told me knowingly.

"I might stay up a bit. I want to think."

She looked suddenly older than I had remembered. In my memories of her, she still has smooth, sun-darkened, and tawny skin over sharp features, but as she eyed my shoulders, her wrinkles were made more obvious. Her smile always seemed natural, but as she forced one upon herself, I wondered how many had been sincere, and how many had been a mask against the thin lines of worry she wore upon her face. A single strand of gray hair hung down on her cheek. Her hands trembled.

Her fingers pinched at the hide of my sleeves. "You've nearly outgrown this," she said. "I'll start a new one for you. It'll be ready by the time you return."

"His nephew…" I said, mumbling. "Ciqala might not be a good man, but with all of us together…"

"Thinner material, since the spring is coming."

"Are you listening, mother?"

"I'll use some nicer dyes." Her thumb snuck a soft circle over my heart. I decided not to push her further.

"I'd love that," I told her. "I'll have to break it in when I come back."

With that, she turned from me and began locating the tools she needed — first an awl, a skiving knife, then others wrapped in a small bit of hide — and busied herself with her hands. It was something to keep her mind on the offensive, as she stabbed at raw leather rather than having to shield herself from old horrors.

I pushed through the entrance of our hut to find Avid half-hidden behind a growing pile of possessions. The light of the cooking fire cast odd shadows against it, making the objects he was handling unrecognizable. I cleared my throat.

"The Rucosti merchants didn't leave us any carts, you know."

"We don't need a cart!" he said, clearly free from the stupor he'd been in before the sunset. "We can grab a saddle as well as a horse, and pack the saddlebags, and use some drag sleds."

I nodded patiently. No matter the concerns of the moment, Avid never failed to entertain me with his plans.

"You've got your bow," I pointed out.

"Yeah. Might need to put an arrow in a grouse on the way," he said, sticking his chest out and deepening his voice a bit.

"Is that salted venison?"

"Well...I might miss."

"And...is that a mound of clay?"

"How do we know we won't need to build a stronger hut foundation or a forge like Graff's?"

"You thought we were building a new village?" I asked. Of course he'd dream of coordinating an entire town's construction.

"Wait. 'Were'? What do you mean?"

"I'm sorry, Avid. Change of plans. You're staying here for now."

He seemed excited — this was his lifelong home, after all. But his curiosity took over. "What made you change your mind?"

I REMEMBER WHEN MY FATHER HAD COME HOME ONCE, AFTER A trip north with his scouting party. I had seen him before my mother had. He was outside of our hut, shooting at a target made from hide stretched over thin tree branches he'd stuck in the ground. In the center of the hide was a yellow spot, made with a dye rendered from feverfew — a type of daisy. We liked to gather them not only for the bright colors they made but also for their capacity to ease an aching head.

Normally, the yellow-dyed feathers tailing my father's arrows would be clumped on the center mark, but as I looked out of the hut, I noticed some of the arrows hadn't even hit the hide.

I had asked him why. I had never been afraid to ask him anything. He held up the bow in his hands and showed me.

It was a Sree-style horse bow, different in too many ways to notice all at once. Unlike the bow I used, which was cut from a single piece of birch and shaved down with a drawknife, this bow was a composite of different materials. My father pointed out to me the strips of sinew on the back of the bow, which faces the target, and the thin layer of bison horn on the belly, which faces the shooter. The material between those two layers was a wooden core. Overall, the bow was shorter than what my father used, but upon pulling it back it seemed to be weighted similarly. The thing was nothing novel, simply different from that to which we were accustomed.

I watched him pull an arrow back with it and noted the shorter draw length, which is to be expected with a shorter bow. My father told me that he had found the bow on his latest expedition. He explained how other clans used a ring on their thumb to pull back the string, and how they shoot on the right side of the bow.

I remember asking him why only some of the arrows in his quiver were fletched with his usual yellow-dyed feathers. He said when you go hunting, it's better to know who shot what. On scouting trips, when you've got more than animals to worry about, sometimes it's better not to know.

It was years later when I realized what he had meant by his words.

I was young, and didn't think to ask how he had obtained a Sree bow and thumb ring.

We spent the evening learning to shoot all over again.

10

A DIFFERENT BREED

"The animals, the plants...seems everything out here wants me dead!"

— TENAL

We left at sunrise. The journey would be made on foot, as horses might betray our need for subtlety. It seemed strange, as our way of life is so centered around them, but according to the veterans in the clan the big animals would only draw unwanted attention. With me were some of the best fighters my people could spare, and I felt out of place among them. I hoped I could count on their aim to save my life.

I looked over to Malik. She had short, dark hair and exacting brown eyes. Her posture reminded me of an elegant creature — perhaps a strong doe — slender, regal, and powerful. She was a few years older than me, and I continually waited for the day when my skills caught up with hers. Until they did, I would lean heavily on my observations to learn how to out-shoot her.

I didn't know the other four as well as Ko and Malik. There was Macha, who wore a spear and bow, and Ciqala and Banar, who had a sword and bow each. Ciqala and Banar shared the pale-brown hair color of a badger. They were both of a strong physique, though Ciqala stood a bit higher, and held himself as confidently as ever. After my experience with Banar earlier in the week, I wasn't overly eager to travel with him. Ikoda had come along, and with her were four of her dogs. Ikoda was a breeder of many animals, and I trusted her creatures would serve well. She carried with her a simple bow and a club.

We journeyed quickly for six hours, and the grasses were already nearing our heads. I found apprehension in the fact that my bow was losing utility as the surroundings turned to thicker and taller obstacles. We were quiet, and I studied my allies. Banar and Ciqala seemed to be battling for the front position, as if it were a position of pride. Ciqala cast his eyes around as if he had no fear, though I noticed his gaze often landed on Malik. Ko was expressionless. Macha seemed skittish.

"They make me nervous," said Ciqala, motioning toward the dogs. They were darting through and around us, sniffing the air and watching the space between the grasses. Ikoda looked as attentive as they did.

"They're more alert than you are," she responded, "and they'll see danger coming before we could."

Banar lowered his flattened hand, and one of the dogs happily pressed its head into it. "At least they're friendly enough. They probably make for better conversation than Macha, eh?"

A few of them laughed, and Macha made a plucking motion from his chest with his thumb, which was considered a rude gesture among my people. The dog licked Banar's hand.

He continued. "Will they protect us? Seems like they take more interest in licking than fighting."

"They'll tear you up just as soon as let you near 'em. Just wait 'till they think you're a real threat."

"I guess you're not a real threat — you can't even scare the dog," Ciqala interjected, looking back at Banar and laughing. "Maybe it's *your* fighting we should worry about, huh?"

There was laughter again, and even Macha gave a soft chuckle as he swatted at the yellow-dyed cloth that hung carelessly from his spear.

"I'd take that as a challenge," Banar spoke with a sudden soberness.

The group became quiet as Ciqala gauged Banar's response and found it to be serious. His brows came together, and he spread his arms out wide.

"Think you can put me down, dog food?"

"Dead as winter."

Their chests inflated with an animal intimidation. The swell to the bellicose caught me by surprise. With one motion, Ciqala and Banar stepped aggressively to each other, and just before making contact, they were flung backward.

Ko stood behind Ciqala, Malik behind Banar, each holding an aggressor back with strong arms and annoyed expressions. The dogs turned sharply and growled at Ko and Malik, their ears flattened and heads low to the ground. Malik looked suddenly concerned. Ko seemed unmoved.

Ikoda shouted with sudden authority. "Down!"

The dogs assumed a sitting position but eyed the action closely.

"I told you, the dogs'll fight quick. They like the idiots," Ikoda said, gesturing to the would-be brawlers. "They want 'em safe."

With the situation diffused, Ko and Malik let their captives go.

Ciqala stared daggers at Banar, who broke eye contact first. Ciqala seemed to have interpreted some sort of silent victory.

Like grandfather, like grandson.

Malik glared at them. "We have a job to do. You fight again, and I'll cut you up faster than the dogs can. If you want to concern yourself with anyone's lethality, let it be mine." Her eyes broke through them already.

Ciqala and Banar turned their attention out at the grasses and continued walking. Malik's words were as precise as her arrows, and I was impressed by her ability to command. But as their eyes left her, I heard her curse under her breath, watched her step slowly to make space between herself and the two quarrelers.

The day brought with it little more to note, save for the moment when Ciqala was momentarily lost, and only briefly tried to find us before calling out in fear. Malik and I exchanged glances, and I had never seen someone roll their eyes so forcefully. Even Ko seemed to grumble something under his breath. I was convinced Ciqala would get us killed. We travelled through varying kinds of grasses, some short enough to brush against our knees, some that grazed the bottom of our chins, and some thicker like the bamboo that grows far to the west.

But time had passed, and the sun, hanging low as it set, cast our long shadows back down the hill we had just climbed. I was expected at all times to know exactly where our home sat in the horizon, but my thoughts become mired in it, jealous of those who stayed behind. I looked east, in the direction of the village, to think of Avid trying to hunt on his own, and my mother foraging what she could among the grasses — wild turnips, berries — or fishing, knowing the salted venison we had may not keep much longer. We were deep into the wilderness. I even had seen a few large patches of trees as we walked west, but the excitement of discovery could only mask the prickling sensation of lands unknown.

As my eastbound gaze imagined the unseen cooking fires of my people, something else caught my eye.

The tips of the feather grass, leaning to the effort of the western wind, were interrupted in their gentle motion. A fissure in the amber waves bowed abruptly to the north and south, an invisible blade cutting at the base of the hill.

Something was combing the stalks toward us.

At first, there was only one. Then, as I was about to speak up, I saw a second, and a third.

Malik's hand on my shoulder thrust me from concentration. I spoke hurriedly and kept my voice low.

"Something is following us."

Just as her head snapped forward with urgency, the movement slowed and stopped. She squinted her eyes.

"An animal?" she asked, without looking away.

"Or several. I saw at least three. We haven't exactly been subtle."

"Think it could be an enemy?" Her fingers silently found the nock-ends of the arrows at her hip.

"No. Whatever they are, they're moving too quickly to be people."

"Those damn fools are going to get us killed," she grumbled. She motioned vaguely in the direction of Ciqala and Banar. "They've spent too much time in the village."

"They've been quieter since you threatened them."

"Give them time. They tend to stay stupid."

I allowed myself a smile and returned to the concern at hand. "We have numbers on our side. Predators won't typically attack a group, even if they're hungry. If we were unarmed and weaker, I'd worry. Predators can sense a good time to strike, but we should be fine."

"Good," she said flatly, turning to make eye contact. "I trust you." She walked back toward our companions, and I watched her go.

There was a simple truth in her voice that made me believe her.

"It's a bit blackened, isn't it?" Ikoda's question was the first thing spoken for a long while. She picked a hair from the charred meat and bit into her dinner.

Macha shrugged lazily from over the fire. "I'm not Kinran. Can't make everything delicious."

"It doesn't have to be delicious. Just *edible*." She was still chewing on her first bite. It was, I'll admit, a bit tough.

Malik sat beside her, eyeing the closest dog nervously. She'd been a bit apprehensive since they'd jumped to defend the others so readily.

"Don't worry. This one's the bootlicker," Ikoda said, grinning comfortably. "Wepe. She hardly lets me be."

"She must be in charge of the rest, then," Malik responded.

"Oh, not at all."

"No?"

"*I'm* in charge of the rest."

Malik acceded. "Well, yes, but—"

"No, really. The dogs have to know I'm their chieftain.

You know that. But the second-most powerful creature in the pack doesn't grovel. The others that bicker, that fight. It's them that are the troublesome ones. Wepe here, she's smart enough to let me stay in charge because it means she's protected if she's a favorite of mine. Not one of the others nips at her. But the other two here," she gestured toward two large, roughed-up dogs, "they're torn up. If they didn't have me, it'd go something like this: One-ear would challenge the bigger one, and they'd rip each other to pieces figuring out who's best fit to lead. They'd hurt, they'd suffer, they'd be bloody. But Wepe's smarter. She'll step back and let those two fight because avoiding the hurt, the blood...that means living. Say one thing about Wepe — she's a survivor. Oldest one in the pack, but you wouldn't guess it. Hardly got any scars on her."

"She doesn't look so weak," Malik observed.

"No, not weak. Just smarter. A different kind of instinct. There's a respect to that, I think, but mostly she's just dependable that way."

"But if she decided to turn on you? If she decided she was tired of you in charge?"

"That's the beauty of animals. They're predictable. They're not people, Malik. People are the impossible ones."

I wasn't in the conversation, but from my place a few strides away I found myself nodding in agreement.

Malik became quiet then, and I recognized the look of someone who had turned inward. Avid had similar moments, but much more frequently. He would say everything he needed to say about a hut or a hand tool, then talk himself up to some new idea on his own and dwell on it for hours. Whatever it was Malik was considering, she seemed to exit the conversation for a while.

~

"Macha, definitely," answered Ciqala.

"You sure?" pressed Banar. "Ko could do some damage."

"That doesn't mean he'll get angry first," said Ikoda. "He could dead-pan give you one to the face. With those fists? Grasses'd take you."

They had been speaking in hushed tones, apparently unaware that I could hear them. It was nearing time for the first watch, and they were putting off sleep for a little conversation.

"How about that Rennik boy?" Banar asked.

Ciqala's face tightened a bit as he thought. "He'd talk. Not sure about anger."

Ikoda spoke up after thinking for a moment. "His mother might seem quiet, or terse at least, but she snaps if she's pushed. Bet he's the same. Stalk don't come far from the seed."

Banar looked up at me from across the fire, as if just taking notice of my presence. The soft light danced on their faces, and the darkness of night shrouded the world behind them. "Rennik," he called, raising his voice a bit.

I looked up.

"You talk?"

"Occasionally."

"You fight?"

"Haven't yet."

"Any good with that bow?"

"Very."

Banar gestured toward Macha, across the camp, just within earshot. "Maybe you could teach this one to shoot. He can't hit the grass from the ridge."

Macha looked up from his dinner and spoke with venom.

"I could shoot that tongue from your ugly mouth if it'd please you."

The trio cheered in unison as Macha became red-faced, settling their debate. I wasn't sure what we had to gain in angering each other. I made eye contact with him, and I answered his grimace with a knowing smirk. Had Macha been of more intimidating figure, his response may have been rightly interpreted as a real threat.

Heavy footsteps introduced Ko to the firelight, and I looked immediately to the group, anticipating their poor decision.

"Hey, Ko," started Banar, but as he formed the biting edge of his sentence, he paled, and his jeering expression fell flat. First him, then Ciqala, until finally all three of the taunters donned fearful faces. At first, I wondered what Ko was doing to scare them so quickly, as I was looking at his back. Then I realized that the group was looking past him, not at him. I followed their gaze to the edge of the firelight, past the boundary of our makeshift clearing.

A set of eyes, like two gleaming opals, reflected the firelight from within the stalks of grass. They were low to the ground, and the firelight was just enough to illuminate the hungry maw that hung under them.

Nagithanka.

Then, a second set of eyes.

Though I had seen plenty of them in my life, I'd never seen them hunt in packs. The Rucosti called them cougars. The older Achare sometimes called them nagithanka, meaning ghost cat. Regardless of what one called them, the threat they posed was serious. I suddenly felt terribly cold, like winter had returned for just an instant. As I surveyed the peering beasts, a third set of jealous eyes showed itself.

Just then, Ikoda's dogs assumed their low growl as they

prowled forward, flattening their ears and brandishing their teeth. They held their heads low to the ground, instinctively protecting their throats. I turned my head, expecting the dogs and fire would be enough to keep the mountain lions away, but there they remained, lightly obscured by the thin grass between us. The stalks threw long, alien shadows across their faces, and I felt truly worried that they would attack. I reached slowly for my bow, keeping my eyes trained on theirs.

It was dead silent.

I heard the creak of a bowstring under tension. Macha had quietly nocked and half-drawn. He pointed an arrow at the predators.

The staring eyes blinked. The beasts backed away and disappeared without so much as a sound. The dogs relaxed and licked their lips.

"Good dogs," whispered Ikoda with a tremble. I looked to see her hand around a long knife on the ground.

A great baritone voice spoke, and I flinched.

"Did you have a question?" Ko, having not moved save to watch the mountain lions over his shoulder, stood over the three men with a quiet strength.

They bowed their heads toward their dinner and said no more.

I LAY WIDE AWAKE AND ALONE. THE REST OF THE NIGHT WAS quiet, and I wondered if the entire trip would be a constant, competitive journey from snide comment to angry quip, over and again until we headed back home.

Home. I was fixated on the image. We had been gone for

one day, and my nerves had yet to settle. I loved to wander, but the circumstances here were new to me. My home was threatened. This was no simple hunt, the end of which had me returning to the village with food on my shoulders and a grateful family in my hut. This was a different kind of self-preservation. The survival of us all. Would I have to fight before I returned home? Was I capable of that kind of violence? Thoughts like these kept me awake. I made a mental note to chew some chicory root in the morning — I had seen some at the edge of camp, and though their purple flowers had yet to bloom this early in the year, I knew their stalks when I saw them. They would calm my nerves a bit.

For now, I had first watch. One of the dogs kept me company, and he lay next to me as I sat with my back against the equipment. The other dogs and scouts slept near the modest fire, comfortable on their thin sleeping rolls.

They reminded me of the animals on the crown of my plateau. They felt safe, well-fed, and completely at ease.

I slowly ran my hand over the dog's back. It was soft — well-brushed, even — but under its softness was a strong and rigid spine. I felt its ribs as its lungs filled, then exhaled to shake the short grass at its nostrils. Its dark animal eyes reflected the fire, just as the mountain lion's had.

The dog had recognized me as a food provider; that much was certain. It rested its weight lovingly on my leg. It had so quickly learned to protect me, and all I'd done was given it a scrap of my food. Was it an emotional attachment it felt, or did it just recognize a cause-and-effect relationship between affection and food? I scratched behind its ears and a long, shameless smile stretched across its face.

Then it shot up in a panic. I had my bow by the time it found its feet. Like before, it flattened its ears, and for a moment I wondered if the beastly mountain lions had returned.

The grasses stood tall, unmoving, silent, and waiting. A lone crow spoke in the distance, a single syllable swallowed by a hungry night.

There was no deep, threatening growl from the dog's chest. Instead, it whined softly and slunk toward the others near the fire. The dogs, each of which were now awake, crept toward the right side of the clearing as if Ikoda had spoken in sharp discipline. They were submissive — apologetic, even. They set their heads on their paws and lay within the protection of their sleeping people. All six of them.

I tried to follow the dogs' gaze, but they all pointed in different directions. Frustrated, I realized they were moving away from the left side of the camp. I looked in the only direction they weren't.

A new set of eyes stared in toward our camp.

Six feet from the ground.

By the dying light of the fire, I could discern neither shape nor color from that which held the eyes, but its form seemed to be that of a man.

Slowly, those eyes turned to look at me. I stared back at them.

An intense cold rushed through my body as if I'd been plunged back into the frozen river of my childhood. It stole the breath from me, and my chest felt tight and icy. I was trapped in my own motionless body. I struggled for air like a drowning man, my lungs working to expel water that was not there. I wondered if this is how it felt to die.

The fire erupted into tall, screaming flames. It shared its deep red with the eyes that killed me slowly.

Then, they were gone.

I gasped for breath. My fingers dug into the dirt as I came

back to land. The heat of the fire felt like life anew, though it wasn't the inferno from a moment ago.

The dog returned to me. It licked my hand and lent me its strength, but I couldn't feel anything.

My fingers were blackened and cold.

And for a moment, it was silent.

11

SOMETHING IN THE DARK

"Rucost has made a habit of exiling privileged criminals. Lowly market thieves may lose a hand, an embezzling guild master will be fined or imprisoned, but if one can elevate himself in the eyes of the nobility, the recoil to their grand crimes may be a lifetime sentence in the wild expanse of Kalanos."

— EXCERPT FROM BRALLIC SEVERIN'S
*KALANOS: A STUDY OF PLACE AND
PEOPLE.*

My heavy breathing and the sudden roar of the fire woke the others. I saw their various reactions through panicked vision, eyes wet from my sudden intake of cold air. Banar and Ciqala rose and reached for weapons. Ko stood high and strode to the edge of our clearing, staring out into the grasses, tense like a fist. Ikoda's dogs threw themselves against her legs, and she worked to calm them. Malik was the only one who stepped to me. She had to repeat herself before I realized she had spoken at all.

"What happened?" she asked with urgency.

I was so fixated on my breath that I did not respond.

There was a short silence, filled only with my breathing and the tension of the others.

"Rennik," Ciqala began, "did you add anything to the fire?"

"No," I choked out.

Ciqala looked doubtfully at the flames that were bigger than those of the modest fire we had made, though their color had returned to a normal shade.

"Somebody," I finally said, quieting myself as I caught up with the breaths I had missed a few moments ago. I pointed at the edge of the clearing. "There."

Malik sprung to Ko's side. "An enemy?" she asked in a whisper. There was the sound of knuckles tightening around weapons.

"I think so. It was staring in at the fire. It...it was like he strangled me."

Ciqala crouched down and inspected my neck. "No marks," he stated doubtfully.

"He didn't use his hands, he just looked in at me."

Everyone seemed to be thoroughly confused, and Ciqala took another look around.

"Macha is gone," he said. He turned back to me. "Rennik, Macha must have been up and walking. He's probably taking his business a healthy distance away. The man eats like a hound."

"No!" I responded quickly. "No, you were all asleep! I saw you all — Macha was just here — I saw him!"

"Just like you saw this enemy?" He spoke to me slowly, as if I were a child. "Rennik, we're not looking for one man.

We're looking for a horde. I think if we were close — and we're not — we would have noticed an army by now." He stood from his crouched position and addressed the whole group. "The boy probably fell asleep on his watch. Had a bad dream. Saw Macha and got confused." He turned to me again. "Next time you get a little scared, try not to wake us all up."

The rest of the group glanced severely in my direction, then settled back into their places.

I wanted to scream at him, to tell him that I had almost died, but it was obvious that my words would get me nowhere against Ciqala's hard reason. I would have shown any anger at all had I not been so overwhelmed with the night's events.

How could I explain to them what I couldn't explain to myself?

The group worked itself back into sleep with the exception of Ko, who began his watch. He sat and fixed his eyes on where I had pointed. At least someone was taking me seriously. I remembered that Ciqala was the only member not taking watch tonight.

I took another look around the camp and wondered when Macha would be coming back.

I realized then that I would have a sleepless night.

DAWN DREW WITH IT A WARM SUNRISE THAT LIFTED THE DEW from the tips of the tall feather grass quickly. The sun's dim morning rays speared through the stalks like little walls of golden light among the grasses that were starting to green for the first time this year. Birds were singing, and the breeze was light.

The state of my mind failed to match the scene at all.

"He didn't come back," I said sternly to Ciqala as he roused from his sleep. I had gathered more confidence in the night. "I know what I saw. Someone is out there, and they attacked me. And now Macha is gone."

Malik's eyes searched for Macha, and when she did not find him, she cursed under her breath. She began packing up hurriedly. Ciqala stood, his expression shifting as he tried to reason what had happened.

"He left," he said at last. "The coward. He went home. He must have seen you sleeping on your watch and left when he had the chance." He shook his head and began to help Malik.

Ikoda approached me, her eyes wide. "You sure, Rennik? You sure you saw someone?"

I clenched my jaw. "Yes," I said quietly. Ikoda reached down and wrapped her arms around one of her dogs nervously.

I walked over to where Macha had been that night. The sleeping roll he had brought along was gone, as were all of his possessions. If it weren't for my experience last night, Ciqala's claims would make sense; however, it was obvious by the amount of disturbed dirt that he hadn't walked away.

He had been dragged.

I searched the immediate area the drag marks led toward and found absolutely no trace of disturbance. No grass was bent or broken; no dirt had been moved. There was simply no indication of where to look next. It was as if Macha had simply disappeared.

It was Malik's turn to haul the large pack, and she was just heaving it up on her shoulders when I approached her.

"Malik," I started, "there was somebody here. I wouldn't say this if it weren't the truth!"

She eyed Ciqala from the side, and he studied her in

return. "Listen," she said in a hushed tone, "I don't like him any more than you do. He's...capricious. But he does make some sense. You just have to pick it out of the rest of his crap. I don't think we'd have seen any threats just one day from home, and if we did, it wouldn't be one man combing through the grasses. I'm not even sure one man can live alone out here." Her voice carried a soft, almost apologetic tone. "And to be honest, I'm tired of arguing with him."

"Tiring of an argument isn't reason enough to not challenge him. And he's got a habit of getting lost."

"That's why you're here," she said. "He swings a sword. You navigate."

"I also track; there aren't *any* footprints where Macha slept. He was pulled into the grasses by something. The tracks just disappear after that."

She considered this for a second. "Rennik," she said, keeping her eyes down, "I know you're nervous about everything, but you've got to stop this." With that, she followed Ko as he pushed through the grasses to the west.

There are certain invisible things between people, and like the unknowable spirits in Achare stories, one can only see the footprints of their existence. I felt there was something between Malik and Ciqala that I did not understand, but I couldn't place what it was.

I shook my head. I knew how it sounded when I told them what happened, but if they weren't going to have it, I wasn't going to push it any further. My vigilance here would have to be my own.

The days ahead would be lonely and maddening.

∿

"I CAN'T BELIEVE HE LEFT," BANAR SAID, REPEATING WHAT HE had been told earlier.

"I can," replied Ciqala. "The man never speaks. He was too nervous. Probably looking around constantly, on edge the whole time. Makes sense now that he's gone. Some men are too fearful for this sort of journey." He eyed me from the side.

Macha didn't seem to have a problem threatening you last night. If he had any fear at all, it wasn't a fear of you.

Leaving was tempting. It would be easier to travel without these fool fighters, but then again, there was the threat in the grasses, the aggressive mountain lions, and worst of all a missing fighter. Macha wasn't a huge Ko-like figure, but he could certainly hold his own. I feared for what had become of him.

"It's for the better," Ciqala continued, "I wouldn't want someone like that watching my back in a fight. Fighting in a group is all about knowing you can depend on the man next to you. You get good men, you won't lose."

"How are you so sure we'll be fighting at all?" Malik asked, piping up after a long silence. "We're a scouting party, not a warband."

"Scouting party, warband. Call it what you want — names won't matter much when you're forced to defend yourself. Hell, we could be sent to pick flowers, but as soon as we're fighting for our lives, we're no different than the group they'd call a warband." He shrugged with unearned confidence. "Sure, our intent right now isn't to seek combat. But when it's you and a man that wants you dead, the only thing on your mind is coming out on top and alive."

"Our scouting parties," Malik continued, emphasizing her words, "haven't been attacked in years."

"Our scouting parties," echoed Ciqala, "haven't had to

look for an entire horde in years. Face it. We're not looking for a new herd of bison. We're not looking for a lone man in the night. We're looking for an army that could run through us like a spear through hide. If and when we find evidence, chances are we'll find a fight." He glanced back at me. "One way or another."

Subtlety really wasn't his strong suit.

Malik looked like she wanted to say something else but decided not to. She appeared to have truly given up on him. The sun, filtered by feather grass, hit her in beams, the little walls from this morning having stretched upward with the day's passing. I found myself staring, noting how strong her shoulders were from shooting. She stepped higher on the hill, and her brown eyes scanned the plains beyond its peak. Her gaze leapt among the moving landscape like a hawk searching for its prey. I didn't know what to say, but I knew I wanted to talk to her.

She turned and saw me looking. Embarrassed, I glanced away. I moved to look into the grasses and ran my fingers over the back of my arm, studying the scar that was forming. It was still tender, but Gatsi was right; it was healing quickly. Its potential hindrance to my shooting worried me, though I had been able to provide the grouse and rabbit last night by only pulling my bowstring back to my chin. To truly heal, however, I knew that I must avoid overexerting myself.

"I'm worried about my arm," I said after what felt to be an awkward tension. "It still needs time to heal. I know I was brought along to track and help hunt, but I'm not sure I should use my bow until this gets better."

"Makes sense to me," she responded. First I was making claims she thought were false, now I was shirking my duty. I couldn't imagine how little she thought of me.

"Do you think you could hunt for tonight?"

She smiled. "Tell you what. You take my turns with the pack, and I'll hunt until you're better." She began letting the pack of supplies down from her back.

I smirked. "Sure."

I made to pick up the pack and found it to be much heavier than expected. For some reason, though, I didn't want my struggling with its weight to be noticed.

Malik waited to watch me pick it up and scoffed before striding forward. I wanted to smile, to hope she might not think I was crazy. But as I tried, my eyes fixed warily on Ciqala instead.

I was in an open field without an enemy in sight, but with him around, I felt like a cornered animal.

12

THE FOOTPRINT OF ERASURE

"...but perhaps the most terrifying of all creatures in the Kalanosi mythos, more so than their Shivers or Wahkeen, are those who imposter their people. There is, in the old legends of several clans, a nameless and insidious being who will insinuate itself into the midst of man, wearing a deceitful skin in order to appear safe. Legends vary in regards to their motive, but they seem to range from means either violent or somewhat benevolent, though always mysterious.

My sources are unclear as to the extent to which Kalanosi Iket hold their legends to be true, but as in reaction to our own superstitious beliefs, one must occasionally wonder at the kernels of truth in even the strangest of communal fiction."

— EXCERPT FROM BRALLIC SEVERIN'S
*KALANOS: A STUDY OF PLACE AND
PEOPLE.*

During Ko's watch, in the midst of a reluctant sleep native to fear-filled nights, my mind fled the deadly wilds and alighted happily back home. I dreamt of Avid, sneaking to the river to spy on Gatsi, his young mind spinning fantasies to ward off boredom. I dreamt of my mother, plucking away at well-treated hide, patiently crafting a shirt for me and keeping an eye on Tella, and Tenal, pushing his oxen toward the southern horizon, the corners of his mouth propped up by the stacks of silver he's made. I dreamt of a strange man with the voice of a hognose snake, hidden behind a lethal veil of ripgut. When I finally did wake, I found little comfort knowing there were just as many mysteries at home as there were out here in the grasses.

Two days passed with little change. Malik and I hunted, Ciqala thought out loud, and everyone else mostly kept to themselves. There was a tension hanging over Malik, Ko, Ikoda, and me. We had exchanged anxious glances throughout our trip as the unexplained absence of Macha planted its seeds of worry, but with no trail of his to follow, we were powerless to find him.

I wondered how much Ciqala would have to speak to convince himself that nothing was wrong, or how much Banar needed to hear. People do strange things to avoid uncertainty, even if it means ignoring real possibilities.

The next night had passed without incident, though on my watch, which Ciqala and Banar almost didn't let me take, the dogs had acted strange again. They had flattened their ears, stayed low to the ground, and whined while sticking close to a sleeping Ikoda. I had seen them scare off three nagithanka, but there was something out there they truly feared. Apprehension encouraged me to stave off sleep, but it came anyway. I had woken the following morning with a start.

The next day was filled with Banar complaining about the smell of smoke. I didn't smell it, and I had trouble believing that his nose hadn't yet gone blind to the smell of our campfires. But even Ko seemed to meet his claims with a certain silent wariness, as if to agree that the scent was there.

We set up camp on the third night. As I settled into first watch, Ko sat himself next to me.

"You should speak more," he said in his quiet baritone. "Those who don't speak leave room for others to do so. Those who speak more find their words often heard. It's why Banar follows Ciqala so closely. His talk gives him the seeming of a leader. He should not be a leader."

"You think I'd do any better?" I asked him doubtfully.

"Yes. I do. You are practical and cautious. He ignores threats. He spoke of depending on good men. A good leader knows his men are his best resource. That means his doubt in you is a weakness by his own standards. He fears you are correct. He is no better than those in the village who wish they could ignore the dust."

"And what about you? You don't doubt me, then? You believe what I saw?"

Ko looked out into the darkness. "I've followed good men with strong minds deep into the grasses before. This isn't the first time someone has...seen something strange. Ciqala doubts a member of the group. You trust your senses. I tend to think better of people like you."

"Then why don't you say something? Why should it be me when you've got experience out here?"

"I'm not a man of words. I like my axe. I'll defend my people 'till the dirt takes me. But I'm no leader."

"I'm not sure a revolt is a good idea here."

"Revolt isn't the right word. Not a revolt. People should be led by those they prefer. He goes uncontested and thinks himself correct. Can't revolt if there isn't a real leader. Just natural competition."

"But I've spoken against him already. What else do you suggest I say?"

Ko shrugged. "I'm not one for speaking. The words will have to be your own. You'll just have to say things in a way he'll understand."

"I think the only thing he understands is anger."

"Hmph."

"This trip will only last a few more days. We'll be back soon, and when we are, the only leadership we'll have to worry about is the chieftain's. I can go back to living my own life. I'll never have to talk to Ciqala again."

"I wouldn't be so sure." Ko stared across the fire at our sleeping companions. "That kind of pride can be hard to kill."

"How so?"

"You've met his grandfather."

I nodded. Chaska was hard to forget.

"His great-grandfather was an ass, too. As was his father. Their family has produced two chieftains and a dozen entitled asses. The family acts like they deserve something better than everyone else. Your father and his fought constantly. I usually stepped in to stop it. This time, I think I better let nature take its course."

"Is that why my father and the chieftain didn't get along? Because he butted heads with the chieftain's brother?"

"No. The chieftain is his own man. Dremma gave him brains."

"You want me to fight Ciqala? Is that what my father would do?"

"What I want is for someone reasonable to make the calls."

"And you think that's me?"

"Well, it's not me," he stated, eyes boring deep into Ciqala's sleeping body. "And it sure as hell isn't him."

"They've got spears longer than their horses, and they stain the fletching of their arrows with blood."

"Haven't they got swords, too?" Banar asked between bites of venison.

He and Ciqala were taking their watch together. I lay on the ground, waiting for the sleep that had been eluding me for the past few nights. Banar dug into the dirt by the fire with his sword. His eyes were focused on the ground; Ciqala's slipped to Malik's sleeping figure now and then. Though Ciqala's eyes traveled a well-worn groove to her, I didn't feel as though his attention was born of romantic attraction. As they went on speaking, I considered the things I'd yet to know.

"Some do," Ciqala continued. "The bigger clans have a broader reach, see, and they have access to settlements closer to Rucost where true blacksmiths are more common."

"They trade for weapons there?"

Ciqala laughed. "Trade? No. They take. They train in mounted combat with their blades, but mostly they stick to bows and spears. Takes a wicked accuracy to shoot from a moving horse, you know."

"They all train like that?"

"Well, many do. The Sree and the Wahto are the biggest. They're the two that fight with each other constantly."

"Everyone knows that," Banar interjected.

"But think. They've got the best fighters — they have to, otherwise they'd be taken over by the other. But smaller clans like the Yohri and the Kor just have a small portion of their people dedicated to a sort of militia. Kind of like us."

"Think anyone from the Achare can shoot like that?"

"From our village? Unless Kinran gets into a cook-off with the barbarians, we can't put up much of a fight. Maybe if we had the right leadership, we could hold our village where it is."

"What makes them so much better?"

"Some say they've got demon's blood in them, and it's why they shoot so quickly, too. But that's an excuse for the simple-minded."

I could practically feel Ciqala gesturing at me.

"In all my scouting trips—"

"How many is that?" asked Banar earnestly.

Ciqala seemed irked by the question and ignored it. "I've never really noticed what makes them better. Truth is, I don't think any one of us knows. Most who'd see it surely wouldn't live to tell the tale."

"Actually," I rolled over, "they shoot from the right."

Surprise was written on Ciqala's face. It gave me pleasure, but unlike him, I knew how to hide my emotions.

"What do you mean?" asked Banar.

I turned and grabbed my bow and an arrow.

"Normally," I instructed, slapping an arrow against the left side of my bow, "an archer shoots from the left. It aligns the shaft of the arrow in a straighter line with the dominant eye. Unless your left eye is better, of course."

I aimed for a piece of venison hanging from the makeshift rack in our clearing. The pain in my arm was searing but speaking out against him was worth it. My eye fixed on the target quickly and I thought about letting go, but I decided against ruining the food. Instead, I jerked my shoulder a bit as if I were going to shoot. Ciqala jumped at the false shot, and I almost couldn't hide the reciprocal smile on my face.

"But archers from some of the other clans, like the Sree and Wahto, shoot from the right."

I slid the arrow against the right side of my bow and pulled back below my ear. I held it there for a moment, then slowly let the pull go.

Ciqala laughed. "Why would they shoot from the right?" he jeered at me, "Wouldn't that make them less accurate?"

"It's less accurate for us, yes, but it's not about *our* shooting, and it's not entirely about accuracy. It's about speed. Watch."

I nocked an arrow normally, on the left.

"To nock on the left, the archer makes extra movements to place the arrow and move his hand to the other side of the string."

I moved the arrow to the right of my bow. Holding it there, I took several more arrows from my quiver, placing the ends between my fingers. They stuck out of my fist like claws.

"They keep their arrows in-hand while they shoot. It means they can nock and aim much more quickly than our clan could because our shooting tradition is so different. Our people learned to shoot to hunt, and their people learned to shoot at each other. Different needs called for different shooting styles."

"But why shoot quickly when you sacrifice accuracy?" Banar asked, his brow furrowed in thought.

"I would have probably missed because I'm not used to shooting that way, and because I don't have a thumb ring. They're practiced in it. The other clans' archers also shoot with a protective ring on their thumb that pulls the string back with a sort of pinched grip. They're supposedly the fastest shots in Kalanos."

Ciqala spat bits of food as he spoke. "Supposedly? You're saying this could all be wrong? How do you know any of this, anyway?"

"My father was a scout. He would come home, train me to shoot, and tell me about the things he saw out in the grasses. He actually brought a Sree horse bow home once and taught me how they shoot with it."

"Your father?" Ciqala asked. I could tell from his tone that he was about to say something he might regret. I thought back to Chaska in the village, and how I hadn't hit him like I should have.

Ciqala continued. "So here we have the boy who thought he saw someone in the grasses, telling us about his father, who also thought he saw someone out in the grasses, impractically shooting with the same hand they hold their arrows in?"

"Watch your tongue."

I hoped my tone and expression would catch him off guard, but he resumed his glare.

Banar stood and smirked behind his friend as he spoke.

"Where's your father now, Rennik?" Banar pointed his sword out into the grasses. "Hasn't come back yet?"

I didn't take my eyes off of Ciqala. I could feel my heartbeat in my chest and the grouse feathers between my fingers. I had a quiver full of arrows.

It would only take one.

"You say he *was* a scout. He *used* to come home." Ciqala's words dripped out of his mouth like blood.

I couldn't help but picture it. Just between the ribs. Like an animal, his heart and lungs worked tirelessly beneath his shoulder blade. My own heart pounded for his silence.

Banar spoke again. "And now we have you. The son of a man who couldn't even defend himse—"

Banar didn't finish the word before I drew and pointed.

"What are you doing?" he asked nervously, gripping the hilt of his sword tighter and widening his eyes.

"There's something here," I responded. Not even an archer with a healthy arm can hold the string back for long. My arm felt as if it'd tear again, but I trusted my eyes. Something had just moved at the edge of the clearing. I let a small amount of tension from the bow, ready to pull back again in an instant.

A pregnant darkness pressed toward us; the pressure of an unseen intrusion pricked at the hairs on my arms.

Banar's eyes shifted between my drawn arrow and Ciqala, who was stilled by the sudden severity of my focus.

"Come on, Rennik," Banar's voice wavered anxiously, "this is just the other night again, isn't it? Or maybe being caught in that blizzard ruined your heari—"

"Stop talking."

Ciqala reached slowly for his sword. "I see something too," he said, keeping his voice low. His eyes darted to mine to confirm suspicion.

The tips of the feather grass shook to the left, but this time it was a sound that caught my attention.

The creak of a bowstring being pulled just outside of our clearing.

Ko woke Malik behind me.

The dogs let out their low warning growl and prowled forward.

I felt suddenly claustrophobic as tension rose like the tides. My vision only went as far as the clearing — about twenty feet. An archer needs his distance. Bows were excellent when the shooter was the hidden one, and I usually was. My breathing grew loud and rapid. I could hear my heart in my ears. I wasn't a fighter.

I shouldn't be here.

We waited, drawn and ready.

There was the slap of a bowstring, and the sound of a loosed arrow pierced the air. A shout came from outside our camp, and Malik drew again.

A voice shouted from behind us in a quick Kalanosi cadence, speckled with a strange accent.

"Fall back!"

And all at once, the grass began shaking with the movement of retreating figures.

I scanned the grasses for signs of an enemy but found none.

After mere moments had passed, it was quiet again. Ciqala began adding to the fire aggressively to brighten our camp.

"No one sleeps tonight. It's only a few hours before sunrise," he said hysterically. "This is all the evidence we need, right? We'll go back home and stay where it's safe."

No one responded. This wasn't the first time a scouting party had experienced violent contact with another clan. Though I couldn't help but feel the fear that comes from knowing I could have been shot moments ago, I wasn't yet sure this altercation constituted uprooting our village. For now, I agreed with Ciqala.

Malik looked at me wide-eyed, her fingers still split around a nocked arrow. "You think they'll come back?"

I took a deep breath and thought a moment. "I don't know," I responded. I wanted to talk, and to distract myself from this sudden feeling of apprehension, but I knew that silence would be paramount for the remaining hours of the night.

∾

WE LEFT AT THE FIRST SIGN OF MORNING, AND WITH THE SUN grew my impatience for Ciqala's leadership.

"We're safe to move," he was saying to Banar. "They went further west. They had to."

"Why do you think they went west?" I asked him. I had been biting back an argument all night, and my lips could no longer keep the words in.

"It's the only thing that makes sense," he replied, looking at me like I was an idiot for asking.

"Did you *see* them go west? Did you hear them say something? Have you seen even a single thing that makes you think so?"

"It's where they came fro—"

"They probably know we're Achare. If that's true, they'll know we're going to go back east, at least eventually. If they wanted to hurt us, I think it's more likely they're waiting to ambush us on our way back."

Ciqala mocked my voice. "Did you *see* them go eas—"

"No!" I shouted. "No, I didn't! It's why I haven't insisted that they did! My guess is as good as yours, but until we know where they are, we can't just commit to assumptions!"

"He's right." Ko's deep voice came softly yet powerfully from over my shoulder. It was the kind of intimidation that can only come from a strong man speaking quietly.

Ciqala swallowed hard, and for the first time, he looked frightened. "They went west," he asserted again, though with a bit of shaking in his voice. "We're safe to go home. We'll find Macha on the way back and stay where we know it's safe."

Something inside me snapped. I stepped over to him and grabbed him by the shoulder, turning him violently to face me.

"You *still* think Macha just went home?" I shouted. My

chest swelled with anger, and my eyes grew wild. He slapped my hand away.

"He's a coward! Of course he—"

My fist collided with his jaw. The impact shook me. I was no fighter, but Ko was right. I was leaving too much room for Ciqala's leadership, and he needed to be challenged. Ko said I'd need to talk in ways he'd understand, so now my words would come in the form of a fist. He fell to the ground and looked up at me wide-eyed.

"He was taken," I continued. "It could have been any of us and you ignored that threat."

He tried to stand, but I put a foot on his chest and pressed him into the dirt. Banar backed away and said something to me, but my ears were deafened by a fury that pounded into them like rushing water. I hardly heard myself as I continued shouting at him.

"You're terrified! You don't have what it takes to lead these people through the grasses! You'll say whatever you need to make yourself believe what's convenient, but let me make the truth perfectly clear: we were almost *slaughtered* last night. Someone is out there that doesn't want us coming back from the wilderness alive. You ignored the threat and it almost got us killed. Macha might already be dead!"

"And what would you have done?" he shouted up at me, teeth bared like an animal.

Before I could answer, everyone's attention snapped to the west. Malik, Ko, and Banar rushed into the grasses. I let Ciqala out from under my foot, and after looking back at me briefly with hatred in his eyes, he too leapt into the wild.

The soft sounds of nature quickly crept back to me, and with it I heard shouting.

Ikoda.

I burst into the grasses. As I ran, I found that I had no

answer to Ciqala's question. What *would* I have done differently? I shook the thought away and focused on running.

Keeping my head low, I threw my arms ahead and pushed the stalks behind me, carving a path as I listened for signs of the others. My arm burned slightly as the grass rubbed past the now nearly-healed wound.

And suddenly, the grass was gone.

I erupted into a massive tract of open space. The earth was gray. The sun cast no shadows as its heat and light met the ground unimpeded. To my right were the others, staring as I was, mouths open and eyes darting quickly upon an unfamiliar landscape. Ikoda was here, dogs at her side.

I knelt down and dragged my fingers lightly through the soil. It was loose and weightless, but under its cover was something rough. Brushing away a light layer, my fingers uncovered the deep imprint of an unshod horse hoof. Then another.

I brought the soil up to my face. I knew the substance as soon as I laid eyes on it, but to see so much of it here was unsettling — a reminder of the dangers we faced.

I looked toward my scouting party, all of whom looked expectantly toward me. The soil fell easily between my fingers and onto the ground.

"It's ash," I said.

I stood and stared out at the mile-wide clearing ahead of us, the distant half of which held the edge of a bison herd. The clearing was massive and seemed to swallow the air itself.

"It's all ash."

Wildfires are a common danger in Kalanos, especially before the dry season has ended. They can ignite with the strike of a lightning bolt, or a careless hunter lighting a fire without clearing ample space. Without the rainy season to dampen the earth and grasses, the dry stalks catch fire quickly and spread at an alarming rate. With little to stop its growth, the fires can effortlessly level several dozen acres of plant life, if not more.

But there seemed to be no reason why the fire had stopped where it did. The grass at the edge of the clearing was just as dry as it could be without becoming too brittle to stand.

"What are they doing?" asked Malik, gesturing toward the bison herd. The huge creatures were ambling around the clearing in a close congregation, sifting through the ash with their snouts and snorting loudly.

"They're looking for new grass," I replied. "Plant life that grows from fertile ash is healthier than normal, and especially so when it's young. They love the stuff."

As I finished speaking, the bison at the head of the herd rolled something larger from the ash with its nose. It was thin and looked to be several feet long.

"A tree branch?" Ciqala asked.

"I haven't seen any other trees around," replied Banar. He was right. Trees that do grow in the plains of Kalanos typically bunch together. We would have seen more.

"True, but it would explain the lightning strike that started this fire." He spoke as if it were known. If the cause really was lightning, he had a good point, but he was only making another assumption.

As we spoke at the edge of the clearing, Ko began striding toward the herd. I thought it unwise, as I had seen a hunter spook a herd of bison before. Even I had trouble with just one. I didn't intend to die in a stampede today.

"Ko!" I spoke quickly, raising my voice just enough to be heard. "What are you doing?"

"That's no tree branch." His hulking frame shook as his breathing quickened and he walked closer to the herd. Several bison at its head grew wary and backed away, keeping their eyes on Ko.

Then, he stopped.

Silence came upon us, and we waited as the huge man stared downward. He knelt to the ground and closed his eyes meditatively.

I made several tentative steps forward before realizing that he was praying.

He turned to face us.

"This fire was no accident."

I felt the fear from the night before sink back into my chest. As Ko returned to the group, he stopped a few feet away, looked down, and kicked something out of the ash. Several objects settled on the surface, resting in plain view.

Bones.

Silence befell our group like a heavy weight.

"Who would do something so reckless?" Malik said, her voice trembling.

Generations ago, clans would use fire in battle both offensively and defensively to control the movement of their enemies. If done properly, the fires could be contained before burning more than either clan intended. This, however, was the problem; attempting to control a fire among the grasses takes just as much luck as it does skill. The difference between a controlled grassfire and a cataclysmic wildfire is a teetering balance that even a master would have difficulty maintaining. Casualties often occurred on both sides of any battle if fire was involved.

Because of this, the use of such fires worked its way out of tradition for all clans. The risk simply outweighed any perceivable benefit.

"This was a clan," Ko said, leaving Malik's question unanswered. "And a small one. I don't imagine they had many enemies."

"But who would..." Malik repeated, letting the last half of the question add to the weight above us.

Suddenly, Banar drew his sword.

I followed his gaze and saw a series of trails moving through the tips of the feather grass to the southwest.

"They're back," I announced, drawing my bow from over my shoulders. I wasn't looking forward to seeing the faces of those who nearly attacked us last night.

"We should run," said Banar, backing toward the grasses as his eyes filled with panic.

"No," I responded, almost solely to try on the role of command, "they found us in the grasses before, they'll find us again. We have a better chance if we lead them into the open where we can see them coming."

We moved quickly toward the center of the clearing. As we ran, I kept my eyes trained on the grasses in every direction but knew that under my feet were the bones of a now-dead people. I eyed the bison herd warily, knowing their reaction was the difference between life and death. As I looked, something shone in the midst of the grasses. It looked like a piece of bright metal reflecting sunlight, but I could discern no further detail.

We stopped near the center of the clearing, biased toward the north, hoping to keep enough distance from the southwest edge to draw them into the open. Stopping too close to them would give them cover within shooting range. Strategy aside, I couldn't help but feel like I was on the prey side of my own hunting tactics.

"There!" I shouted.

They emerged from the grasses to the south with arrows nocked. They were quick, silent, and outnumbered us at least two-to-one. Contrary to traditional dress, they wore patchwork leather armor, which was in turn decorated with the dyed feathers and horns typical of the larger Kalanosi clans.

As they closed their distance, my eyes caught more movement in the grasses to the northwest.

"More are coming around!" I shouted.

"We can't let ourselves get surrounded," Ko shouted. He turned and looked at me, eyes glazed over and wide with the fury of an experienced warrior. "Fight, Nakai!"

Ko hefted his axe and launched forward. He had called me by my father's name. Hearing it caught me off guard, but it was enough to put me in motion.

With that, we followed.

This was all new to me. I decided I would focus on Ko and Malik, trusting their instincts in battle over my own.

Arrows pierced the air ahead and fell short of our position; our enemies had started their assault. Ash erupted in little clouds that were swept into the wind as their arrows pelted the earth.

Malik stopped her charge, knelt forward, and drew all in one motion. She loosed an arrow that buried itself in the leg of a charging enemy. He fell.

One down.

As I slowed my pace, I drew an arrow. Its nock came easily to the string. The grouse feathers grazed my cheek as muscle memory brought the knuckle of my thumb to the back of my jaw, under my ear, ready to make the same shot I'd fired since my father had taught me how.

I saw the chest of a charging man clearly in the morning sun. His heart would be drumming quickly as he ran. I heard my own in my ears.

I pictured the bone of my arrowhead lacerating his chest and ending his life, the red feathers in his hair burying themselves in the ash at his feet.

I thought of my home and wondered if he thought of his.

I thought of this man's family.

I thought of Avid.

The tension of my string lessened as I slowly let the arrow forward.

Malik fired next to me and hit another man.

Two.

A man covered in white war paint broke from the group and began running toward Malik and I, spear in hand. As he came forward, I knew his eyes were fixed on me.

He brought the spear over his shoulder and prepared to throw.

I froze.

Just as his arm began to launch the spear, he stopped. His eyes lost focus. His legs struggled to keep his forward momentum, and he fell into the ash. Buried in his back was one of Ko's throwing axes. I could see him in battle, over the dead man's body in my vision. He nodded at me and continued to fight as more enemies came from the grass to the south.

Three.

There were ten left ahead of us. I watched Ko swing his axe down against an enemy's spear, then up to slice through the armor on his chest. He fell.

Four.

Banar and Ciqala met their challengers head-on and fought together.

Suddenly, Malik shouted.

I turned to look and saw her clutching her arm, cut by an arrow that had grazed it. Blood seeped around her fingers.

"I'm fine!" she shouted. She drew again and fired, ignoring what must have been immense pain.

I saw movement from the corner of my eye.

They were already behind us.

"Move!" I shouted as I pushed Malik away, several arrows raining into the dirt where we had knelt.

I rolled to the west and took in my surroundings. I was not a fighter. I had no instinct here.

Looking back to the south, Banar and Ciqala were being quickly outnumbered.

Ikoda and her dogs leapt ferociously at the men around them.

As I scanned the battle, I saw Ko fighting four men on his own. His axe struck out like the claw of a cornered beast, beating down spears and evading their attempts at surrounding him. Man after man fell to his ferocity. He was a force of nature.

Then, there was one. The man I hadn't shot at before.

The man with red feathers leapt through the battle among his fallen allies, striking out at Ko with his spear.

He stabbed forward, and Ko spun left.

Ko swung across, and the man rolled under.

It was a dance of strength and speed as Ko's muscle lashed out at the red-feathered man.

Ko's axe caught the man's calf. He fell to the ash on one knee.

Just when his opponent knelt, Ko's body jolted. An arrow

had cut neatly into his back. But Ko, with all his raw strength, continued to fight.

Following his backswing, Ko brought the axe up and across to the man's head, but as he did, the man threw a handful of ash upward.

The man deftly ducked under the swing as Ko's blind eyes took him to panic. He swung wildly.

Then the red-feathered man thrust his spear through Ko's chest.

He was facing me. Blood poured from his chest. The red-feathered man pulled his spear back, and Ko's eyes locked on mine. The man who had fought with my father — the man who would have died for my father.

The man who had saved my life just moments ago.

He fell to his knees, then into the ash.

Tears welled up in my eyes and veiled my vision from the storm around me. It was my fault. Ko died because of my inability to defend my own people.

Malik shook me from my stupor and pulled my attention again to the archers behind us.

It was a chaos for which I had no solution, a blizzard that would not become a breeze.

I spun around, an arrow nocked with no destination.

My people fought for their lives to the south.

Enemies charged and fired from the north.

My home lay days to the east.

And to the west...

The bison.

I would not die here on the ashes of a peaceful people. I would not let myself be blown into the horizon with what remained of their charred bones.

I looked toward the edge of the seared clearing and

loosed an arrow. A bestial cry filled the air as it struck a bison in the middle of the leery herd.

Then, all at once, the ground began to shake.

The charging men halted and everyone, ally and foe alike, turned to see the stampeding herd launching forward, and even more erupt from the grasses to the west. I wanted a distraction, and I knew they'd stampede.

I didn't think it'd be directly toward me.

As the creatures thundered toward us, a cloud of ash filled the western sky. We left the dust of the dead behind and sprinted to the east.

I glanced over in the direction of the others and saw Ciqala run his sword through an enemy before fleeing with Banar at his heels. Ikoda and her dogs ran toward the southern edge of the clearing, splitting from the other two.

The red-feathered man lowered his head and attempted to run with his allies in the same direction as Ciqala and Banar, struggling with his injured leg.

Shifting my gaze ahead, I quickly realized I had no plan of escape. I had recently been in danger with a single bison, and I couldn't even outrun her.

Now there were hundreds, and I knew our speed wouldn't be enough.

As I ran I found myself next to Malik. I looked behind me at the half-ton beasts rampaging toward us and I turned away from the herd's path.

"Run north!" I shouted at her.

We angled our way away from the direction of the stampede, hoping to dodge its path within the seconds it would take for them to meet us.

Their roars were low and deafening as they filled the air, a cascade of bestial battle cries over the brontide of their thundering hooves.

The first of the bison careened between Malik and I as we ran diagonally across its path. Its thick muscles powered past at a shattering speed and I could smell the musty stench of its leathery hide mixed with the dirt in the air.

Malik lunged forward to me at its passing, and we found ourselves adjacent to the storm of the stampede.

It was difficult to maintain balance on the surface of the shaking earth. It felt as though the dirt itself was being pulled out from under my feet.

We passed an enemy clad in leather armor just before he was met with the horns of a pursuer. He was thrown forward and prostrate, and directly in our path. We leapt over him as he screamed, then was promptly silenced by the crushing weight of the herd.

Within seconds there were bison ahead of us, and we found ourselves running not in front of them, but in their midst.

Luckily, because of our northeastern path, we were close to the edge of the herd's broad path. Wary of the beasts around us, we weaved around certain death. I leapt away from the head of a bison and had to shove off from its massive, heaving side to push myself to safety.

We soon found ourselves diving into the grasses to the northeast of the clearing, no longer among the herd, but continuing to sprint clear of it nonetheless. Our path led us uphill, and when we reached its crest we finally stopped.

The charging bison were now running away from the clearing and to the southeast, clearing a huge path through the feather grass as they went.

Our breathing was labored and coarse as we choked on the ash and dirt in the air. I looked out into the clearing, and as the wind took the ash with it, I saw the bodies that had been trampled into the earth. They were beyond recognition and covered in dark ash and dirt; I had no way of knowing if our allies had made it out.

Nineteen.

I thought of Ko and dropped to my knees. I fought back my sobs. I must have looked pathetic.

"We would have been slaughtered," I managed to choke out. "We were going to die."

I'm not sure who I was trying to convince.

Malik was silent as she stared in bewilderment at the scene of the battle to the southwest. My fingers dug into the dirt as I clutched the earth in frustration. I wanted to save the others.

I may have killed them all.

13

THE COST OF COWARDICE

"Said Drakka to the wolf pack,
    'on all things I must feed.
    Each but the strong will come along,
    though all will soon meet me.'

The Wahto die for their grasses,
    the Yohri for their trees,
    but some will say 'I'd rather stay!'
    From Drakka's jaws, they flee!"

           — CHILDREN'S SONG OF DRAKKA

After watching the newly lifted cloud of dust drift to the east, tracing our inevitable journey back home, we spent hours silently searching the land near the ash plain. I could tell from the heavy silence between us that Malik was either too shocked or too angry to speak with me. By noon we had given up hope of finding anyone and took solace in the chance that the others had made it out alive and headed back east. At my suggestion, we stayed clear of the wide trail the charging herd had cut, knowing that the enemy would likely follow it for an easier route, if they intended to come east at all.

Hours passed.

"That was cowardly," Malik said suddenly, turning on her heels to face me. She spat the words out like a hot and angry coal she'd been carrying on her tongue. "You could have killed all of us."

"We were going to get slaughtered, Malik," I responded defensively. "I had no other choice."

"You did have a choice. We could have stayed and fought. We could have avenged Ko—"

"Why?" I asked. The word was abrasive — salt in cut gums. I already hated the things we were about to say. "Why avenge someone when it'll kill you — do we all just keep looking for revenge until everyone is dead? I could have shot Ko's attacker before they even stepped toward each other. I had that chance."

"Why didn't you shoot him?" she asked incredulously.

"Because I'm not a fighter, Malik! I'm not going to kill someone, and I'm certainly not going to die in battle! When I die, it'll be at the hand of nature — a nagithanka, or a fall from my plateau, or, I don't know, a stampede of bison. I'm not going to die with a spear through my chest. That's not who I am, and that's not something our people can expect of me!" The last of my words surprised me as I said them. I wasn't even sure I *meant* them.

"Our people can't depend on you to defend them?" She looked at me like a stranger she already hated. "You are a coward, Rennik. You wouldn't raise your bow to save your own people."

"I'm not a killer."

"You've killed creatures in self-defense."

"That's not the same—"

"It *is* the same! If one of those men had tried to run you through with a sword, you wouldn't have attacked him first if you had the chance? You wouldn't even have saved your own life?"

"I don't know!" I shouted, scaring a flock of birds to the south into flight. I stood, simply breathing for a moment.

"It's your life or theirs," she continued. "It *is* the same as a natural predator. Living things exist in a constant struggle, and if you don't fight to live, you're allowing your enemies to do so."

"I don't know," I repeated, slowly deflating. "Maybe it is my fault. I don't know much about fighting, so maybe there was some sort of option there that I didn't see. Something my father would have seen."

"You were brought here to guide us and help us survive, not to make decisions that get us all killed!"

"I wasn't going to allow myself the chance to die by their hand, but regardless of what you think, staying in a battle we'd lost from the beginning isn't my idea of survival. I was sent here to track and navigate. I didn't come out here to die."

Malik stood in silence and stared daggers at me. "This isn't just about *you*. This is about the survival of our people. If you can't kill to save your own people, when can you?"

"Ko was the strongest man I knew," I continued. "If he was killed, I knew we wouldn't stand a chance. I made a decision, and from what I can tell, it saved my life *and yours*. And if you want to talk about killing, go back and take a good look at that field of ash. How many bodies did you see trampled into the earth because of my actions?"

Malik looked to the ground and let out an exasperated sigh. "I don't know, over a dozen."

"And how many people had died there before?"

Her response was an angry silence. She began pushing through the grasses again, away from me. I followed and talked at her back.

"We were fighting on the ashes of an entire people — hundreds of people, maybe. We were stepping on the dead. I may not have been thinking about killing our enemies, but I was thinking about those who had already died. I wasn't about to join them. I didn't *want* anyone to die, and I wasn't going to sit idle and wait to die in battle myself. I may have hesitated at the threat of a human enemy, yes, but I ended up acting in self-defense and now I'm alive."

"And what happens when those people show up on the ridge outside of our village?" She turned to me again, her tone changing from anger to desperation. "What happens when our people are the ones threatened, and you don't have a herd of bison to do your killing for you?"

I had no words for her. Like Ciqala's question earlier that day, I found I had no response, but I knew I was tired of not knowing.

Malik spoke more quietly than before. "Come on. Let's keep walking."

I joined the path behind her and let my anger mingle with hers in a silent tension that hung in the air.

The daylight had passed before we spoke again. We settled down for the night and ate some small game we had seen on the way. We had little energy left for a real hunt, and our voices were left weak and hoarse from breathing in the ash.

"Those men," she said, looking toward the fire, "they were all from different clans."

"How do you know?" I couldn't look her in the eye.

"The man who killed Ko, the one with red feathers, was dressed in traditional Sree decoration. But the others near him were Wahto and Turin."

"How could that be? The Turin aren't that violent. And I thought the Sree and Wahto hate each other."

"They do, but I know what I saw. I think the threat out here in the grasses is greater than what we've seen before. If those clans are working together..." she let her words hang silently.

"And what about that armor?" I asked. "I've never seen anyone from Kalanos wearing armor before."

"That's a mystery, too. There are surely leatherworkers around that can make it, and plenty of hide for tanning, but it seemed out of place. Kalanosi fighters always dress lighter than that. Who knows — things change, I suppose."

I tried to swallow the dust and ash in my mouth. I thought of home.

"Do you think we should move?" I asked.

"Rennik, the sun has set."

"No, not us, I mean our people. When we return. Do we need to move the village?"

She thought for a moment. "Yes. I think we do."

Before we could continue, movement from the edge of our small clearing caught my eye. I stood and spun quickly.

Two of Ikoda's dogs came slinking into the firelight.

14

THOSE LEFT BEHIND

"Rucosti horse racing was forever changed when a handful of studs from the Sree were obtained by a few courageous collectors. The resulting generation of half-breed horses, the 'Kallemude', were the first of the swift and levelheaded racing horses that dominate our sport to this day."

— EXCERPT FROM BRALLIC SEVERIN'S
*KALANOS: A STUDY OF PLACE AND
PEOPLE.*

We combed the grasses the next morning for signs of Ikoda and found none. The two dogs that had come to us kept weaving in and out of the tall feather grass, directing a search of their own, but each time they came back to us without success. They were trusting of Malik and I, but they couldn't seem to shake a certain nervousness they held.

We had failed to find the heavy pack of supplies back at

the ash field, so whatever supplies we did use had to be scavenged from fresh vegetation, small game, or the sparse patches of trees we found on the way.

We were gathering what bits of wood we could from such a patch when Malik spoke again.

"I thought you might kill Ciqala yesterday."

"What? No, I told you I can't—"

"I know, I just...you hear stories of people losing their minds a little out here. The grasses have that effect on people. They forget themselves sometimes."

I pulled on a branch as Malik hacked at it with her sword. There were surely more efficient ways to gather wood, but it's what we could do with what tools we had; the hatchets were in the pack we'd lost. She told me the sword would likely be ruined by the time we'd returned home. The dogs lounged anxiously in the sunlight that filtered through what little canopy hung above.

I watched her handle the steel blade easily. It couldn't have been more than thirty inches long, and it ended with a slight curve at the top. The swords that were used by my people were a mixed bunch. Some were made by Graff in his clay forge, since he'd been taught by foreigners, and others were obtained through traders from the south. Swords were more of an exotic weapon for us, so people tended to teach themselves how to use them, and the blades were as varied in their design as they were in their origin.

"I can't say I hadn't thought about it," I responded after a while. Malik's mouth curved into a small smile.

"Well, I think we all did at one point or another. I was just surprised that you hit him. You seemed so blinded by anger, I thought you might actually do it."

"To be honest, I'd never been in a real fight — I'm still not sure I have been. But he had been talking about my father, and ignoring Macha's disappearance, and treating me like a child. All of those things just added up until I couldn't take it anymore. And I've never been out in a situation like this, where we could really be killed. After we were almost ambushed that night, I realized how much my life really was in the hands of the people around me. I didn't want to die because of Ciqala's lacking wisdom." I raised my hand to her. "My knuckles are still swollen from hitting him."

"You should probably stop hurting yourself."

I allowed myself a modest smile.

"Like I said," she continued, gathering a few thin logs into a small personal pack she carried, "the grasses have a strange effect on people. Come on. This wood should last us two more nights. We might not get any more worthwhile trees until we get home."

We walked for miles, speaking of small things as we went. After our argument the day before, I was surprised by the tone of this one. I wondered what made Malik suddenly decide to treat me well. Maybe the burden of anger is too heavy to carry this far.

The feather grass was slowly decreasing in height as we traveled, meaning we were getting closer to home, even if it was still days away.

Building a fire in the grasses took the know-how not to burn the entirety of a field, but also had its benefits. We didn't have to worry about smoke at night, as no one would be able to see it from a distance. Typically, in other places in the world, one would have to concern themselves with the light their fire gave out. Here, as long as there were no high vantage points near you, the surrounding tall grasses muted the firelight and made for a relatively safe environment.

When the sun had set, and the dogs had settled near the

fire, we sat in silence and cooked the two hares we had recently killed. I know I should have felt less at ease without the full force of my travelling companions around me, but being alone with Malik was more comforting than having to worry about the trustworthiness of the others.

People are a strange sort of animal. Malik and I had come so near to death, but on our second night since then, the tension began to fade. Like a child in the night, we pulled the blanket of conversation up over our heads, pretending it could do anything to keep us safe. Sometimes the easiest lies are the ones we tell ourselves.

I noticed that Malik was scanning the edges of our small clearing closely before she spoke.

"You really saw something that night?" she asked.

"Which night?"

"You know which night."

I nodded slowly and kept my eyes on the meat of the hare. One of the dogs — Wepe, I remembered — looked up past Malik to stare longingly at my dinner.

"I suppose it could have been the men we fought," she said. "They found us a few nights later and didn't strike until after they had watched us."

"It wasn't them," I responded sternly.

"How can you be sure? Who else would be out here?"

"I don't know. But whoever it was did something I had never experienced before. Or I guess it did something I *had* experienced before. An exact memory."

"You've said 'it' and 'him'...which is it?" She looked at me with either confusion or concern. It was hard to tell which. I shook my head to say "I don't know" and proceeded to explain the memory.

"When I was little, I fell through the ice of a river and almost died. It's actually a wonder I kept all of my limbs."

"Believe it or not, I know the basics of the story," she said. "But I'm sure your version is closer to the truth."

"It was while we were ice fishing, my father and I. But I remember feeling helpless and unable to breathe. It was so cold that I couldn't feel my arms and legs. I wound up with all of these bruises all over my body from the rocks in the river, and it took me weeks to heal — I was pretty young."

I reached out and gave the last bit of my hare to the dog nearest me. Its coat was thick and warm. I scratched behind its ears.

"When I made eye contact with the person the other night, it was like I relived the experience of drowning. I saw all of these flashbacks to my father's face, and I could picture my pregnant mother sitting next to me, crying and praying while I recovered. The pain from the bruises came back, exactly where they had been before. I truly thought I was going to die, but just before I did, I remembered the fire my father had built to save my life, and the fire in our camp just sort of erupted — you might remember that — and then the person was gone."

Malik stayed quiet for a while.

"I know it sounds ridiculous," I continued, "but that's what I saw. And that's one of the reasons I hit Ciqala. After I was reminded of how close I'd been to death, I realized how easily it could come. I was just scared, I think."

"So this person tried to kill you with his stare? Or your memories?" she offered.

"I don't know what they tried to do. I just know what happened."

She took a deep breath and changed the subject.

"Your father. I've heard he was a good man."

"He and my mother were wonderful together. He taught me how to survive on my own and how to provide for others.

He loved to laugh. From what I've learned more recently he looked out for his companions pretty fiercely." That last statement stung as the image of Ko falling into the ash came back to me.

"And he was lost in the wild?"

"He was killed in battle."

A wash of understanding came over Malik's face. "I'm sorry," she said. "I didn't know."

"It's fine. There's still a lot that I don't know. But he was a scout, like you, and he encountered some remnants of a Sree war party. He didn't make it back from that one. They brought his body back, though."

She looked like she didn't know what to say. The dog closest to her stretched out and laid its heavy head on her lap, where it promptly closed its eyes again.

"You lost your father out here too, didn't you?" I asked.

"He and my older sister. They didn't die in battle. They went out on a hunting trip. My father was practically obsessed with bison furs, and he never took too much or anything, but he certainly enjoyed himself when the need was there. I happened to have hurt my leg a few days before, and he didn't want to risk taking me."

"What happened?" I asked, hoping I wasn't overstepping my bounds.

"They just...never came back. I never found out what it was. I guess they could've been attacked by a predator, or injured, or..."

Malik trailed off and turned her head to the east, redirecting her attention. Her eyes watered in the light of the fire. I decided that I should feel lucky for having the opportunity to burn my father's body and find closure for his death.

"What were they like?" I asked.

She sighed and turned her attention to the fire. A soft smile appeared in the warm light.

"She was amazing," she answered. "My sister was such a good tracker. You remind me of her a lot, actually. She taught me how to navigate using the stars and landmarks. When we were younger, she would take me out to spend the night in the grasses — dangerous, I know — and she would quiz me on the constellations. And when we were done, we'd come up with our own and draw them out for each other."

"You made your own constellations?" I asked, openly grinning.

"Yeah." She looked up and pointed. "There," she said, "see the Doe's Tail?"

"I do," I answered tentatively. It was the first one you teach children to find.

"Well, take that bottom star and trace it down and to the left — my left — and there you've got the broad side of the Clumsy Bear."

"The what?"

She laughed aloud, a sincere laugh with sadness behind it. I shifted to her side of the fire, an action the dog wasn't too happy with. It readjusted its position and curled up next to me again.

"See?" she pointed. "Its head is up at the top right, and its arms are sort of flailing."

I didn't see anything, but answered with a vague, "huh."

"Well, when we were little, we went camping once, and apparently while my father and sister were out getting food, they left me behind so I could keep the fire ready. I was too little to really help with the hunting back then. They said when they got back, the tent was knocked over and I was sitting under the fallen tarp crying. They asked me what had happened, and even though I had obviously knocked it over on accident, I told them a black bear had come along and done it.

"My sister had to hold back laughter and asked me to tell her exactly how it happened. I said to them that a black bear came through, drawn in by the fire, and had tripped on a log because he was clumsy, and fell on the tent. He was so embarrassed that he took off right away."

"My mother only saw a black bear in Kalanos once, and it was so far south it may as well have been in Rucost."

"I know, I know," she replied, "I was little, I wasn't a good liar. But when my sister and I had to come up with some constellations, she wanted to bring up that gem of a story and immortalize it in the sky."

She continued to stare straight up into the stars.

"Was your father angry?" I asked.

"About the tent or us ruining the stars for him?"

"The tent."

"Of course not. He laughed harder than my sister did. He was a good man, just...busy. My mother ran off and disappeared when I was very young, so my sister and I were a handful. He was gone hunting and trading a lot."

I scratched aimlessly at the ground with a stick from our firewood, and I felt younger than I was, playing in the dirt.

"But I had my brother for a while after that," she said. "Hashil."

"I remember him, I think."

"He died a few years back. Not to the grasses or anything. He just got sick." She looked up at me briefly. "He was close with Ciqala, actually."

I considered how to phrase my next question. "They... actually got along?"

"I know, it's strange, Ciqala being the ass he is. But really, he was a lot nicer around Hashil. My brother was about a year older, I think, and he looked like he'd end up being Ko's size. They were a lot closer than people realize."

Our gaze returned skyward.

"Sometimes I worry I'm spoiling my brother," I told her.

"Why's that?"

"We had to grow up pretty fast, you and I, so I'm not sure if he's just growing a little differently than me, but when I was his age, I was alongside my mother keeping the family alive. I was playing the role of an adult, and he gets to play actual games with friends."

"Well, to be honest, I'm not sure many parents would've given you a chance anyway. You should've heard the elders talk about you in the chieftain's hut."

"I suppose your right," I said sullenly.

"But it seems unfair, doesn't it? Having to grow up quickly."

"These grasses are merciless...my father, your family, Tella's family," I started.

"Tella?" Malik interrupted, "that insane woman at the edge of the village?"

"Yeah. I suppose she is the insane woman. I don't know, I've gotten to know her a bit more lately."

"She's staying with your mother, right?"

"She is. And she's definitely a bit strange, but more so I think she's just..." Malik waited while I searched for my words. "...sad."

"Sad?"

It seemed simple, but it was something that hadn't yet occurred to me.

"Her whole family was killed out in the grasses. They were gone for days, apparently, and I think maybe she saw something that changed her, or maybe the grief changed her, but lately I've been thinking of her as not insane, just...changed."

"Well, I was sad, and I don't talk to the sky," Malik chuckled. My face remained stoic, and Malik stopped laughing. She cleared her throat and continued.

"The grasses seem to just...swallow people whole."

THOSE WHO LEAD

"Cut fat away from venison; dry to jerky.
  Render bison suet to tallow over quiet fire.
  Powder jerky, onion, chicory root, and two pinches takar.
  Mix tallow into powder, kneading with hands.
  Store in dark place until ready."

— KINRAN'S SPICY VEGETABLE PEMMICAN

Tall pillars of smoke from cooking fires led us home a few days later. It was evening then. Even if I had somehow not recognized the details of the surrounding landscape, or seen my plateau growing close in the distance, the smell of salmon with wild onion was a trail I could follow in the dark. I detected no trace of venison in the village's aromas and assumed that my people must have had a good day at the river.

Laced among those smells was the scent of takar, a spice

that is commonly used by my people. It was — or maybe still is — endemic to Kalanos. I had heard stories from the older villagers that traders once swapped high-value tools, furs, and weapons for just a small amount of takar. One small clan, though, traded a handful of seeds and cultivation advice to merchants from Rucost, in what one old man described as "the most idiotic trade in memory". After that trade, the merchants became less and less interested in the spice, and we began to hear from the Turin that Rucosti folk were coming into the southern plains, planting takar, and harvesting it in mass amounts. This is likely why the Turin hold such a grudge against the country to their southern border.

The taste of takar wasn't easy to compare to anything else, but it kicked like the seeds of a mild pepper, and the smell always reminded me of home. Even if it was no longer of any value to the rest of the world, it was something small that meant the world to me.

Against the darkened eastern horizon, I could see our scouts still lit by the deeply setting sun, like silhouettes in reverse. Our approach gained their attention quickly, and they disappeared beyond the ridge, presumably alerting others of our return. By the time we had arrived, Gatsi was waiting.

"Rennik," he greeted me, his face serious. "Stop by your family, and I'll be there to retrieve you very shortly." He gave Malik a polite nod, turned, and walked away.

Of course I'd wanted to tell him what had happened in the grasses, to let the pressure out of my head, but there was something odd about his behavior that told me to wait. It was rare that he was so terse and to-the-point. I brushed it away in favor of seeing Avid and my mother. The dogs trotted past us in the direction of Ikoda's hut.

"May as well follow them, and see if there's anyone to find," said Malik. She jogged after them.

Alone, I hurried through the doorway of my hut and halted abruptly.

The first thing to greet me was the smell of dinner. Exactly what I had predicted from outside the village. My mother and Avid sat with the kind of lethargic satisfaction that comes from a full belly.

My mother looked up quickly and froze when she saw me. Her jaw quivered, and her eyes looked worn and sleepless. She tried to say something, but no words came. I strode forward and caught her in a tight embrace. Her tears were warm as they met the skin of my neck.

"Rennik!" Avid's voice shouted as he ambushed me from behind. "I knew you'd be back! I told mother you were too hard to spot in the grasses — no one would ever see you!"

I escaped the clutches of my family's embrace and saw Tella sitting quietly in the corner. Then, something new in the doorway caught my attention. It was a hanging bit of sage and a series of small papers, hung out of the way so that it was hardly noticeable.

"I assume that's yours?" I asked, gesturing toward it.

She simply nodded. It was an old and nonsensical tradition; demons don't like the touch of sage, and if one such creature enters, the papers are meant to scatter and confuse them. As if that kind of fictional creature could be stopped by a few scraps of paper.

One of the dogs that had split off strode into our home, panting with its head lowered, obviously unsatisfied with the journey to his master's hut.

"Is that one of Ikoda's?" my mother asked.

"It is," I answered plainly, wondering how best to continue.

"And where is she?"

I hesitated to speak, and my mother interpreted the silence well.

"So you did find something," she continued, worry painted on her face.

"We fought with others. Some were Wahto, some were Sree. Some were from smaller clans. They were fighting all as one."

My mother and brother shared a look of shock.

"We lost Macha," I said vaguely, "...and Ko."

My mother let the air out of her lungs slowly as her eyes continued to tear up and grow distant. "That man was a great friend of your father's."

"And of mine. He saved my life. We even spoke on the journey. I..." The silence grew as I struggled to admit my failure to my family. "...I could have saved him. I didn't." I dropped my head with the weight of the shame.

"Rennik," my mother started. "You were taken on the journey to guide, not to kill. No one will blame you."

"How many were there?" Avid asked, failing to keep the excitement out of his voice.

"Almost twenty, I think."

Their mouths opened in disbelief.

"Did you..." she started. "Did you kill them, Rennik?" She seemed to be almost afraid of the answer.

I hesitated. Memories of broken people pressed into the ash came to me. "No. No, of course not. That was their job. Not mine." I hoped she could not hear that I was trying to convince myself as well as her. "Have Ciqala and Banar come back?" I asked.

"You're the only one so far. Has something happened to them?"

"We were all split up after the fight. Malik and I searched

for them but found nothing. We journeyed home with just the two of us." The dog nuzzled my brother curiously. "Four of us, counting the dogs."

Just then, Gatsi's head appeared as he brought the hut's flap up with one hand. "Rennik. With me." He stepped outside and waited.

"I'm glad to be home," I said quickly as I embraced my mother once more. Before stepping through the door, I turned back to her. "Don't let Avid name the dog. We don't need another mouth to feed."

I left, but nearly forgot to put away my bow and arrows. After the trip into the wilds, it felt strange leaving them behind.

THE CHIEFTAIN'S HUT WAS LIT FROM THE INSIDE BY A COOKING fire. Its walls, made of animal skin and cloth, were braced by ancient mammoth tusks. The tusks had been a gift from the Turin years ago, when I was still very young. Now they stood vigil to the elements outside and acted as testament to the longevity of our home. I found the tusks both unnecessary and somehow grim, but I wasn't about to say anything of the sort.

The slim opening of the hut's entrance and several other spots along the lengthy walls let out little strips of vibrant yellow light, and from the outside I thought it looked somewhat like two hands cupping a flame. Gatsi led me in with the same sober countenance he'd had all evening.

The inside of the hut was furnished with a nearly conflicting collection of objects. Among jewelry of wood and bone were the pelts and teeth of the chieftain's greatest hunts. The furs of a wolf, a mountain lion, and even that of a black bear were among the others on the floor of the home. The man was a passionate hunter, and I respected his tenacity in that regard, though his predilection did border on the excess. I had heard he was a ferocious fighter as well as a hunter. On the floor was a small bed made from the pelt of an oryx.

Sitting along the tops of the pelts were his daughter's toys, some gifted by villagers and others homemade. A bison carved from bone, a crown of early-blooming snowdrop flowers, a doll made of straw and fur — playthings scattered atop the once-living predators of the wild. I felt a genuine respect for the fact that, just from standing in their home, I could see both the things they owned and that from which they came.

The man who owned this collection stood from his seated position and approached.

"Rennik!" he said happily in his deep warrior's voice. He took my hand in his meaty paw and shook it with all the strength a respectful greeting could warrant. "By the beast, you look more like your father each time I see you. Come, sit. We have much to discuss, and there is much I want to know."

My father and the chieftain were close, once, before he was chosen to be our leader. It was something I had gleaned from listening to conversations when I was a child. I'd never been entirely sure how severe the rift between them had grown by the time my father died, but the chieftain had never wronged me or my mother, so I carried no coals for him.

His wife was present, as well as his daughter, who couldn't have been more than five years old.

"Cordah, my darling," said the chieftain to his wife, "why don't you take Nivan to another hut while we discuss. I know Kinran had an excess of fish tonight — why don't you join her?"

His wife smiled and took the hand of their daughter, who promptly dug her feet into the ground.

"But I want to talk, too!" she argued, her voice as confident as a miniature Avid's. "I have important things to say! I want to help!"

"Nivan," said the chieftain, grinning at his daughter, "Little Owl, when you and your mother return, we will talk of all your ideas for the clan. We'll need to practice if they're going to want you to lead someday."

The small girl shrunk into her tiny voice. "Okay, father. But do I have to listen to Kinran's stories?" she addressed her mother with the question.

"Sometimes the oldest stories carry the most truth, Little Owl."

The girl groaned, and instead of leaving with her mother, she stormed out of a smaller doorway near the back of the hut. As she did, I noticed a wicked-looking scar on the side of the girl's neck.

"Please, Rennik. Sit. Eat." I helped myself to some salmon. The chieftain sat on a wicker hassock, lording over his kingdom of pelts. I sat on a fine bison skin on the ground. Gatsi remained standing. His countenance discomforted me still.

I suddenly donned a deep uneasiness. After settling in, I found the earth beneath the pelt to be uneven. The bumps in the dirt felt almost like a spine, and now that I was inside, the mammoth tusks that framed the hut looked more like a massive ribcage. We were inside the belly of a great beast, and the winds blowing against the hide walls were the breaths it took into its chest. It cultivated an anxiousness in my own. I tried throughout the coming conversation to focus on what was being said, but I couldn't shake the feeling of being trapped inside something that blurred the lines between the living and the dead.

"Tell me," he started, "are we threatened?" His smile fixed into a serious concentration. The chieftain always spoke plainly when he needed to.

"We walked west for four days. That night — the night of the fourth — we were nearly ambushed. The grasses can be much taller in that part of Kalanos, so we didn't get a good look at them. Malik shot one before they attacked, and they retreated. The following morning, we came upon the charred remains of another village. Ko found human bones in the ashes. In the same moment we were attacked by a large group of enemies, numbering around twenty, to my memory."

"Sree? Wahto?"

"Both. Some Turin, too."

"Why have only you and Malik returned?"

I wanted to tell him everything. I wanted to tell him how I'd been tortured by the gaze of a stranger, how Macha had been swept away, how toxic Ciqala's leadership was, how I hit him. But I decided instead to speak as plainly as he was. He wanted only the facts he could use without too much consideration. Terror and uncertainty would likely muddy the waters of his clear mind.

"Macha was lost on the first night," I said, avoiding specifics, "and Ko was killed in battle."

His jaw clenched with the smallest mote of shock, or maybe fear, but he did well not to show it otherwise.

"The first night," he echoed. "You found trouble that close to home?"

"Not exactly," I offered. "We aren't sure what happened." He didn't look satisfied, so I gave in. "Ciqala thinks he may have tried to run away from the group."

The chieftain seemed to accept this answer solemnly.

"After the battle, we were all separated. Malik and I managed to stay together," I continued.

"How did you survive when you were vastly outnumbered?"

"I forced a nearby herd to stampede. It was the only thing I could think of that would get us away from the fight and back here alive."

The chieftain nodded to himself in thought. "You may have been smart to do such a thing," he said finally. "Your father had the instincts of a true survivor. It's why I sent him on such trips. It seems I was right to think you'd act similarly."

At the second mention of my father, I swallowed hard and brought my chin up a little. The chieftain continued.

"He hated me for — no, perhaps not. I do not think it was a hatred that he had for me. He was always against my decision to send him with the scouting parties. He had no interest in fighting men, but I knew him well before they asked me to lead. I would venture so far as to call ourselves friends. I knew he was a survivor, and that our scouts needed someone level-headed to keep them alive. In my position, the decisions I make need to address what is best for my people. It pained me to put my friend in harm's way — it truly did. But I believe your father saved the lives of many capable fighters, whether he knew it or not."

He looked into the fire and took a long, reminiscent breath. The silence that grew within the hut afforded me a moment to rein-in my emotions.

"And now I wonder, Rennik. Do you hate me for my decision? Do you hold it against me that your life was threatened out there in the wilds?"

The question caught me off-guard, and my mouth

worked through a brief and silent stutter. I took a moment to think before responding. It was true that I could have been killed. I saw a good man die. I was somehow drowned and frozen, even in the warm air. I wondered from whom the chieftain sought forgiveness — from me, or from my father? I responded with the phrase I had leaned on lately.

"I don't know." I had to wrestle the words out of my mouth.

The chieftain smiled with one sincere corner of his mouth and chuckled quietly.

"You are so much like him," was all he said in response. He turned to Gatsi. "Funny how blood can turn a man into his father, even from the grave."

I had almost forgotten Gatsi was there. I turned to look at him and studied his reply.

He forced a small smile and said, "the virtues of men are put in place at a young age. The child is often pushed in one direction by his earliest years. The rest of his youth is composed of miniscule adjustments to that path." He hesitated briefly. "But blood seems to be strong in some families. This much cannot be denied."

The chieftain smiled, obviously feeling as though his statement had been affirmed.

There were moments in the past where I had seen Gatsi briefly stumped by some task or riddle. Each time, he would furrow his brow, and his nostrils would flare and shrink slowly and repeatedly. His eyes would find a high point on which to focus. He would take a deep breath, and by the time he exhaled he would produce his answer. This entire process rarely took more than a few seconds.

From the time he had found me on the ridge, it looked as though he were trapped in that first moment of his signature calculation. It suddenly came to me that I had never seen this expression of his for this duration, nor had I ever spent this much time in his presence without hearing him speak. I wanted to know why, but I couldn't find the question to ask, and I was sure it wasn't the time to do so.

"Rennik," the chieftain continued, "you are not a fighter. You take pleasure in being close to home. Do you, a man of the village, feel threatened by what you saw?"

"Yes," I answered honestly. "I do."

"Then we'll have to begin preparations to move. I will speak to Malik and some of my trusted men tomorrow to plan a route before informing our people. We'll leave the following morning. I'd ask that the both of you keep this information to yourselves for the time being. Panic before tomorrow will be counteractive to our migration. Hopefully by the time we leave, the rest of your party will have returned."

Gatsi and I both agreed to keep quiet about the plan.

"For now, Gatsi, why don't you tell the story of our hunt. The time Nakai and I thought we'd be coming back as corpses."

Gatsi exhaled loudly. "It's your story. Won't you tell it better?"

"I'm a shit storyteller and you know it."

Gatsi looked intently into the fire and said nothing.

The chieftain narrowed his eyes in some combination of concern and suspicion.

"Well, then why don't you tell the story of the first clan," he asked.

This time Gatsi glared at the chieftain, who merely grinned in return.

"Fine, fine," the chieftain submitted to the old storyteller, "I'll try my best to remember the details." The chieftain looked at me. "Has he ever told you the story of Sedda?"

"Senga," Gatsi interjected, correcting him.

"Right, Senga. Senga was the leader of a clan who were expert weavers—"

"They weren't expert weavers," Gatsi corrected again. "They were learning to plant and harvest." He sighed, regained his composure, and began telling the story in his own way.

The chieftain smiled as if he had just won a small battle.

"They weren't expert weavers," Gatsi repeated. "They didn't sew materials. They sowed seeds into the earth.

"Our ancestors, long before there were Achare and Wahto and all the other clans, had been searching for a perfect piece of land to call their own. Their leader was chieftain Senga, who was strong, charismatic, and led her people well. They had discovered in small ways how to plant and harvest, and it granted them the potential to become sedentary — *if* they could find a place that allowed them to do so.

"After exploring coastal cliffs of the south, the high steppes of the north, forests to the west, and even the deadly Inkwood to the northwest of that, they were nearly killed off. As it happens, as cunning as we like to think we are, people have trouble rapidly adapting to new environments. It takes time, and time is often hard to find. Time," Gatsi paused dramatically, staring into the flames, "is to be coveted."

His tone shifted with what seemed to be a caveat, and he and the chieftain made the kind of eye contact that comes with knowing something secret.

"But the sick needed medicines in a strange land, and the children needed food among unfamiliar plants and animals. The people were desperate, and death was inching nearer every day. Then, just as their food was dwindling, they came upon a deep and lush valley. The soil was fertile, and the seeds the people had carried with them rooted to the earth well. So much so that the crops were quick to harvest — it seemed the plants were enamored with the valley. A man in whom the clan placed trust convinced their leader that they should stay.

"And like the plants, the people of Senga's clan were comfortable in the valley. She was proud and thankful that they had at long last found fields upon which they'd settle and live. A place to truly raise the next generation. The stroke of luck was as fresh as the soft breezes that were guided through the valley walls. There were even fruit-bearing trees scattered around pools of clear water fed by an underground spring. They wanted never to leave.

"But as time passed, a strange series of insidious threats sunk into their land. The tenth year's crops rotted. The animals they had tamed grew sickly, and the walls of the valley began to erode and collapse. The sixth year was even worse. Senga knew the place was no longer safe, but her people were reluctant to leave. They had become complacent, and the skills needed for their nomadic lifestyle had partly atrophied as hunters had turned into farmers. They were simply too scared to leave it all behind.

"But the people respected their leader. She told them that their true home, the world of their ancestors, was broad and limitless, and lay in all the land beyond their valley. They needed to travel again until a safe place was found, or simply never settle at all. When one man stood and asked where such a true home should be, she pointed to the horizon and told him they'd find solace in a place where the valley meets the sky. And thus it was that they left their static life and took to finding the impassible horizon."

What followed was the heavy silence of a tension I did not understand.

"This story seems ancient," I pointed out. Gatsi had trained me to be critical. "How have I never heard it before?"

Gatsi and the chieftain were silent in response, Gatsi with his eyes on the fire, avoiding the chieftain's stare. I tried a different question.

"Then that is why we move? That's why it's our tradition never to settle?"

"Yes," Gatsi replied. "That is why. But tradition is often based on necessity, long-forgotten as it may be."

"Then why have we been here for so long? What has kept us from moving? We haven't planted much here, besides a few small gardens and Frai's little spice field."

"An excellent question, Rennik," the chieftain cut in. "But it seems as though we'll resume our tradition soon enough."

Gatsi kept his eyes on the fire, his face kept stone-still. He did not meet the chieftain's gaze as he was spoken to.

"Gatsi," he said, "if you will, stop by Kinran's on the way back to your hut. Tell my wife and daughter to return to me."

Gatsi left promptly and without a word. The chieftain watched him go, then turned to me.

"Go to your family, Rennik. Sleep well tonight. I may call on your advice tomorrow."

I thanked him and left the hut, secretly grateful to escape the graveyard that was the chieftain's home. I had taken no more than three steps before Gatsi placed a hand on my shoulder and turned me to face him. The sun had long since set, and we spoke briefly in the darkness of night.

"I want you to be ready for the grasses first thing in the morning. Do not tell the chieftain. There is something you need to see." He hesitated. "I want to show you the real reason we've stayed here all this time."

THE NEXT MORNING FOUND ME STARING OUT AT THE HORIZON for a long hour having lost the comfort I'd had with the surrounding wilds. Two weeks ago, I could comb through the grasses while tracking animals that couldn't be found without confidence and skill. I would do so without feeling threatened by anything more than the occasional predator. Even then, I knew the nature of such predators, and knew how to scare them off or survive by other means.

Now, I found myself wondering what horrors lay in hiding just under the surface of my perception. My father was dead. Ko was dead. Macha, Ikoda, Ciqala and Banar may have joined them. The grasses used to be a place of comfort to me, even if I couldn't see past a few feet when I crouched within them. This newfound fear warped them and turned the familiar into a thing of terror.

I wondered where Ikoda was, and what had really happened to Macha. I wondered if the people I'd seen in battle were right in front of me, kneeling in the grass just at the base of the ridge.

Gatsi found me, and at his request we began walking to the river. I was glad for the company.

"Where are we going?" I asked.

"You'll need to be patient," was all he explained. "And you'll need to save many questions for later."

I told him about our journey and asked about the strange person I'd seen on my watch.

"You said you felt...cold?" He kept his expression flat, but I thought I saw the smallest spark of apprehension in his eyes. "It is possible," he continued, "that Macha had just been taken by some enemy party. But it isn't just his disappearance that bothers you. It's how it happened. It sounds familiar, no?"

"It sounds like a Shiver," I said. It was the first time I'd admitted it to myself. "But..."

"But?"

"That can't be right."

"Why not?"

I shook my head. These were simply the sort of things that didn't happen.

"What *is* a Shiver? Aside from myth," I asked.

"Some answers are hidden even from me, Rennik."

I was doubtful, and without knowing what question to ask about it, I went instead with a question I'd had for days. "What about your smoke? You and Tella, it looked like you had used the smoke somehow."

"If a man is alone in the wilds," he explained, "and hears a twig break nearby, what would his first fear be?"

"Someone is approaching."

"Of course. And if someone were approaching with malicious intent, and the man had simply chosen not to listen for signs of approach, he would be clueless."

Gatsi stopped speaking as if the explanation were finished.

"...and?" I asked.

"There are more ways than one to hear something approaching, Rennik. And one must occasionally think to listen if he is to listen at all."

"The clans, you mean. You think the enemies are approaching?"

"The smoke would not likely warn us of human visitors."

"What other visitors would there be?"

"Time will tell."

"This is sorcery," I said.

"It seems as such when only two people can do it, hmm?

When it is strange? But here *we* are, the only two in the village anywhere near proficient in reading. Reading is not sorcery. It is only a skill. A lack of participants doesn't qualify something as magic. I will ask you to not mystify that which is unfamiliar, and instead consider these sorts of things as rare skills."

"Tell me where we're going." This time I said it with iron in my voice.

"To answer your questions."

"Oh," I said, rolling my eyes, "is *that* what we're doing?"

The river was a wide one, running through the hills a mile to the east of our village. It was one of the many sources of food nearby, as the fish were plentiful and the mussels were an easy gather. The river itself had many side pools that would trap freshwater shellfish constantly, so if my hunting was unsuccessful for a long period of time, my family would likely live off of what the river offered with just a bit of luck.

We approached the river, which was flowing a little higher than usual. The lands far to the south of us must have seen warmth and heavy rain — a sign that the full brunt of spring was approaching. We traveled north along the shore. When we stopped, the bank opposite ours sat about a half-mile away, though in places to the immediate north and south the river's width was lesser. As the river flowed through the distant regions to the north, however, it widened to be entire miles across before draining into the sea. This is something I'd heard from others and never seen myself.

Gatsi and I had reached a part of the shore neighboring a collection of rocks that plateaued above the river's surface. They formed a natural pathway to a sort of islet in the river that sat closest to our shore. The islet itself was only about a hundred feet long, and only about fifty feet across as its shape ran lengthwise with the water's current. It seemed like the kind of whimsical scene my brother and his friends would treasure. In fact, the mulberry tree they frequented was just over a half mile, south on the bank. Gatsi removed his leather shoes and prompted me to do the same.

"We'll need to show respect in a place of such power," was all he said in explanation. As usual, I had questions, but followed anyway.

Dominating the islet was a massive tree. Its branches, reaching both high into the air and far over the water, gave it the shape of a huge verdant sphere. I didn't need to travel under its winding, spider-like boughs to know that smaller wildlife would find easy sanctuary in its branches, but it was exactly in this direction that Gatsi was leading me. We stepped carefully along the flat rocks, water lapping at the skin of my feet and between my toes until they were met with the short, lush grass of the islet.

The foliage above us drew complex patterns of contesting shadow and sun on our faces and upon the earth. Breezes rustled the leaves, and the boughs that held them were steady against the soft wind and the weight of various small animals traveling the many paths of the tree's branches.

"Here it is," said Gatsi with a reverent voice, though surprisingly I detected an undertone of fear. I scanned the mighty tree and noted its craggy bark, rigid and leathery leaves, and wide-spreading branches.

"It looks like a normal oak."

"It *looks* like a live oak," he specified. "The kind that only grow closer to the warmer lands south of here. But this isn't an oak. It is called the Delkhi, and it differs from an oak in many ways. I've seen only one other in my travels, and it was much further north, where the earth was all sand and stone. It doesn't appear to have a preferred environment. The specimen to the north was...different."

"So it's a hardier oak," I simplified. As usual, I sensed he wasn't telling me something, but I found myself tiring of his cryptic responses.

"No," he responded, "very far from it. Normally, with a little work, one can strip or flake some of an oak's bark away. The bark of the Delkhi, however, is impossible to mar. You will not find any knotholes or imperfections in its trunk, and its leaves have no veins," he said, softly cupping one such leaf in his hand. It was a flat, waxy color that lacked any of the normal texture a leaf should have. It looked somehow out of place.

"How does it survive without veins in its leaves?"

"By mysterious means. There is much about the Delkhi that is unknown, or perhaps unknowable, but what I know to be true is that the leaves and bark are a façade."

"They're not real?"

"A camouflage, by definition."

I wracked my mind for a logical explanation.

"Its roots, then?" I asked. "It depends solely on the soil rather than sunlight."

"A reasonable assumption. But I can tell you from experience that its roots are...unique. I'm not sure it depends too greatly on soil. For nutrients, that is."

"Then I'm not sure how this tree can live. It seems to defy everything a tree does."

Gatsi smiled his signature wide grin that let me know he's in control of the conversation.

"Correct. This isn't a tree at all, Rennik."

My brow furrowed, and I waited for Gatsi to explain further. He merely kept his gaze on the tree and remained silent.

"Well, then," I said impatiently, "this must be the largest liverwort I've ever seen."

"Not a liverwort, either," he responded coolly, refusing to

acknowledge my sarcasm. He took a deep and somber breath. "This, Rennik, is a living, conscious creature that has taken on the seeming of our world, not unlike a predator that uses the grass for cover, or a hare that changes its fur to remain unseen in the winter months."

I took a tentative step backward and eyed the thing cautiously. With so many questions filling my mind, I stuttered as I struggled to pick one. I was suddenly overtaken by a fearful uncertainty, the kind one feels when familiar things are made strange.

"*Our* world?" I asked. "What do you mean?"

"I suppose I mean the simpler world." His tone was even and serious.

"This thing is conscious?"

"Something like that. It communicates, to put it simply. Its behavior is actually quite similar to what we see in all living things. Everything it does stems from its will to survive."

I suddenly found it difficult to speak. "What could something like this do to survive?" I managed. My head felt light. The air seemed to hum quietly. "What threatens it?"

"Its roots spread far, through much of Kalanos. You've noticed beasts acting strange lately. I believe this is the product of the Delkhi's fear. But it can give great things. Rare skills—"

"Your smoke?"

"Yes. Like my knowledge of the smoke."

A heavy anxiety built itself in my chest, an amalgam of the frustration I felt with the uncertainty of the Delkhi tree and something undetectable — some unperceived and dominating weight that sank into me like a stone.

Gatsi saw my struggling and smiled.

"The animals are...afraid?" I asked weakly.

"No, Rennik. It is the fear the *Delkhi* feels that is instilled in them. A forced empathy."

"Gatsi, I..." I began, but found myself wavering, my vision swimming like the eddies in the river. My knees buckled, and I caught myself on the branch to my left.

"Be calm, Rennik. Take deep breaths."

I did so.

"Give me your bow and quiver. You won't need them tonight."

I obeyed.

My hand found the skin over my heart as my chest tightened. I couldn't speak.

"You must set this fear aside."

I fell to my hands and knees. The patterns of sunlight warped and darkened until they shifted into a starry night sky eclipsed by oaken branches. The stars above spun slowly as I fell into vertigo.

"Let yourself go."

Gatsi's voice reverberated among unseen walls.

The stars swam like the embers of a burning fire.

Let yourself go.

16

THINGS UNSEEN

"Dreams are a way in which we speak to ourselves, and like all languages, fluency takes time."

— GATSI

The fire was too large for the space it filled, but the extra heat had been a necessary risk. Its orange light flickered among the simple furnishings of an animal-skin hut. The occupants were a sinewy man, shivering though unblanketed by the many furs they owned, and a woman, rocking on her knees with worry and working a bit of string through hide.

"Do you remember that man named Itka? From that group of Yohri we traveled with?" The man broke a silence that had tensed between them like a muscle under pressure. He held his blackened fingers to the fire as he spoke.

She did her best to ignore him.

"He had a boy, a courageous little thing, that would sneak out into the grasses at night. He'd come back in the morning with wild tubers or whatever other edible plants he could find. Itka would be furious, but the boy kept insisting that he wanted to get his own food. He had such a fierce independence about him. He'd have kept going out even if it killed him."

"It did," snapped the woman. "It *did* kill him."

The man nodded. "So it did. But if that boy's family had been killed first, he would have had a chance. It's a dangerous world, and even though Itka forbade the boy from leaving, I think a quieter part of him *wanted* the boy to go out. He wanted him to learn, to feel fear, to know how to live on his own."

"And instead he *died* on his own," the woman countered. She punched the needle through the hide with a vigorous force. "They found his body trampled. They only knew it was him because of his size. I'm sure it was easy to tell — no one else that young would have ever been out in the wilds by himself." She punctuated the last statement by glaring at the man.

The man bowed his head apologetically. After a long while he turned his attention to a third presence in the hut. A boy, hardly noticeable under the thick layer of blankets, shivered against a cold that wasn't there.

"You left him," the woman said suddenly, her voice faltering like broken stone.

"I couldn't find him." The man defended himself, raising his voice, repeating the statement for what would not be the last time that night. "I ran up and down the southern portion of that river for hours, Raisha. Wherever he was, I didn't find him."

"He walked back through the snow on his own, Nakai. He had so many chances to die — he *should* be dead!" She threw the hide against the wall of the hut and cradled her belly — her second child, warm and ballooning from her body.

The man's tears welled up and fell as the woman stormed to the other side of the hut in frustration. "Damn this storm..." she muttered, her words drowned out against the screaming winter winds outside.

The boy stirred. He called for his father, his voice laden with the gruffness of ice.

The man stood over his son and tucked him tighter into the blankets and pelts.

"I'm cold," the boy said in what was nearly a whisper.

"I know, son. You'll be better soon."

"Aren't you cold from saving me?" His small and shaken voice was hardly audible over the wind.

The man stood frozen by a guilt colder than the river's water and decided, against his gut, to let the boy believe. The boy fell back into a deep sleep.

"I'm sorry, Rennik." The tears came more heavily now. "I'm so, so sorry. I'll never leave you again."

The hut grew dimmer. The small family's belongings disappeared into shadow, and the space was instead filled with long shelves, a lesser fire, and a man with gray hair at his peak. He tended not to a frozen boy, but to a rain-soaked girl, shivering all the same.

The man helped the girl with her warm soup as he spoke softly.

"Now," he started, "I know you're cold. But I need you to tell me what has happened." He tried to coax the words out of her, though her voice seemed to have been taken by some sort of trauma.

"You're safe now," he continued. "You're going to be completely okay, but I need you to describe what happened."

The girl's eyes were fixed somewhere distant, as though she heard nothing of what the man said.

He leaned in and cradled her small frame. "Perhaps you need more time, but I need you to tell me what you saw." He looked as though he were about to give up.

"Birds." Her whisper was nearly indiscernible against the heavy vibrato of her shivering.

Gatsi leaned in. "What kind of birds. Big? Small?"

"Big."

"*How big?*" he asked.

They disappeared, and the hut darkened and lighted all over again.

Years passed. The girl shifted into a taller frame, though scarcely different in any other dimension. On this day she carried an overwhelming smell of smoke. It overtook the hut, still cluttered in its shelves and niches, though it had moved with the village to a new location. One in which it had sat for years.

The same man, grown older, stood at a small table, staring down at a cluster of small dowels next to a copper plate. He addressed her as she entered.

"That was dangerous, but now isn't the time for lecture. What is it you've seen?"

"Dangerous," she repeated. "See people. Horses." She hesitated between each new word.

"Other clans?"

She nodded.

"Fighting each other?"

She shook her head. "Fighting with each other," she said.

"They're fighting together?"

"Together."

"Are they coming this way?"

"This way."

"How much time do we have?"

She furrowed her brow and produced no answer.

"Who has brought these clans together?"

The hut shifted once again before she could respond. A single ember glided up on the lift of the hot air in the hut and became the only speck of light on a field of dark landscape.

The ember was a distant campfire, well below the eyes of a crow through which the scene was perceived. Around the campfire feasted men dressed in red feathers and paints, their leader sitting nearest the flames. Next to him sat a woman in white paint and another man, though he was the most disparate of them all. His skin was unusually pale and his hair a bright gold, and he wore no colors. Behind him lay the disassembled leather straps of a metal chest piece, glinting in its many angles from the firelight.

They spoke in the Kalanosi tongue, though the pale man's accent betrayed his fluency. He did not belong there.

"What of the Turin?" the red-painted man asked.

"I have yet to hear back from my ambassador," replied the pale man with gold hair, "though I doubt they can refuse the offer."

"My Wahto fighters and these Sree are many and capable," said the woman in white. "If they refuse, we will force them to join us."

Another woman sat silently near them. She wore a violet string braided into her hair. Her hatchet-like face was studying the conversation intensely.

"Wahto, Sree, Turin," the pale man answered. "A good start, but I think *all* will join our cause. And soon, we will all fight under a common flag. My king — *our* king," he corrected, "will be incredibly pleased with you all when we find the individuals we seek."

The crow dived into the grasses, and sunlight poured over a new landscape.

The sky stretched wide over the plains of Kalanosi ancestors.

The fire was roaring as the men and women left their camp. Several stayed behind to keep its blaze alive. The hunters stayed low, keeping their heads under the snowy grasses. Their target would not be difficult to find. Its path was wide, and it stood an entire man's height above the tall grass.

The vulture who watched stayed close, anticipating a fine dinner.

Suddenly, a massive tusk swept through the grasses, tearing stalks and men from the earth. The mammoth's cry was angry and desperate. It had traveled alone for days since these people had attacked its herd — what small amount of its family had been left of it. This beast would not fall as easily as its brothers and sisters had. It was the last true fighter of its kind; it was the last of its kind at all. The mammoth fought with the armor and vigor of an unnamed and existential terror.

It killed two and flung itself into a sprint.

Spears and arrows lashed out from the grasses, though few could penetrate the creature's thick hide. It turned and swung again, catching the legs of a woman and sending her dozens of feet back, spilling the arrows from her quiver like shattered bone.

Suddenly, a spear tore through its chest.

The mammoth rose rampant and crushed the assailant with its massive feet. Blood poured over the tangles in its brown fur.

It took to run again, but found its strength sapped. Its

eyes grew wide and panicked, anger leaving them like the breath from its great lungs.

Its eyes closed as it fell to the earth, dirt pluming like tufts of upset ash. The beast, nearly the size of their homes, gathered air for the last time and trumpeted once into the swallowing horizon.

The hunters returned to the camp before nightfall.

Then, they were gone. Their tents and drying racks simply cleaned from sight. The last light of the resting sun disappeared in strips.

The fire darkened and blackness overwhelmed all things.

The subtle glow of the moon washed slowly over a floor covered with animal pelts as a tent flap was moved slowly and silently. A single second, and the stranger was inside the hut.

The girl whose eyes lent this memory lay unseen beneath the thick fur of an oryx in a little bed on the floor. She wanted to speak, but her fear was heavy. Instead, she sank into the safety of the fur.

The stranger stepped lightly through the darkness of the hut, around the fire which had long been extinguished. Its coals no longer shed their waning orange light. No smoke rose toward the hole in the ceiling of the hut. It was a dead fire.

The stranger stood beside her parents' bed of furs. He lifted the lid of a small wicker box, and with his hand rose the thin head of a snake.

The father in the bed felt no pain, no indication that he had been bitten.

The stranger did not see the girl under the tan and black pelt.

The girl was just as paralyzed as her father's lungs were soon to be.

Her fearful hands crushed the crown of flowers she had held when she fell asleep.

She ducked beneath the covers until she saw nothing.

She tried not to breathe.

Sunlight burst upon a limitless field of feather grass.

The thick pelt of the oryx now moved with the rest of its herd, combing the stalks, searching for food. Life beat its path under the creature's pelt.

The herd stepped lightly over the split and bloodied shaft of a spear whose burial shroud was its own yellow cloth.

The stalks of the grasses erupted into rapid growth and became thick trees with heavy foliage. Their trunks curved up and away from a massive object boasting the semblance of an oak — a singular and unassuming part of a sprawling forest. The sun shone over this far-away land with twilight beams. At the base of the seeming tree sat a long-dead animal, its meat half-devoured. Roots were wound tightly around the corpse to ensure their feast.

The horizon was curtained by the crowded trees. The wildlife was relaxed; a doe waltzed between trunks without fear, and a raccoon chased birds among the tree branches playfully. Breathing slowly, its fur tossed lightly by the breezes that weaved through the forest, a large wolf lounged at the tree. Its nose was buried under its curled tail as it assumed the instinctual sleeping position of a creature who knew the cold well.

Among the untainted wilderness was a woman. With a sword at her side, she knelt down to the roots at the surface, tracing her hand over them. Her hair was long and was the same reddish color of the bloodied animal at the base of the tree.

She murmured something to the roots, then turned and looked me in the eye.

~

I woke and gasped for air. My skin felt frozen, and I began to shiver uncontrollably. My eyes pained against the blunt force of the midday sun. I was hungry.

My head was fixed upward, and as I tried to move I found myself bound. Something rough in texture was keeping me in place.

The roots.

I had been caged by a series of roots at the base of the Delkhi. My muscles strained against the rough grip of the bark, but I remembered Gatsi's mentioning that it was unbreakable. Did the roots move on their own? Had he known this would happen?

I heard a loud purring just in front of me.

I forced my eyes downward as far as they could go.

A mountain lion, large and unafraid, stared into my eyes just a few inches away. From its mouth hung a dead and bloodied rabbit, its lifeless stare pointing into the distance. I could smell the mountain lion's wet, musty fur and the bloody heat of its breath. I became suddenly aware of how vulnerable my throat was in this position. The creature's maw could easily fit around my entire neck. I began to panic, and I thrust with all my strength against the snare of the Delkhi. The bark tore at the skin of my neck and arms, but I struggled until the effort left me tired and breathless. I braced for the mountain lion's attack.

Instead, the giant cat simply strode to the side, keeping its eyes on mine for a moment longer. It left my vision, and I heard it drop the dead rabbit at the roots of the Delkhi.

The roots began to stir.

My arms, chest, and head found physical agency as they were released from the snaking clutch.

I rolled forward onto my hands and breathed heavily, now that I was able to do so. The mountain lion had spread itself out and lounged in the spotted, beaming sunlight near the roots. Its length in this position was astounding. The rabbit lay motionless where it had been dropped. The predator seemed to take no interest in me and licked the blood from its lips carelessly before yawning. It seemed at ease, but my basic instincts disallowed me to feel any comfort while I was near this killer animal.

I glanced down at my arms to see rough, abrasive wounds snaking toward my shoulders. It was obvious now where Gatsi's wounds had come from.

Looking straight ahead, I saw bison scattered along the shore I had come from. Birds chatted playfully among the branches above. A small turtle crept onto the shore and blinked slowly. Most importantly, a storm was gathering in the distance. This sunlight wouldn't last for long.

I knew I could try to wait for the bison herd to move on, but that could take hours if not an entire day, and I was already feeling the effects of an extreme hunger, to which I was admittedly unaccustomed. That, combined with the rational fear of a storm in the open plains, was enough to get me moving.

I struggled to my feet using a large branch for support. Judging by the sun's position, I had been unconscious for almost an entire day. The dreams I had experienced, the strange things I'd seen, were all clouding my mind — clouding the part of me trying to focus on getting through an entire herd of lounging bison. I shook the dreams from the surface of my thoughts and began to step lightly over the rocks in the river. My feet were soaked, as the river had risen slightly since my trip to the island. I could see my leather shoes sitting at the back of a reclined bison.

I made a little noise before reaching the shore. I figured that letting the creature know I was there was better than spooking it when I was a foot away. It raised its head lazily, took a slow look at the approaching human, and laid its head back down. Warily, I crept up and gently took the shoes. I put them on and made my way through the herd.

The air was hot with their breath. At first I was apprehensive, as any sane hunter would be, but the bison seemed to consider me no bother. I allowed myself to relax and cut a path through the herd.

As much as my ease increased, I would never feel completely safe without my bow. It wasn't about self-defense or the inability to hunt for food, though those thoughts are certainly paramount. I think it had more to do with the fact that it was one of the last things I had of my father's. It wasn't really his, but he helped me craft it when I was grown enough to use a man's bow. I suppose that really made it *our* bow.

Uprooted from reality and alone, I walked the fields back to the village.

17

INTO THE DIRT

"There are some Shivers that keep the spirits of their victims in their heads, in a kind of pocket, so as to call on their knowledge when they need it. Imagine spending your death being interrogated by the one who killed you."

— GATSI

There is a certain feeling in the keen observer at the precipice of a storm. The air is rarefied and becomes electric. The hair on one's arms begins to stand on its own, and the heart races in terror of a force of nature that can effortlessly whelm most anything in its way. As children we were told this feeling means that the Wahkeen are in the midst of choosing a man to strike down.

I buried this disquiet deep in my chest and continued into the village. As I did, I couldn't help but hear the conversations around me.

"In his sleep?"

"Too young to be fair, I say."

"He was a great man. Did you see his wife? Her hands couldn't stop shaking enough to braid the grasses. Poor dear."

"And that young girl."

I thought of the dreams I'd had at the foot of the Delkhi — the man with the snake, the girl who saw it all.

Could what I had seen be true?

After walking toward Gatsi's hut, I slowed my steps as the potential reality of my visions dawned on me.

"Rennik!" yelled Avid, suddenly behind me. "Gatsi told me to find you! He wants you to meet him in the chieftain's hut!"

"Avid, has something happened?"

"You haven't heard?" he asked, surprised for a moment. His words drew the last of my composure out from my body.

"The chieftain is dead."

THE ENTRANCE TO THE CHIEFTAIN'S HUT WAS BULWARKED BY his wife, his young daughter, and a skein of villagers. They sat in a tight cluster, braiding the grasses. This was a process of working long, thin stalks into a traditional ornament that would hang around the wrist of the deceased's loved ones. It was meant to symbolize the time of grief. The grasses would be wrapped into a tight and complex weave, and over time would dry out. It was said that by the time the circlet fell apart, it was no longer time to grieve, and the wearer was symbolically free from the weight of the loss. To unburden oneself from an emotion was to "let it go to the grasses" as the ornament fell apart and returned to the earth.

"But those grasses will be around us forever," my mother had told me once.

Gatsi saw me coming and stepped out of the hut. Even though everyone knew I spent much of my time with him, I wouldn't have dared entered the home without his escorting me, lest I offend the grieving widow and the privacy of the family. As I passed the group of villagers, I gave a solemn bow of my head. Gatsi led me inside. I couldn't feel the steps I took, only the anticipation of what I was about to see.

On the side of the large hut opposite the door lay the body of the chieftain. Over him was gently cast the soft fur blanket of an oryx pelt. His eyes were closed, his face was relaxed, and overall, he seemed very at peace.

I felt my hands begin to shake.

"Rennik," Gatsi chided, "I know you must be hungry and confused, but you need to be calm. We have much to—"

"I saw it happen," I blurted out. I hoped the people outside had not heard me.

A wave of understanding poured over Gatsi's face.

"Rennik," he said in hushed tones, pulling me deeper into the hut. "You saw the chieftain pass?"

"Yes," I managed, my voice wavering.

"Did he convulse? Did it look to be his heart?"

"I think he was murdered."

Gatsi's hand slowly left my shoulder, and after a few seconds of stunned silence he darted around to study the body.

"How was it done? Did you see who did it?"

"Gatsi, tell me what I saw isn't true. Tell me it didn't happen."

"I need you to tell me *what* happened." His voice was rushed. "Only then can we discover the truth."

I swallowed hard and willed myself to step closer to the

body. With one trembling hand I reached out to where I saw the snake strike.

On the inside of his elbow were two miniscule puncture marks, nearly indiscernible from the natural blemishes along the rest of his arm.

I collapsed backwards and landed on the bison pelt. The bone-like earth beneath it hurt and I scrambled up again, struggling to maintain any sort of composure.

Gatsi's face was close to the body, examining the arm. I chimed in with an explanation.

"It was a sn—"

"Krait," he said, correcting me before I had even finished.

I tried to quell my panicked breaths. "What?" I asked.

"These are the marks left by a krait. It's a kind of snake."

"I've never heard of it."

"You," he said, "contain a deep internal catalog of Kalanosi wildlife. What does this tell you?"

I thought for a moment. "This snake isn't from Kalanos," I answered.

"Precisely."

"Then where?"

"Rucost." The reach of his knowledge amazed me at times. "Krait venom paralyzes muscles, especially in the face. It also keeps the heart from beating and the lungs from pushing air. The bite of a krait can be completely unnoticeable. It makes for an effective means of assassination."

"How could this have happened? Traders?"

"My first thought, too. But I can't imagine their kind bringing such a dangerous creature on a long trip. Hardly a likely sell to a small and peaceful clan, from their perspective. But the snake wouldn't come out here on its own."

A sudden realization hit me. "Gatsi, there's something I

never told you. When I cut my arm out in the grasses, I heard voices talking. Voices I didn't recognize."

Gatsi looked at me, eyes trembling with a mixture of calculation and worry. "Someone is near, Rennik. Very near." He looked back to the snakebite. "Someone who doesn't want to be found."

I thought back to the people from our fight. They were too far away to have done this, and most of the people in Kalanos who were dispositioned to kill someone would do so face to face. This was cowardly.

"The girl," I remembered aloud, "Nivan. She saw." I glanced down at the floor to see the scattered bits of the snowdrop-flower crown.

"I will speak to her and her mother in a moment or so. Right now I'm more concerned with the questions you surely have." He resumed his work with the body. He was preparing the chieftain for his funeral.

There were many things I should have asked first, but my mind was fixated on the dead man.

"There was something between you and the chieftain that night. I'd never seen you act that way. It seemed like you didn't want to tell that ancient story."

"The story is not ancient," was his response. "The people in the story are ancient, yes, but their story is relatively new."

"I don't understand."

"Don't think, Rennik, that you're the only person to have seen distant things at the foot of the Delkhi."

I rubbed the deep scratches the bark had left on my neck and waited for him to continue. He sat across the body from me and spoke with a deeper voice.

"Tell me what you saw."

"I had strange dreams at the base of the tree." I studied

his face for his reaction and saw none. "Of you, of my mother and father after I fell through the ice, but..."

"But what?"

"They couldn't have been real, Gatsi. The things the tree showed me were wrong. I know I saw the chieftain's death, and that obviously happened, but...I still remember falling through the river — I remember my father saving me in the woods the night I almost died. At the Delkhi, it seemed like my father *didn't* save me."

Gatsi kept his eyes tied to his work on the body and spoke carefully. "There are many things with which we find familiarity that are merely inventions of the mind, Rennik. The Delkhi seems to have quite a knack for disillusion."

I was taken aback. "You're saying my father didn't save me?" I grew angry and red. "You're going to tell me that my memories of him pulling me out of the water, building a fire, and warming me back from the edge of death are some sort of an illusion?"

"The mind of a child is full of the desperation to make sense. It invents things to compensate for the unknown instead of simply accepting it, *especially* in a state of hypothermia. You were just a boy, Rennik. You were so young..." he trailed off, eyes closed in remembrance. "To your parents it was a small lie. They didn't have the heart to tell you the truth."

"Then what was the truth? How could a small boy have survived in that cold? And how do we know the tree's visions are true and my memories aren't?"

"It was a truth your parents didn't even know," he said. "The Delkhi saved you that night."

"What? That doesn't...No, you're wrong! My father pulled me from the river! I *know* he saved me!"

"It seems to have a great sympathy for children."

"What?" I asked.

"The Delkhi. Only certain people can do what you did last night, Rennik. Can see what you've seen. And it seems to be limited to those who have been connected to the Delkhi prior."

"How could that tree have saved me? What could it have done?"

"It's not a tree, Rennik. You'd do well to remember this. And much of nature obeys the Delkhi. It's well within its ability to warm a small child."

Confusion was doubtlessly painted across my face. Gatsi saw this and tried a different route.

"Surely, in the visions, you saw more than just your own life. Surely you saw things well beyond the reach of your perception."

"Yes," I said softly. "I saw you and Tella, I saw a mammoth hunt...I saw Macha's broken spear."

"And these visions were seen from the eyes of children, animals, or from no one at all," he predicted. "Those in whom the Delkhi takes interest. The reach of the Delkhi is broad. It controls much of the region we inhabit and the creatures within it. And it's not just you — it seems to favor all children. It's as though it gives them a second chance, if they need it."

"So these elders with their superstitions...they're right to fear me?" I asked, defeated at the thought.

"Fear? No. But their wariness is rooted in tradition, and much tradition is rooted in truth, even when it's forgotten."

An inkling of understanding stained my thoughts, though I had no way of articulating it. I did, however, make one immediate connection.

"Tella," I said.

Gatsi nodded.

"She was so young, and gone for so long," he explained. "There was no way she had the knowledge to survive on her own. You saw this, and I can confirm it as truth, just as you've seen the truth in the chieftain's murder. What else?"

"They hunted down a mammoth. I think it was the last one...it was horrible."

"I'm sure."

"And a foreign man eating with leaders of the Sree and Wahto."

Gatsi's eyes went wide.

"What?" He asked incredulously.

"He had golden hair and pale skin. He talked about a king and said something about joining clans together."

"He is the one who has joined them together? Who is he? Are they headed here? *What king did he speak of?*" His voice was fast and panicked.

"I...I don't know, I don't think I saw anything like that. He said they were seeking certain individuals. Gatsi, I'm sorry, but what happened to me? If these visions were true, where did they come from?"

He took a deep breath and gathered himself.

From the floor of the hut, he brought up a bowl of dark, pulpy paint. With his thumb he dragged the dark-green color upon the face of the body, drawing a traditional warrior's funeral paint. I suppose in death, even a chieftain is no greater than the warriors and hunters from which he came. After a few silent moments, Gatsi continued.

"Like I've said, the Delkhi's reaches are far. It seems to connect people with all of that over which it has power. Memories, current things being seen. It can let one see what it sees through the eyes of animals and children."

"There were animals. A mountain lion, the bison herd,

and others, just relaxing near the tree. Do they use it somehow?"

"I think the Delkhi uses them. Or perhaps they benefit mutually, like an egret on a bison's back."

"Where does this thing come from? Is it dangerous?"

"I don't know where it comes from, and it may be dangerous, but mostly it seems to protect. In fact, that's why our people settled here and stopped migration for so long."

"And that's why the herds stopped here as well."

He nodded.

Thunder rolled in the distance.

"How do you know so much of this thing?" I asked.

"I mentioned yesterday that I had seen one far to the north. It was there that I experienced visions of my own."

"What did you see?"

"I think the things *you've* seen are much more pressing at the moment, Rennik."

"Tella and I both came close to death as children. You're suggesting this has something to do with it. Something similar happened to you, then?"

"Yes." He clenched his jaw. His hand grazed his neck in a seemingly unconscious gesture. I waited for him to continue, but he didn't. I decided not to press the subject.

He dipped his finger back into the paint and continued the designs down the arm of the body, hesitating before painting over the bite marks.

"Did the chieftain and his men come to a course of action while I was gone?" I asked.

"Not quite," he answered. "They couldn't agree on what to do. Several of the men hadn't known your father and doubted the counsel of a stranger's son. They questioned the chieftain's plan to migrate. Malik did her best to try and convince them, but they didn't want to risk leaving the home they've grown to know."

"And now that he's dead?" I asked.

"They will surely scramble, and when men are scared, they latch on to the familiar. In this case, the familiar is this village. They won't want to leave, Rennik."

I noticed Gatsi's jaw clench in anger.

"I thought settling here would protect our children." He spoke softly. I realized then that the anger he felt was directed at himself. "I thought the Delkhi might keep us safe. It's why I convinced the chieftain to stay here."

"So that's where that tension was coming from. He blamed you for our complacency."

"I believe so, yes."

"But maybe the Delkhi is still protecting us." I considered for a moment telling the village about the Delkhi, but there must be a reason Gatsi hasn't, and they already distrust with their superstitions. "Maybe the only way to keep us safe is to warn us of what is to come. If it can't stop the other clans, it can at least help us to avoid their path."

"Perhaps, Rennik, but you need to understand that this is our valley. I am the man who wanted to settle in one spot, and these are the people that won't want to leave."

"But who is our Senga? The chieftain is dead. Who is left to convince them to flee a threat they haven't seen?"

Gatsi handed me my bow and quiver and looked deep into my eyes, saying nothing. His face carried a vague worry.

"Are there any others?" I thought to ask. "Other people who are...*connected* to the Delkhi?"

Gatsi seemed to consider his answer carefully. "I know of a Turin woman. She—"

His response was cut short as the hide of the hut's entrance suddenly burst open.

"Rennik!" Malik's voice surprised me as she came to a halt.

I turned to look at her, my heart leaping to action with the alarm in her voice.

"It's Ciqala," she said. "He's back."

I EXITED THE HUT TO FIND TELLA TO MY IMMEDIATE RIGHT.

"Going to kill Rennik," she said with quiet urgency.

"What?"

A sharp and sudden pain erupted on the left side of my face. I fell to the ground clutching my jaw.

Ciqala stood over me, face wrenched in anger. Tella must have known he was coming and repeated his words.

He looked terrible: his face was dirty, he had bruises on his arms, and he was disheveled from his trip through the wilds.

"Get up," he demanded.

A crowd must have followed him; a large strand of villagers formed a half circle among the huts, wary and curious all at once. Banar took a few steps out of the crowd before Malik put a threatening hand on his chest.

"This isn't your fight," I heard her say.

I rolled to my side and slowly stood up, stepping back several paces. This time, I wanted to fight, but the pit in my stomach hadn't left me yet. I hadn't eaten since yesterday's breakfast.

"Ciqala," I managed through a pained jaw, "we can talk about this."

"No," he responded. "We can't. That one was for the morning you hit me." He stormed closer to me. "And this is for that damned stampede."

I dodged several punches as he launched forth. We circled together. He tried to land a blow and I weaved away, both of us contained by the spectators and huts around us. The sky curled and snapped behind him.

He feinted left and caught me off guard. Again I felt his knuckles, this time against my ribs.

"Rennik, just fight back!" Malik shouted from somewhere behind me.

Something broke inside of me when I heard Malik's command. Her words somehow unhinged the floodgates keeping my anger back, and I felt the catharsis like a river's sudden freshet.

I took a painful breath and countered.

I landed three good strikes — a lucky start for someone who doesn't know how to fight. His hide shirt provided some protection, but under it I knew he could bruise just as easily as I. The skin of my knuckles tore in small ways against the rough and weather-worn material, but I couldn't feel it at the time. I only pictured my fists against his ribs.

I continued my assault, and he took several steps back. Then, as I leaned too far into a punch, he ducked and kicked my feet out from under me.

I fell hard onto the dirt and felt the breath get knocked out of my lungs. The arrows spilled from my quiver, and my hand fumbled around the dirt for one of them. In the midst of my rage I didn't stop to think that I could kill him — it just came through me, more water in the surge.

My fingers grasped the grain of an arrow's wooden shaft.

Ciqala knelt down and clutched my collar, lifting my chest off the ground. His face eclipsed the sky, but from what I could see, the clouds were quickly darkening.

His knuckles crashed against my jaw, and the arrow fell from my hand.

"You killed Ko!"

He slammed his fist into my face.

"You killed Ikoda!"

Another punch. My vision swam. I choked on my breath and felt suddenly cold.

"You coward!"

Then, just as he brought his arm back to strike again, a collection of shouts came from the direction of the crowd. I turned to look, and through my swollen eyes I could barely make out the scene.

Avid and his friends were sprinting full force at my attacker.

They tackled him with a group effort, and he fell from atop my chest. Their fists collided with him like hail on a hut. It hurt to smile.

"Get off!" Ciqala yelled helplessly. But he was flailing under the repeated attacks and could only try to push them away without hurting them. There had to be at least eight of the boys. Weak as they were, they were holding him down well. I thought it might only be a matter of time before Ciqala was forced to strike at them.

Villagers moved to intervene in a body to ensure the safety of the children, and I felt myself being dragged away.

18

VISITORS

"It is said that the Achare are a jovial and lighthearted people..."

— EXCERPT FROM BRALLIC SEVERIN'S
*KALANOS: A STUDY OF PLACE AND
PEOPLE.*

Some clans, like the Turin, lay their religion thick upon their people, and it is that belief that keeps them from tearing each other apart. The threat of punishment from their goddess dissuades theft, murder, and other undesirable things. Other clans, like my own, have always put their faith in the strength and competence of a leader. We sometimes recognized Dremma in moments of terror, but the chieftain was always assumed to know what's best, especially since he spoke plainly and was reasonable. He left no room for interpretation, like belief would. If there were ever an issue, he was strong enough and respected enough to put a stop to it. This system of trust — of faith in *something* — is a glue that holds large groups of people together, or so Gatsi has always said. When the glue is removed, people panic, and some will begin to act irrationally. If a village is a kind of creature, our chieftain was the heart; strike it through, and the rest of the animal dies with it.

It was a short span of time that led to this. The sun had set, and the chieftain was killed. The sun had risen, and suddenly the peace he kept had died along with him. Everyone in the village knew it on some level. Ciqala knew that few would stop him from attacking me, as their words carried less authority than our dead leader's. There was no one there to make the decision to stay or run from the potential threat of violent clans. Or, if someone had suggested it, he or she may not have been respected enough to find their words so eagerly heard.

Ciqala was convinced that we had no enemies so close to home. That belief was threatened when Macha went missing, and instead of reconsidering the reality of the situation, he did what he needed to do to justify his keeping the same belief. I understood now why he acted the way he did. The belief that Macha simply got up and left was easier to accept than the alternative. It certainly didn't help that Ciqala was a charismatic speaker. People liked to listen to him, and when one hears their own words echoed back to them, it's easier to be confident — even falsely so. Perhaps the mind works like an animal and protects itself when it is threatened.

But was I any different? Once the belief that my father had saved me from the cold was challenged, anger pumped feverishly through my veins. Perhaps our only anchors in life are the fragile beliefs to which we cling.

These were the thoughts that filled my head after I had woken up, when I wasn't distracted by my painful black eye, swollen lip, and stinging ribs.

I had lain awake for hours.

At my feet was a new shirt, and after a little mental effort I remembered that my mother had started to make me one before the trip into the grasses. I struggled briefly to bring it within arm's reach and examined it.

It was buckskin. Light blue dye traced the chest, shoulders, and arms in thin designs, and the lower half boasted a darker red dye stemming from the chest as well. Fringes fell loosely from the hem and cuffs. I tossed it lightly toward my things, wincing as my body responded to the action with pain.

I rolled over to see a sizable bowl of fresh mulberries next to me on the floor of my hut. Avid knew how to pick the good ones, that was certain. If the Achare could ever settle down permanently, I'm convinced he'd make a living cultivating food-bearing plants or building things. I ate the mulberries slowly and tried to relax.

Within the hour I heard someone come through the door of my hut. I sprang up, but spasmed with sudden pain that tore across my ribs.

"Still jumpy?" asked Malik. She was smirking, but I could see an uneasiness underneath.

"I suppose I am," I managed. We were quiet for a while, neither of us entirely sure of what to say.

"Has it started raining yet?" I asked her.

"We're in a bit of a break from yesterday's storm."

How long have I been out?

"But right now it's just misting a little. Most people are taking advantage of the pause and are out doing what they can before the next storm comes. Looks like it might start coming down even harder pretty soon. More lightning in the distance and all."

The dog that had been following me nuzzled my hand. I stroked its neck lightly.

"I wish it didn't hurt so much to hit people," I thought aloud, noting my bruised knuckles.

"You get used to it."

I kept my attention on the dog.

"I thought these dogs were supposed to be vicious. Where were you?" I asked the animal, tussling its ears. "You were no help." At this point, I wasn't sure whether I was talking to the dog, or to Malik. She seemed to pick up on what I was saying.

"It wasn't my fight, Rennik. And if I hadn't shoved Banar back a few times, he was going to jump in as well."

I guess I hadn't seen him interfere after the fight started.

"What about the other villagers?" I asked. "No one else stepped in. They just watched. I've been living among them my whole life, even giving out extra food when we had it, and they just stood by while I was beaten senseless."

"They were scared, Rennik. They *are* scared. Since the chieftain's death, no one really knows what to do. You should hear them in their tents, shouting and arguing. Tales of our scouting trip have gotten around, and between the heavy rains and thunder are heated debates regarding our lack of leadership."

I tried hard to scowl, but my black eye turned it into a helpless wince.

"How are the boys? Ciqala didn't hurt them, did he?"

Malik smiled again, this time wholeheartedly.

"No, he didn't hurt them. He's pretty beat up, but mostly from you. He's got a nasty black eye, maybe even worse than yours. Once Avid's pack got to him, the rest of the clan followed in to break everything up. Funny how it took a bunch of children to remind adults of what they should do."

"Yeah. Funny."

"Rennik, there's something else..." Malik trailed off. She closed her eyes momentarily as she brought her hands up from the floor in a tentative motion.

My bow hung in two pieces from her fingers.

I was overwhelmed and couldn't speak. The deep and angry breaths that took hold of my body hurt my ribs. I snatched my bow from her and cradled it helplessly.

"After the villagers got Ciqala to stop, he grabbed a nearby adze and took his anger out on your bow. After he split it, he started to swing at some huts. He was all bloodied from the fight, and people were afraid to approach him when he had something sharp in his hands, but eventually they got him to stop. He made a fool of himself in front of almost everyone, though."

"I helped my father make that bow when I was a child." My hands began to shake.

"I'm sorry," was all she said.

"I might kill him."

She was silent in response.

I held the pieces in my trembling hands. I felt the section smoothed by my left hand after thousands of shots. My fingers grazed the string notch at the top where my father had to fix a small mistake I had made. A mistake I never made again.

As I pictured Ciqala's face, there were several mistakes I decided I'd never make again.

"Why are you here?" I asked Malik. She seemed surprised by my sudden question.

"What?"

I repeated myself.

"I figured you might be awake," she said, taken aback. "Someone needed to bring you your bow."

"I made the worst decision I could possibly make out in the grasses. I put our lives in danger. We should probably be dead. No one believes me about that first night. Why don't you hate me like the rest of them?"

"They don't hate you, they just..." She looked thoughtful for a moment and looked down at her hands. "After our encounter with the other clans, and after we escaped from that stampede, I was angry with you. I could have beat you into the dirt with my fists."

"Sounds familiar."

"But after we argued, I stayed up for most of the night thinking about it all. At first I was furious that you could even sleep after making that decision, but..."

"But?"

"But I started to question what would have happened if you hadn't," she admitted with the last bit of an exhale.

"Ko could have lived, apparently. Ikoda might not have been lost."

"No," she responded, "that's not true. I saw Ko die just like you saw him die. He was gone long before you loosed that arrow. It's just something Ciqala is still saying to make you seem like a coward."

"Still saying? Not *said*?" I asked.

"I told you that people are arguing. The chieftain's death left a hole that needs to be filled. Some people think Ciqala should take the role and make the decisions for our people."

"Surely there's someone better."

"You are so damn daft sometimes!" she sputtered. "It's like you send any decision you're presented with out into the grasses to die. Except for the one you shot into that damn bison."

I was surprised by her sudden criticism.

"It's you, Rennik. *You're* the other person."

"What? How am I possibly qualified to lead the clan?"

"People respected your father, at least for the most part. You've proven you care about the village — you've fed pretty much everyone at least once, if they needed it. You were seen talking with the chieftain, and they know he approved of you to some degree. Most of them trusted his judgement, at least."

"There's no one else?"

"Well, everyone would expect Satra to take over, but..."

"She hasn't returned," I finished her thought gravely. "But people really think Ciqala should lead?"

"Some do, some don't. It's split evenly for now, but that won't last long. Ciqala hasn't been unconscious like you have."

"I'm pretty sick of being unconscious."

"And I'm pretty sick of Ciqala lording his false claims all over the village. He's been lying left and right, exaggerating everything that happened on our excursion. And I've been trying to undo it all. It's hard when the rain is coming down in sheets. I've been trapped with an odd selection of families while the ocean pours from the sky, and when it lets up, I've got to move around as much as I can to talk to whomever I can. And the whole time, Ciqala is doing the same thing."

"Then why don't you step up? Why can't *you* lead?"

"Don't try to shirk this responsibility — people don't know me like they know you. I have no reputation beyond the people I'm close to. It's you who people know, whether you realize it or not."

"Most of the older people don't like me. They never have! They despise me for surviving in the wilderness as a child, and now that I've done the same as an adult, they want to trust me?!"

"The chieftain was removed, too. It's not like he was best

friends with everyone. You need a certain detachment to lead, because it's not about being loved — it's about being trusted. After Ciqala's rage, people are starting to look to you for the first time. And don't forget that you're the one that lived. *You* came back first with the information we needed."

"So did you."

"The decision is yours, Rennik," Malik said, deflecting my comment.

"You keep referring to my decisions, but apparently I don't have one here! I don't want to lead, Malik! It's not my place!"

"The question isn't whether or not you want to lead. The question is whether or not you want *him* to lead. It's us or them."

I was quiet for a time.

"So who will it be?" she asked, still frustrated. "You, or Ciqala?"

I found my lips moving instinctively to form the words "I don't know," but caught myself before they found the air to give them flight. Instead, I pressed my lips tightly together and decided that this time, I did know.

"Me."

"Then you'll explain to everyone tomorrow that we need to leave."

"Yes," I said, though I wasn't sure I wanted to. For once in my life, I wanted to know something for certain, but I couldn't shake the nervous feeling in my gut at the thought of leaving home for good.

Malik nodded. "Great. I'll keep speaking to the villagers, then. They sent two more scouts on horseback to patrol the areas a day out. We should be hearing back from them soon."

"Where's Gatsi?" I asked her as she moved to stand.

"Honestly, I haven't seen him. The last time we talked was

during a pause in the storm. We were talking a bit, but I was in a hurry to get to the next hut and drum up some support against Ciqala. I hadn't thought about it, but I haven't seen many people at all. Everyone's sort of shut-up in their homes until the storm passes, stewing on what has happened."

I tried to move again in vain.

"He said you'd be out for a while, though," she said. "You bruised a rib or two."

"When are we burning the chieftain?" I asked.

"We can't until the rain stops."

"I'll be there."

"Rennik—"

"I said I'll be there."

≈

"THE YOHRI?"

"No. They're next to the Inkwood. I'm asking about the people to the south of them. Keep thinking trees."

"The Ikar!" Avid guessed again.

"Good, but Gatsi will expect you to get these right on the first try." I knew that the words "Ikar" and "Inkwood" might be easy to mix up.

Avid was preparing for one of Gatsi's famous quizzes. He wasn't taking as big of a role in Avid's learning as he had in mine since Avid had me to help raise him, but Gatsi was still making sure the important things would be learned the right way. This time it was the names, locations, and overall personalities of each major clan.

"Speaking of Gatsi, have you seen him lately?"

"No, I guess not since the fight," Avid answered after thinking for a moment. "And I've been in my friends' huts since the rain has been so heavy."

I hadn't moved from my place of rest, and I was well into the second bowl of mulberries he had brought me. I decided I'd need to look for Gatsi myself when I was well.

"Okay," I continued drilling him between mouthfuls of mulberries, "tell me about the Turin."

"They're religious."

"Is that all?"

"They believe in the Mountain Mother."

"Yeah, they're pretty touchy about her," I added.

"Gatsi says they're hard-headed."

"That's actually pretty fair. They're a big clan, too. Some of them were fighting with the people we fought, but I'm sure most of the clan is still on that mountain."

"They're not usually too violent though, right?"

"Right. But keep going on the Turin."

"They gifted us the tusks that hold up the chieftain's hut. Will we leave them behind when we move?"

"I suppose we'll have to. But why did they give the tusks anyway?"

"We sent our scouts and fighters and lots of food to them when soldiers from Rucost started raiding their people. They live south of us, just above Rucost's northern border. They don't like Rucost because they keep trying to settle parts of the Kalanosi plains there. There's not really anyone to stop them because none of the clans claim to own the lands, but Rucost has laws that say they own things."

"Right."

"Why does that mean anything?" he asked.

"What do you mean?"

"Laws. Do they just write things down on paper, and it's suddenly true? Can they just write that they own Kalanos, and they do?"

It was a good question. Smart.

"That's what it means to them," I answered, "but their laws don't mean much to us."

"If you can just disagree with a law, does it really mean anything?"

"Everyone in their kingdom has to believe in it. Well, almost everyone. If more people believe in the law than break the law, it means they can punish the ones who contradict it."

"Why don't lawbreakers just move into Kalanos, where there are fewer people to stop them?"

"That," I replied, "is a very good question. But enough about them. Tell me about the clan to the east. The big one."

"The Rask. They used to be part of the Wahto a long time ago, but they split off when one leader turned the clan toward violence. They traveled east and now they live on the cliffs above the ocean. They're good with boats and they survive mostly on what they get from the sea."

"They're pretty nice folk. You've never had crab, have you?" I asked.

Avid shook his head.

"It's supposed to be good. Traders tried to bring some here when you were really little. It had been sitting in the heat for a while, though. No one wanted to risk trading for it. You can't really keep seafood fresh on a four-day trip. What about the clan in the center of the plains, near the river?"

"Nice try. That's us," he replied. I thought I might trick him with a simple question.

"And we are..." I condescended.

Avid rolled his eyes. "The Atch-*air*," he answered sarcastically, mimicking a Rucosti mispronunciation. He really was like me sometimes. "We traditionally migrate all around the central plains and can live off of the creatures there or along the river. We trade more than most clans because our central location makes us accessible to many others. Our migrations haven't happened for over ten years."

"Why not?" I was curious as to what he'd say.

"Dalon says it's because there are Shivers in the grasses that can't come over the ridge, so we settled here to escape them. He says the Wahkeen used to nest here — that's where the ridge came from."

"There are no such things as Shivers," I responded. "Or Wahkeen."

"Are you sure?"

"Let's just agree that your friend Dalon might not be an expert."

"Are we going to leave the village? Just us and mother?"

"Do you think that's best?" I wasn't quizzing him anymore — it was a sincere question.

He thought for a while. "I think a lot of people have been mean to us, and they don't deserve people like us to save them, but..."

"But?"

"It just doesn't seem right, leaving them. Dalon, that Malik lady, Tella. They might need our help."

I cleared my throat. "Tell me about the clan to the north."

"The Wahto?"

"No, The Wahto are north-west of us. A little south of them are the Sree, and even more north and west of the Wahto are the Yohri, remember. I'm talking straight north."

"The Kazel."

"Right. Tell me about the Kazel," I prompted.

Avid looked up, trying to remember. I wondered if he was catching some of Gatsi's mannerisms.

"They're a bunch of sandy-brained idiots who let their convoluted and yeastless philosophies trample any rational thinking that happens to worm its way out of their foolish, blabbering mouths."

I shot up, ignored the pain, and looked at Avid incredulously.

"What?" he said defensively. "That's what Gatsi says."

I chuckled and remembered him saying something like that to me years ago.

"That might be what he said," I explained, "but let's try for something a bit more...objective."

Avid sighed and started over.

"They live on the fringe of the desert to the north. Their migration patterns dip into both the desert and the plains. They're very..."

I raised an eyebrow while Avid chose his words carefully.

"...spiritual."

"Good enough."

WHEN I HAD INITIALLY BEEN LAID DOWN IN MY HUT AT THE beginning of that day, I had expected an evening of quiet. I wished I could have stared silently at the small drops of rain sneaking down the inside of our walls, racing toward the earth and out, magnifying the textures to which they clung. I wished I could have enjoyed the subtle aroma of the sage Tella had hung at the door, and the petrichor in the air left by the rain. It truly was my favorite smell.

However, just as a hunter's ears attune to the finest detail when sitting still in the wilds, I began to hear the symphony of sounds around me, such as the soft, low billowing of my hut's walls against the wind. I heard much inside of my home, but I heard even more from outside. In the pauses between downpour and gale, distracting footsteps wound around the village, and birds swooped around the top of my hut, surely looking for a potential nest with spring about to arrive in full. But prominent above all were the voices. Most clearly, the woman who was talking with my mother at our door.

"But he *must* speak. The scout, Malik, told us he knows the safest paths away from the coming horde," the woman said.

"He's hurt," replied my mother. "And we don't know for sure that there's a horde coming. I'm sure he'll be out eventually — I've never seen him inside for this long, and it's only been a day and a half. He won't stay in any longer than he has to."

"But we *do* know they're coming! Malik said the ones they fought will return to their leaders with news! That man, Ciqala, he shouldn't have hurt Rennik like that. What your boy did out in the wilds saved lives!"

"Yes, I've heard that version of the story."

"It takes more than muscle when you're out there! You've got to be quick-witted! Can't be slow to the decision!"

"Yes, you're right." My mother was trying to get a word in, but the woman was persistent.

"You're sure he can't talk now? We need to know if the huts should be taken down soon."

"I'm sure he can't talk. He can hardly get on his feet."

"The chieftain is gone — just tell me, is Rennik going to lead us?"

"I need to tend to my son," my mother said authoritatively, avoiding an answer. "When he is able to do so, he will speak."

A long pause ensued before the woman spoke again.

"Sleep well, Raisha."

"And you."

My mother stepped back into our home and closed the flaps of the hut behind her. She circled her heart. For many, it was a symbol of recognition, a reminder that we are built to survive; for my mother, it was a habit she developed when her bones became a bother and getting out of bed was a struggle once or twice a month. What little light crept in from the clouded evening was cut out and the room became dark. She strode over unsurely and looked down at me.

Her deep eyes were intense as she studied my face. For a short while she did not speak.

"You've dug yourself quite the hole," she said finally.

"I'm not sure what you mean," I replied.

"Half the village thinks you're going to save them. The chieftain's dead, as all of our chieftains are. Satra is probably dead, too. They'll be quick to accept a new leader in the midst of a threat. They seek someone else on whom to stack the responsibilities. And the blame."

"You don't think I can do it?"

"No."

I wasn't sure how to respond. She had never before been so blatantly negative with me.

"And I don't think you do either," she continued.

"Malik seems to have confidence in me—"

"Malik is just as scared as the rest of them. She saw you make a decision that saved her once, and when people are fearful, they'll place faith in what they've seen before. And to most people here, you look like your father."

"What would my father have done?"

"*He* turned down the opportunity to lead. He knew we were nomadic at heart. Knowing we must keep ourselves moving is one thing, but becoming the man that moves others is...different." She swallowed hard and struggled to continue. "But he helped people, so they expect you to help, too."

"Then I'll help them," I replied, my tone becoming terse.

"You don't know what you're doing, Rennik! They can't expect you to lead! You're making a mistake."

"Then what do you suggest we do?" I asked testily, sitting up on my elbows. "We can't let Ciqala lead our people to their deaths! He's a brute and a fool."

"And you're no different?"

"I'm no brute!"

"Then perhaps I've raised a fool!"

I winced in pain as I tried to sit up taller, swinging my legs across the floor.

"Why do you have so little faith in me?" I asked, exasperated and wanting to cut the fat out of a sour conversation.

"I have faith in you to stay alive," she said. "I have faith in you to hunt well and to provide for your family. We could leave. We don't need to stay for them. I've never seen you lead, Rennik. I hardly see you talk to the people you now call your own."

"I don't need to be their friend. These people and I share a home."

"This isn't our home! We're nomads! We've been wandering for generations. We call no place our home — our home consists of the people around us — the *living* people around us. We should have left this place when you were a child!"

"Then let me lead them away from it! Let me be the man who reminds them of our place!"

"I won't allow for a leader that doesn't believe in what he says."

"What are you saying?"

"You don't really want to leave. I know how to read my son. You've grown up here. You're complacent."

I found myself unable to disagree.

"In more ways than one," she added. "You come from a family of wanderers, a lineage of those who plant no flags to claim land as their own. You know this in your words, but you don't *feel* it. You want to stay in this little bowl of ours with its short grasses and its easy hunting, but more deeply you want to stay as you are. You spend each day with your family, eating, hunting, talking, learning — it's an easy life. It's spoiled you. You've become complacent and now the village looks to you to lead them away from everything you've become. You are not the man they think you are, and pretending to be something you're not is only going to get you killed."

"I'm not afraid to leave," I replied. Even as I said it, I found myself in a pool of doubt.

"Yes, you are," she said sternly, just before her shoulders deflated and her posture became one of defeat. "But you've been nocked, and fate has pulled you to its cheek. An arrow can't stay still for long."

"You think I don't want this?"

"You're not listening. It's not about what you want. The hand of the archer doesn't ask for volunteers. You've been selected by their worry, not their logic."

"I can change. I want my people safe—"

"*Your* people?"

"Yes! My people! *Our* people! If it takes a different man to save them, then I'll change. I can be a different man!"

She stood and took a deep breath — the kind that carries the weight of a thousand things left unsaid. I wondered what it was she wanted to tell me. Instead, she spoke simply.

"I love you, Rennik. I don't want you dead, too."

I watched her leave. Under her breath she muttered something about my father that I'm sure she didn't intend for me to hear.

At first I was angry, having heard my mother assail me with so much doubt. I was confused, and rightfully so.

Then a memory came back to me. Not a memory of my father, nor of my mother or Avid.

I remembered beating hooves, and a beast's fury and hot breath an instant behind me. I remembered running for my life while I pounded through the grasses toward a patch of ripgut.

I thought of the young bison calves I never had the chance to see, and suddenly I understood my mother in a way I never had before.

IT WAS A LONG EVENING THAT BLED INTO A LONG AND fractured night; my sleeping was so inconsistent that I had no way to keep track of the passing time.

The storm had begun again, and rain was pounding against the walls. I sat thinking about my incipient attempt at leadership. This recovery, this sleep, would have to be my metamorphosis, changing me from a quiet man to a charismatic one. The encouragement from Malik and the doubts in my mother's voice clashed like opposing tides in my mind, fighting harder than Ciqala and I had.

Finally, the persistent composition of the rain lulled me into a short but deep sleep. I felt light against the furs beneath me. I let myself go to the grasses.

In my dreams I saw an otter, a beaver, and a great oryx, all holding their heads high with pride. They were framed by the branches of a mulberry tree. Around their feet poured the patient waters of the river near my home. They traveled toward the setting of a distant sunset painted with a violent collection of reds. In the deepest wells of my understanding, I knew it was a sunset that would not be seen for some time.

But I knew I would be there to see it. Suddenly, the horizon bent, like a bow being pulled just before its arrow launches forth.

I woke feeling sick and gasped for air, nervous for a day that was yet to come. My throat felt tight, rooted to something unseen. I spent the rest of the night wide awake, wishing for distraction but feeling only the dream I had.

It seemed like hours had passed when the distraction I sought came to me in the form of a realization. I would need a plan if the people of the village were to trust me and follow me as their leader. I'd need some idea as to what we should do in response to the nearby threat. Of course I couldn't tell them I'd seen impossible things in dreams at the foot of a tree...

We could not outrun the horde. Just like the charging bison, it simply was not an option, no matter how damning a fact it is. It was clear to me that the only option was for us to hide away.

The storms ended sometime before morning. I had all night to think, and with the dawning of my newfound responsibility came the rising of the sun.

And like the crowing of a bird, a shout shattered the peaceful silence of the village.

RECOLLECTION

"Just as the giant salamander is unique to our rivers, social stratification seems unique to our cities: Students of the Druidic College will tattoo rings upon their arm to signify level of study, an homage to the age of trees. The royal family festoons stages of the moon around their collars, with the full moon upon the King. Kalanosi clans seems to wear no such symbols of status. They are led by chieftain and chieftainess, and the rest appears to be a disorganized mob."

> — EXCERPT FROM BRALLIC SEVERIN'S
> *KALANOS: A STUDY OF PLACE AND
> PEOPLE.*

A pair of horses crashed into the open space near my home — I could tell from the hoofbeats that they were not controlled. The horses squealed in fear, and panicked chatter began quickly.

"Who is it?"

"They're from one of the scouting groups!"

"One of them is still alive!"

"Get him down!"

"No, don't touch him!"

Ignoring my injuries to what extent I could, I stood and hobbled toward the door and into the open. A crowd had gathered already. Unable to see through them, I shambled up to the throng of villagers and placed my hand on a man's shoulder, unconsciously seeking support. The man, whose face I recognized as well as anyone else's, appeared shocked and took a step back from me.

"Rennik!" he exclaimed. "You're better!"

The villagers began to buzz and turned to look at me. As they did, they parted and cleared a path from my position to the horses. Their faces looked to mine for answers. I realized then that this was the first moment of my new role.

Two men were slumped lifelessly from the horses' shoulders, bloodied and broken. One sprouted an arrow from his back, protruding from where his lung would be. Numerous cuts grinned up from their bodies, and now that I stood over them, the gravity of their wounds became clear. The cuts were thin and clean — obviously made by blade and arrowhead. They had been hit by multiple attackers. The horses were mildly wounded as well. Minor injuries on their flanks made it clear that the attack happened while these two men fled the conflict. It's likely they had been chased. I walked over and studied the still-living man.

"Has anyone seen Gatsi?" I asked the crowd loudly. No one responded, and a few people seemed concerned that I had to ask in the first place. They seemed to be waiting for more from me.

From the corner of my eye, I noticed Avid scrambling away from the horses with something in his hands.

"Bring him into Gatsi's hut," I finally said, ignoring my brother. My role as a leader was still new to me, but I tried to make it fit as best I could. "We can help him."

"No," the man near me responded. "Rennik, you're injured. You shouldn't be worrying about anyone else — here, I'll help you to your hut."

I slapped his hand away a little harder than I should have and felt the reciprocal pain in my knuckles and ribs.

"I'll decide what I can and can't do," I responded tersely. "This man is on the edge of death. He takes priority."

The man's jaw dropped a little but tightened quickly. "Then at least let me help you to Gatsi's hut."

"Thank you."

The woman led the horse through the village toward Gatsi's, and the man I had spoken to me helped me walk. As we made our way, more people began to follow, heads turning with worry toward our half-dead compatriot. I wondered how many of those people had known this man since they were children, or if any of his family were nearby. Glancing at the bouncing, unconscious body on the horse, I was reminded again of how lucky I was to have made it back from my scouting trip in one piece.

I led the way into Gatsi's hut and let only a few people in with the wounded man. Having never been inside the hut by myself, it appeared musty and empty to me. It was suddenly an alien place.

I studied the man for a moment. His arms were shredded up to the shoulder, and the back of his neck was cut from a passing arrow; if I hadn't known better, I'd have guessed he'd fallen in a patch of ripgut, though the lacerations would be much more uniform if he had. Cut up as he was, I recognized his face.

"Valen," I said, trying to get a reaction. "Valen, I need you to look at me." His head moved an inch, but no sound escaped his lips, nor was there any motion in his limbs. "Lay him down here," I told the villagers, motioning toward a blanket on the ground.

"Those are weapon cuts," someone broke in. "He's been attacked — they've nearly killed him!"

"Nearly," I responded, trying to keep my voice confident. The people were panicked, and as a leader I would need to exude a certain amount of assurance in my voice, even if I wasn't sure what I was doing. I hadn't exactly healed people before, but I'd seen Gatsi do it enough to know how. My hands felt unfamiliar among the things on Gatsi's shelves even though the sight itself was frequent for me. Never had I found reason to rifle through his things before, but with him gone, I decided the moment was right.

The clay container holding the crystal-like honey sat among other small jars. After briefly cleaning the lacerations of his skin with water, I smeared the honey against the wounds. The stickiness of the blood and dirt were gone, and the honey found its way onto the damaged skin cleanly. The skin on either side of the slices arched up against the invading honey, pressing against the edges of flesh that weren't meant to be pressed. I couldn't imagine how painful this pressure would be if he were conscious. I wrapped the wounds and addressed the others.

"The best we can do now is wait. Unless Gatsi returns and can help him further, we need to let him rest." I pointed to a woman in the doorway. Of all the people in the hut she seemed to be the most prepared to take action; she leaned slightly toward the man and her eyes studied what I did carefully. "Find some clean water, and when he wakes a little, make sure he drinks. If he can't keep it down..." I trailed off, struggling to find the words.

"What if he doesn't wake? What if he can't keep it down?" the woman asked. Her tone did not show a fear of responsibility, as many would have, but rather a need to learn more.

"We'll have to ask Gatsi when he returns," I responded, avoiding the explicit admission that I didn't know what to do. As a someone concerned with hunting, the only medicine I knew was what I'd seen from Gatsi or what he'd done to me.

"The rest of you, find Gatsi, or find someone that knows where he is." I had trouble keeping my voice from sounding nervous. It really was strange that he had been missing for so long. "If you can't find him in the village, check the riverbanks nearby."

The rest of the group turned to leave. Stretching out my fingers, I caught the shoulder of one man — the one who had helped me walk to the hut. He now seemed uncomfortable and ready to leave the scene.

"Go get the other man off of his horse. We'll send him off with the chieftain today." Before he could leave, I spoke again. "And bring me the arrow from his back."

THE CHIEFTAIN WAS TO BE BURNED THAT EVENING. NEXT TO him would burn the body of the dead scout. With Gatsi gone there was no one to prepare the body of the latter, but since we were burning him so soon, I wasn't sure it mattered too much.

After the burning, I would speak to the villagers about leaving, and we would spend the night packing what we could before springing to action in the morning. I fumbled over the words in my head, attempting and failing to compile a decent string of convincing statements. In my mind I believed it was the right thing to do, but still the action felt wrong in my gut. My plan was to convince an entire village to leave their home — quite a task when I had hardly convinced myself. I knew there was no other choice, but my mother was right. Leaving something with which you are familiar is never an easy option.

I was making my way around the village when Avid found me. He told me he had a surprise for me.

"I think it'll help," he said simply. He turned on his heels and walked away, expecting me to follow.

Avid guided me back to our hut. My mother and Tella were elsewhere, likely enjoying the sun as much as they could in light of the foreboding riders that had come in — and in the midst of such turbulent times, I use "enjoying" in its loosest definition.

He crept toward his corner of the hut. There sat a wicker chest containing the few things he owned over an intricately woven blanket of yellows and deep reds. I remember when Kinran made the blanket for him, when he was just a small child.

"I thought about giving you mine, but it might not work well for you, and I figured I should probably have one to work with." Avid reached down into the wicker chest and began rummaging through his things.

"I wanted to give it to you before we had to start packing up. I sort of..." Avid paused to search for a word, "took it. But it wasn't exactly stealing!"

Avid brought up his hands, and with them came a long object wrapped in hide.

"It was on one of the horses that came in. He must have gotten it from an enemy rider or something, and...well, here."

Avid unwrapped the parcel and revealed a Sree war bow, scarred and possibly warped, judging by the first glance.

Taking the bow from Avid's hands, my fingers pecked at the old sinew on its back, and at the bison horn on the belly, facing me.

"Why would you take this?" I reprimanded. "It isn't yours."

"It's not his, either!" He began defending himself in a childlike tone. "Dead men can't have things. Besides, Ciqala broke yours. You need it a lot more than a dead person does!"

I sighed and shook my head. "It's hardly usable. But I suppose I can make another one like it. It'd be nice to have something a bit more dependable. Thank you, Avid," I told him. I wrapped my arm around him in a tight embrace. "This may not have belonged to you, but...thank you."

"You think we'll be okay? You think you can make a new bow in time to save us?" His voice was muffled in my hide shirt.

"I know it." In truth, crafting a bow like this would not be a quick process by any means.

He turned his face downward, pressing the top of his head into my chest. His voice dropped to a whimper. "I'm scared to die, Rennik."

"We're going to get through this. We're going to be far removed from all of this bloodshed. I won't let them get you."

Angry tears welled up in his eyes. "I just don't understand why," he began. "I don't understand why anyone would bother us. We just live here peacefully — what could anyone possibly gain from hurting us?"

My visions from the Delkhi came back to me. The man with golden hair, the Sree and Wahto leaders, the extinction of the mammoths, the chieftain's murder. I felt like I had the pieces of a puzzle with no indication of how to put them together. Or perhaps I was missing something vital.

"You think you can use this sort of bow?" he asked me, eager to change the subject to something more comfortable.

I studied the bow. It had clearly been beaten by violence and time, but I doubted it would be completely useless. Still, I was wary; I'd seen a bow break in someone's hands before and since had learned that such an accident can leave lifelong scars or wounds.

"I'll test it out. This might be fine for hunting in the meantime, but I need to make a new bow anyway."

Avid whipped back around to the pile of his things now tossed about the hut and came back up with a black thumb ring, crafted from bison horn. It looked a little big, but it would work for the new bow.

"Here," he said, placing it in my palm.

My jaw dropped in disbelief. "Avid!" I said. "This is...this is father's ring!"

"Well...you know. He can't have things anymore."

I pulled the string back, glad to no longer be bereft of bow. The draw length was as short as I remember it, and it would take some getting used to shooting from a different anchor point on my face. But I knew that in more ways than one, I was done shooting from my ear.

From now on, I'd fire from the mouth.

"But we come here almost every day! There have to be other trees like it on the river, right?"

"Avid, the thing is huge. I'm sure it'll still produce your mulberries after I take a branch from it." I shifted the axe in my palm and kept my gaze on the tree, sizing up the many large branches that sprung from its trunk. Truly, it was an impressive thing.

"Can't you use any other wood?"

"Not *any* wood, no. It has to be strong enough to resist the pull, but pliable enough to work with. I think this mulberry wood will do very well."

Avid stared at his beloved tree for a few quiet moments.

"It's stood strong for longer than we've been alive," he responded.

"Probably."

"And now it has to lose a limb just because you need it to?"

"Sometimes we have to take charge over nature for the betterment of ourselves. You know this, Avid — you've killed animals for their meat and hide, haven't you?"

"It just doesn't seem right. It's been this way for so long, and now we're going to violate its peacefulness. It hasn't done anything to hurt us."

I noticed at this point that Avid had a few tears pooling in his eyes. I reached over to put a hand on his shoulder, but he pulled away. He had seemed on the verge of a panic attack since the dust had come through days ago.

"I wish the tree could fight back," he said, the tears now running down his face. He stomped at the earth. I hadn't seen him act like this since he was much younger. "I wish the animals and the grasses and everything we try to take even had a chance."

"The creatures we hunt have chances to hide and to run—"

"That's not the same!"

"Listen to me!" I shouted. He was startled and stared defiantly into my eyes. "This is the way life is supposed to work! If an animal isn't fast enough or quiet enough, they don't live. It means they're not meant to live. Its death makes other creatures of its kind stronger as a whole. Haven't you ever seen wolves hunt pack animals? They don't take the strong ones — they pounce on the slow, the sick, the young."

He flinched at the word "young."

Avid knelt at the decline of the riverbank and began punching into the earth. I ignored him and kept speaking.

"Some trees are unfit for what we need, so they're naturally protected from our axes. It's just the way the world is Avid. And I promise you," I said, stopping to make sure he was listening, "this tree will still make mulberries when we're done."

Avid turned to me, red-faced and eyes downcast. "Okay," he whispered.

Within the hour I had taken one perfect length of timber from among the tree's thicker branches, leaving the majority of the tree untouched. It would make for a flawless stave once I had time to carve away at it with a drawknife.

With the battered Sree bow I shot and killed an oryx near the river. Avid and I took all we could from it, as we normally do, but this time I paid special attention to its horns and sinew.

For the horns I broke off the skull plate and carried it all as one piece. Oryx horns are a dark, rich brown and have a ringed texture all the way up. They're easy to grip that way, even if their attachment to the skull plate made the shape of the whole thing somewhat cumbersome. Placing them in boiling water over a fire would allow me to strip the horns from their cores at a later time with little to no damage — likely after we sent the chieftain off that night.

The legs of the oryx provided the sinew. With a small hunting knife, I cut into the underside of the leg, an action not dissimilar to gutting a fish. It was a bloody process, but I wanted to get as much of the work done as soon as possible. Holding fast amidst the muscle and bone are the white, fleshy strips of the creature's tendons. I took as much of the intact sinew as I could. I would need to wet them properly before they could be used.

I planned later to cut the remaining tendons into small segments and put them in simmering water, which will reduce them to a perfectly usable glue. If the water became too hot, it would ruin the desired substance — too cool, and it will take all night. I would use this glue to press the sinew and horn to opposing sides of the wooden stave. Sinew is good for stretching while working to provide tension, and surprisingly to some, horn compresses well when pressure is applied to it. The mulberry wood is simply a solid core and effective absorber of shock.

I decided I'd send some trusted hunters to what remained of the oryx's body when I returned. The extra meat would be useful for times to come.

Avid was surprised at my confidence that I would find an otter at the river, since one doesn't see them as often during the day. I led him right to the edge of the bank, and the otter did not hear our approach against the babbling of the river's eddies. Its dark and silvery fur would be perfect for wicking moisture and absorbing some shock. He asked me how I knew for sure we'd find one so quickly, and I simply told him I'd seen it a while ago; telling him I'd seen it in a dream wasn't my favorite option.

We continued searching, this time for beavers. We killed several. Avid was trying to reason why they'd be in the open this time of day. I ignored his questions for the most part, failing to find words to explain my confidence, and instead instructed him to gather what good meat he could from the animals and prepare to cure as much as he could of the meat overnight. I was personally concerned with the pelts, which, like the smaller otter pelt, would be perfect for keeping things dry. I was exceptionally good at handling beaver pelts, and these would make a fine case for the bow.

As for my own body, it already felt as though my minor wounds were healing up. Much of the bruising on my chest and ribs was decreasing, though the overall soreness remained. I imagined all of this hard work would make for even more soreness the following morning, but we'd have plenty of time to rest once we left home.

I thought back to the dream I'd had last night, with the oryx, otter, and beaver. Somehow I wasn't surprised that it led me here to find the exact animals I needed. It was cause and effect — an easy path to follow.

Before leaving the riverside, I looked in the direction of the Delkhi and gave it a silent thanks.

AVID AND I WERE WALKING BACK INTO THE VILLAGE WHEN Chaska stopped us. In anticipation of his caustic commentary, I tightened my grip on the horn of the oryx in my hand. The skull plate hung at its base just under my knee. The old man halted our approach with his dog close by.

One of the men behind Chaska spoke up threateningly. "Still feel safe without Gatsi to protect you, Rennik? Do you always need the old man around?"

I ignored the comment.

"I hear tell the cowards among us are choosing to follow you," Chaska began. "Suppose they've truly lost their minds?" A small group of older men and women approached to stand behind him, lending their presence to his intimidation. I knew all of them and wasn't sure how to feel about their silent threat. "You see Gatsi through very different eyes, don't you?" he continued. "He taught you to heal, to read and to think, and for who knows what reason. But he hasn't taught you the truth of the world. The stronger will always win in the end. Those who follow you will see it eventually. They'll follow my grandson soon enough."

"Chaska," I started, keeping my tone honest, "you really think you can lift a spear to the Sree? To the Wahto? Don't you see that *they're* the stronger ones?"

Chaska's lips curled and eyebrows arched, continuing the attempted browbeating. "Of all the stories that old man told you, he never told you mine, did he?"

I looked at him impatiently and let him continue.

"I've killed men twice the size of you. I was feared, once, when our clan covered more ground in a month than you've walked in your whole life. It was my spear that kept our hunters safe. Mothers, children, chieftains — they hid behind me just like they hid behind the men I fought with. You're young. You're foolish and fatherless. You have no idea just how strong the Achare can be — how strong we've always been! Even if I'm weak in my old age, my grandson is strong. Ciqala will raise a sword to our enemies. I may be old and slow, but I'd rather die fighting like the proud warrior I am than running like a beaten dog. And I'm sure as hell not the only one," he finished, gesturing in a small way to the villagers behind him.

I tried to imagine Chaska as the strong, young warrior he said he was. I suppose I never did think about who he used to be. My whole life he'd always just been a terrible, sour old badger.

"I may not know the quickest way to kill a man," I finally responded, "but I have the wisdom to know when my life is in danger."

"Wisdom?" Chaska snorted. "Is that what he's been

teaching you? You think the others are going to follow the second-hand wisdom of an outsider?"

"Outsider?" I asked. "What are you talking about?"

Chaska started chuckling as if what he was about to say was obvious, but even the people behind him looked intrigued. His eyes looked like a hunter's before loosing an arrow.

"I remember the day Gatsi came to us," he began. "He was a little younger than I. This was before the chieftain was born, before either of your parents were born. I used to hunt with your grandfather. I was a little older than you are now when we found a stranger standing in the path of our migration. He carried no bow. He had no spear, but he came with an armful of fresh meat as a gift. The old chieftain then — this would be three or four chieftains back — accepted him into the clan."

"You're trying to tell me Gatsi isn't even Achare?"

"I suppose I shouldn't be surprised that he never told you. He was always so quiet about where he'd come from. Acted right away like he was one of us. Told stories about us that I'd never heard. Over time the children all believed him, and they grew up and had children of their own, and they heard the stories, too. I guess I'm the only one old enough to remember the day he walked out of the grasses like a Shiver, fabricating stories right in front of our faces."

"You're lying," I said, my knuckles turning white against the horn of the oryx.

"Ha!" Chaska shouted, "does it really surprise you? He's never acted like one of us. He doesn't even *look* like us! Said he'd come from another clan, named Oonray, or Ornery, or something like that. No clan I'd ever heard of. He was always close with your grandparents, and your mother, too. The day your father treated him like one of our own was the day your father rejected our people. He failed as a man of the Achare."

"Pick your next words carefully, old man," I interjected, stepping closer. The people behind him stepped toward us as well. Chaska's eyes glanced quickly at the skull plate with a tinge of lightly-veiled worry.

"I never trusted Gatsi," he continued, "and I've been proven right to think so. He's run away, hasn't he? At the first sign of danger. And he's taught you to act the same. Never in my life have I trusted a word he's said, and I sure as hell won't trust the boy he raised."

Chaska stepped within an inch of my face and bristled out as if preparing to throw a punch.

The rings on the oryx horn dug into my hand, and I thought I might swing the skull plate like a club right into Chaska's angry, chiding face. I wondered how much he'd feel like a warrior if I beat him into the ground with the bones of a dead animal.

"You think Ciqala will save you?" I asked.

"No. I think I'll save myself. As will most of the others. Ciqala, though, he's a real fighter. Reminds me of myself when I was young. The only mistake he's made is not breaking your ribs completely."

"He won't give a second thought to whether an old, useless toad like you lives another day."

"Nor would I expect him to. He is himself and I am myself. If I can't protect myself, I don't deserve to live. That's how I see it."

"You're old and weak." I didn't mean it as an insult — merely a statement of fact. "It's okay to depend on the clan. You can survive with the help of others."

"I shouldn't need to depend on anyone."

"Then you'll die, Chaska. And when you do, I won't set a flame to your corpse."

"Ignorant child!" he burst. "I was hunting before your mother was born! I know these lands better than you ever will! I've seen fools like you come and go, and believe me, you're no leader. You're a coward hiding behind the opinion of the people, and the only support they give you is out of their own cowardice. Fear breeds fear. This ridge has kept us safe for over a decade, and it won't fail us now. It's the only place our clan has ever settled in. You need to stay and fight for your home. You won't find a single safe place in all of Kalanos."

"Exactly, Chaska. There is no safe place. We have to move."

"Our home is defendable. Our people are more secure here than anywhere else. There may be nowhere completely safe, but you'll be more vulnerable out there. You going to feed all of those people yourself?" he asked, gesturing to the meat Avid was carrying. "You going to hope some of them know how to kill a man? You certainly can't, from the looks of you. You're going to die out in the grasses, Rennik. And all these people talking about following you are going to die, too."

I swung the skull plate.

There was a crunch like crumbling bark as it broke into his nose. A weaker piece of the skull snapped off against the bone under his eye, and he fell to the ground.

It was quiet, save for the old man's hands grasping at the dirt around him, trying to pull himself somewhere other than below my feet.

I stepped around him and pushed through his small assembly. He was on the ground, sucking in air. I felt too sick to look at him. It was shameful to hit an old man, but I couldn't let him go on. The swing of the skull plate started a second before it struck, but in a way, it started years earlier, when he first raged against my family. When he decided I should've died in the cold. When he would tell me Avid was spoiled.

I reached my family's hut. I would boil water for the horns just before we burned the chieftain.

Using the drawknife Graff had given me and the strength of my anger, I began to carve away at the mulberry wood.

I'd lose their trust for striking him — some of them, anyway. They might call me barbaric.

My mind was made up. They were forcing me to lead, but if they didn't like how I did things, they could make their own damn way.

20

DEAD MEN

"The nomadic peoples of Kalanos have a deep understanding of the stars, though their observations are wedded with the mortar of myth. The Wahkeen of their stories borrow lightning from celestial bodies, and in the face of a storm, one may hear a Kalanosi remark that 'the stars are close today.'"

— EXCERPT FROM BRALLIC SEVERIN'S
*KALANOS: A STUDY OF PLACE AND
PEOPLE.*

Everyone I had ever known gathered in the center of the village near the chieftain's hut. Men and women worked tirelessly on a funeral pyre for our dead leader. They had visited several of the scattered patches of trees within a few miles of the village and gathered the wood. Those who did so, many of whom acceded to my leadership, built an extra pyre by my request. Both bodies were almost entirely covered with wildflowers. Traditionally, after the bodies of our deceased are burned, their ashes are spread as the clan travels along; it was always seen as an important rite for one's remains to be scattered throughout the entirety of Kalanos. The smell of fresh-cut birch was heavy in the air. The evening was cold and wet.

I found Malik near me, standing with my mother and Avid. They curled around as I approached, expecting me to have something to say. My mother looked pallid.

"I need you to do something about Ciqala," I told Malik.

"You want me to beat him up for you?"

"No. I want you to lie to him. If he knows where we're headed, there's a greater chance our enemies could find out. We're going to leave the village, but it's not going to be what everyone thinks it is. I need you to make him believe that we're heading south, then east as far as we can go. Can you do that for me?"

"Why me?" she asked.

"You said he knew your brother, right? There's a better chance he'll trust you than anyone else."

She glowered at me a moment before responding. "Fine. I don't like it, but I'll do it." She padded off to speak to other villagers.

My mother watched her go.

"You shouldn't have people do what you won't do yourself, Rennik," she said.

"I don't see another option. He won't listen to me, that's for sure."

"I'm only saying that dirty work should be personal."

"You've seen Chaska's face," I responded. After another moment, I added, "We're all making sacrifices. People will just need to trust me."

She brushed a hand under the cuff fringes of the new shirt she had made me.

"You won't win them all, Rennik," she said. "Many of these people — most of them, even, — may not come with you."

"I know."

"And what will you do if they won't listen? What will you choose to do if all of your people want to stay here and die for the sake of some dirt they've grown to like?"

"I'll leave anyway," I said. "I'll take you and Avid to safety."

My mother considered my answer for a moment. "So tell me," she continued. "Does valuing the right decision over the will of your people make you a good leader, or a terrible one?"

"It means I live. It means that I'm going, and if they want to remain here and die, then they'll do so. I'm their chosen leader, not a king of Rucost. I can't truly tell them what to do."

"You weren't chosen to be a temporary trail guide, Rennik. A leader will have to concede now and then."

"I can't concede to the dead."

My mother simply nodded, ending the conversation.

As the people gathered, I made my way to the chieftain's hut. Once there, a few older members of the clan, Ciqala, and I carried the body on its wooden riser to the place where the pyres stood. Ciqala and I did so wordlessly, more so from our shared enmity than of the respect we had for the chieftain. The body of the dead scout had already been laid upon its own pyre.

We placed the chieftain down. I resumed my position in front of my mother as a thin mist began to float down from the sky. The setting sun painted the horizon in a gray-stained gradient of oranges and blues.

Across from me stood Ciqala, and behind him were all of those who, whether consciously or not, stood in turn behind him to show their support. Chaska and Banar were hovering beyond his shoulders. The old man's face was swollen and black, and he looked as though he would kill me with his stare — the one eye that *could* stare, that is.

A sideways glance revealed a similar phenomenon behind me. I briefly wondered who had more Achare at their back. More immediately at my presence stood Avid to my left and the dog to my right, settling in just under my hand. A horse's nervous whinny sounded from somewhere in the village.

Normally any funeral, especially for the chieftain, is punctuated by a memorial speech from Gatsi. With his absence, no one was quite sure what to do. The grizzled warrior who held the torch looked from Ciqala's face to mine, unsure of how to proceed, and unwilling to break the somber silence with a question. The entire event seemed empty.

Without an answer, he stepped forward, took a deep and audible breath, and lowered the torch to the pyre. Perhaps we had waited too long to speak.

The kindling and smaller pieces of wood caught quickly. The second pyre lit just as well. Thick billows of smoke began to rise — more than I would have expected from the pyres.

I noticed Tella to my right. Her head was pointed straight up at the smoke, and her eyes glistened with worry.

The flames danced from around the head of the chieftain and warped the images across the pyre. Swimming amid the invisible movement of rising heat was Ciqala's hardened face, staring straight back at me. Banar followed suit. The people at his shoulder fixed their gazes on the burning bodies.

Entire minutes passed before Ciqala's face twisted with an old anger that thrust him into movement. He stepped halfway up the ridge, turned to look down at us, and began.

"Just two days ago, our chieftain died peacefully in his home. After a decade of work, he had made his hut and family something to be proud of. He passed away surrounded by the things he built. He was in the presence of his daughter, Nivan, who was born and raised next to this very ridge. A ridge," he continued, pointing out at the surrounding landscape, "that frames every sunset we've seen for years. A ridge that has guided the harmful winds over our huts and allowed us to settle. We've made this place our home — look among us at the children who have known no grasses but those we see each and every day. Look at the children whose bellies are filled by the nearby herds and generous river. It is true that our ancestors traveled. This was and is our tradition, but is tradition not born purely of necessity?"

People seemed to be listening intently. I stood quietly within the crowd, knowing my time to speak would come.

"I know nothing of our distant history beyond the simple stories we've all been told — the stories we've been telling the children in this village their whole lives. But perhaps our ancestor's urge to travel was not simply mindless movement. Could it be that there was something they sought to find? Would it not be wise to know a destination when it is reached? There's a reason we've lived in the ridge's sunset shadow all these years. We know it. The herds know it. And whether or not we want to admit it, our enemies know it. We have met our need, and we will travel no more."

Ciqala paused, letting his words sink in.

"We belong here. I will not stand before you and tell you to run. I will not ask you to leave the safety of your home."

He slid his sword from its sheath and pointed it west, toward the sunset.

"I ask you to defend the very place our clan has been seeking for generations! Our ancestors traveled their whole lives, time and again, to find a place to exist in peace — to find the very dirt upon which we stand. And now," he continued, shifting the sword's point toward me, "our greatest threat comes not from the grasses, but from our own home. Rennik would have you flee. The boy would lead you away from all that our clan has earned. Let us defend our legacy!"

The crowd gave a murmur of approval as Ciqala shouted. His blade gestured now at the dead scout burning near the chieftain.

"Let us avenge the men our enemies have slain!"

A louder agreement rose from the villagers.

"Let us become what our ancestors sought to be!"

He was met with zealous shouting.

Ciqala looked down at me from his raised position on the ridge, brandishing the same grin he wore when he beat his fists into my face.

Malik stepped up to the ridge.

"And how many of you have *seen* our enemies fight?" she shouted. The crowd quieted and faces turned back to listen. "I was on that scouting trip, same as Ciqala. I saw our enemies charge from the grasses and cut our best fighter down. Ko was slain because he had no chance to run, and I'm willing to bet that if he could take his life back, he would. He bled into the charred remains of a dead clan. His last breath was soured by their ashes. They may have had no chance to leave, or perhaps they were stubborn, like many of you. We'll never know about them, but I don't intend to be turned to ash. I don't want the bones of our children to be charred to black.

"The only reason I'm alive today is because Rennik was able to see beyond the battle. He knew when we were beat, and saved me — saved Ciqala and Banar, too, though they won't admit it. For those of you who intend to keep your lives, it's him you'll want to listen to."

"He's going to take our only chance from us!" shouted Ciqala before I could speak. "Every man or woman who follows him is just another coward who won't lift a spear to save their own people. Our fighting force will be weakened for every healthy hand who leaves."

"Your fighting force is going to die, Ciqala!" shouted Malik.

"If you take even a single man from our home," continued Ciqala, stepping down and meeting me eye-to-eye, "you'll be weakening the rest of us, and condemning us to die. Our blood will be on your hands, Rennik. Like the blood of my grandfather."

His words carried out and above the village, swallowed up by the hungry landscape.

I stayed quiet for a moment, letting the crowd's silent focus turn to me in anticipation. The apprehension settled in, and I felt my mouth grow dry and my throat become constricted. As soon as the nervous beating of my heart was the only sound in my ears, I began.

"You know little of our history," I started, meeting his gaze. "You said this yourself."

I turned and walked among the crowd, looking each man and woman in the eye as I passed.

"I stand with you — not above you — as a man who has spent most of his life in the village. Years learning how to hunt its game, learning your faces, and learning your laughter." I hesitated as I searched for the right words. "And learning from Gatsi the truth behind our stories, and the origins of our people."

Now that I had begun speaking, the words poured from me more smoothly than I knew they could. It was an alien feeling to be voicing myself this well. Somehow, I felt fear under my confidence.

"You've estimated correctly, Ciqala, that our ancestors sought safety in the lands of Kalanos. The tall grasses contain many threats, and it is the unperceivable that keeps us so still against this ridge. But it was not quite the seeking of safety that put motion to their feet — it was the knowledge that to remain still is to welcome the threats to come.

"It takes a certain kind of courage to walk into the grasses at night; the cowardly can't bring themselves to leave behind all that has grown familiar. We've convinced ourselves that this ridge is safe, but how quickly could a Kalanosi horse charge its rise? How many arrows will fire from its peak before you realize that the dirt and stone below us won't offer any protection? The power we have is not within this place. It is among our people!"

"We've never once been attacked here!" came a shout from somewhere in the crowd. A momentary muttering of agreement rose from the silence.

"I wish I could tell you the chieftain died peacefully," I said, my voice lowering in volume.

The buzz died down and the only sound left was the crackling of the fire and the soft push of the wind against the grasses.

"I wish I could tell you that, but it would not be the truth. I've learned more than most of you about the nature of harm and healing. I was with Gatsi when the body was prepared. I spoke to his daughter about that night. And it is for those reasons I know the truth behind the chieftain's death."

The dryness in my throat increased. I did not know how the people would react to my next statement. I stepped toward the burning body and looked into the flames.

"The chieftain was murdered by a foreign invader."

The expressive people among them reacted with gasps. Many simply furrowed their brows and clenched their jaws, some tipping their proud chins up, focused on the next words to come. Nivan and Cordah embraced each other in reaction to the brutal reminder.

"You're lying!" interjected Ciqala.

"It's true!" shouted Avid. "Gatsi said it himself!"

"And where is the old man?" demanded Ciqala.

"Listen to the boy!" shouted Cordah amid the sounds of her husband's burning body.

I ignored Ciqala and continued.

"Someone killed our leader, and I believe it was with the intent to distract us from something. Think of all that has transpired since his death — in the midst of a storm that pinned us in place, our own indecision has kept us just as still. It benefits his killer to keep us here, and that is exactly why we must leave this ridge."

It was at this point that some of my people nodded in agreement while others became softly indignant.

"Ciqala," I addressed him directly, wielding the arrow pulled from the dead scout's back. "If you truly wish to stay here and attempt to fight against certain death, I won't stop you. But I will beg the rest of you," I turned to scan the crowd, who now stood more in the light of their burning chieftain than that of the quickly setting sun, "to please, think of your people. This ridge will be your cairn, and your bones will sink to the earth, unmoved by the wind just as your feet are unmoved by the call to survival!"

"You would have us flee?" shouted a woman's voice from the throng of firelit faces, accusation and disgust heavy in her tone.

"I would have you live!" My voice became lower and louder — it no longer sounded familiar to me. Grasping the arrow that had come from the scout's back, I thrust it into one of the pyre's logs, my hand grazing the flames for a moment. "I would have us invoke the traditions we've forgotten. In a short span of years, we've let our wanderlust disappear. Whatever string of discovery pulled our ancestors — my own father — into the unknown has long since escaped our grasp and our vision.

"For those among you who choose to clutch at the life promised by the rising sun — for those of you who still contain any shred of our ancestors' wisdom — you will make yourselves ready to leave this disnotable piece of land by morning. You will bring with you only what you need — light loads of food and water, and any tools you can carry easily."

As I spoke, a deeper baritone affected my voice. My lungs became strong and pushed the gale winds of persuasion from my throat. Thunder rolled overhead.

And yet my neck began to tighten against the rough texture of an invisible force. It felt as though the stony grasp of an unseen beast clutched at my throat to squeeze the life from me, but instead instilled me with power. I moved to speak without meaning to.

It was then that I recognized the abrasive presence of the Delkhi. It wanted us to leave, and I was the push.

I couldn't breathe. My body turned suddenly cold, and I stepped instinctively toward the burning bodies for warmth.

The faces of many of the villagers shifted then into a placid countenance, and they listened. Breath continued to burst from over my tongue.

"The mothers and fathers of every man and woman in Kalanos once found within themselves the need to travel. Our ancient chieftain, a strong and wise woman called Senga, bestowed upon her people the knowledge that complacency would kill them. She beckoned them forth into the distant grasses and sands, cast them into unceasing motion upon the cliffs of the Rask, found them homes in the wild mountains to the south. Our people — all of the clans of Kalanos — survived not by rooting into the earth, but by keeping it underfoot. They were wise enough to know that a home is not a place, but a people, and that the only place we belong is where the valley meets the sky. Our only home is on the horizon, and it is to that end we must travel now!"

The invisible grasp on my throat clung tighter, and the last of my words poured from me like the last bit of moisture from a waterskin. I stood in a desert of my people, seeing no trees by which to navigate nor oases to give me rest; instead, the nourishment of my speech came from some unseen well-spring and erupted from me with a force I couldn't control.

I suffocated in the cloud of words that would be my people's salvation.

"We will learn to breathe from distant breezes! We will nourish ourselves on the bounty of the passing lands! We will live in spite of those who want us dead! We will leave with the rising sun so as to see it time and time again!"

Tella screamed.

"*Rennik!*"

The massive cloud of smoke above our heads suddenly collapsed and buried each of us in violent black tides. Strong winds pushed against the crowd and seemed to stem from the bodies of the dead. Panicked shouts erupted from each side of the pyre, and I felt Avid's hand grab my own. I couldn't force my eyes to open. The winds cut against the bare skin of my arms. My foot reached back to steady myself against the force, and though I tried, I couldn't scream from my own constricted throat. The small papers Tella had put in our doorway fluttered high into the sky.

Then, just as soon as the smoke had come, it vanished over the ridge and into the grasses.

The bodies of the chieftain and scout were gone.

I stood motionless, eyes intense at the silent crowd. The stalks of grass in the edge of the firelight swayed behind their stone-still bodies. Tella was already staring into my eyes, looking hopeless. Everyone turned to stare at me.

After another long moment, the grip on my throat melted away and I regained the ability to breathe. I gasped; my fingers were blackened and cold.

"Beckoned them," Tella whispered, voice filled with awe, gazing deeply into the sky.

Unable to understand what she meant, and sick of the weight of the villagers' stares and their silence, I stormed from the barren pyres and back to my home.

I boiled the skull plate at the point where the horns were connected. Under normal circumstances, they would be near impossible to separate from the bone, at least without doing damage.

Fire made the separation possible. Fire weakened its constitution. With the boiling of the water rose my frustration with Ciqala, with Gatsi's disappearance, and with the clan as a whole. My breathing increased and anger erupted up my spine.

I stood and pulled violently on one of the oryx horns, ripping it from the plate. The other horn followed easily.

The work kept my mind off of what had happened at the funeral. I was glad for the escape. After I nearly choked in front of my people, working with the horns allowed me to convince myself of my own agency. I wanted to cut the leash around my neck and feel like I was free to move myself as I wished.

But deeper inside, I felt like a rabbit at the roots.

21

WORDS FROM THE OTHER SIDE

"A dog will be loyal as long as the food lasts. People aren't much different."

— MALIK

My heavy frustration kept me awake for the entire night. My mother and Avid had come home shortly after the funeral, but neither had spoken to me. Avid had stared at me briefly before hurrying inside. At some point in the night, Tella had walked straight past me and into the grasses, appearing somnambulate but surely just acting within her idiosyncratic normalcy. My hands began to blister and callus against the grips of the drawknife, but I paid the pain no mind. Simple work relaxed me — or at least it was supposed to.

Just as the sun started rising, Avid emerged from the hut and sat across from me.

"How soon are we leaving?" he asked.

"Soon. I actually need you to come with me while I gather everyone who wants to join us."

Avid nodded in understanding but made no move to stand. After a few moments, I gave in to the silence.

"Was there something else, Avid?"

"They think you're magic."

I was startled by the comment. "What?"

"Everyone who saw you speak last night. You did some strange things, Rennik. I..."

"Like what? I just spoke. There's nothing strange about that." I thought back to the feeling of the Delkhi's roots the night before, but tried my best to believe it was something only I could perceive.

"Right, but it was *while* you were speaking. Your voice changed and got low and loud. Your eyes sort of...I don't know, they got more intense, I guess. Your neck tightened. And then the smoke..."

"Avid. I was just trying to be loud. My eyes didn't change. I didn't do any smoke magic — who do you think I am? Tella?"

"Tella does smoke magic?!"

"No, Avid, I just...I don't know. I don't know what the smoke was about. I don't know why my eyes looked different. I'm sure it was just the firelight. It must have been a strong fire, since the bodies burned away so quickly, right?" It was easier to redirect his questions than answer with what I thought was the truth.

Avid only looked to the ground.

"You seem scared, Avid."

"So do you."

"I know there's a lot going on, but you need to get focused," I told him. "I need you to come with me to gather everyone who intends to come with us."

He shook his head as if to rid it of confusion, then stood up confidently.

"I can do things on my own, you know," he stated, his voice rising.

"I know that," I responded warily. "I wish you'd speak your mind, Avid."

"Let me get the villagers together. You probably have other things to do. You're with me when I hunt, you're with me when I'm home — I can do this on my own."

I wondered briefly if this was truly an attempt for his own agency or if he was somehow scared of me after what happened. Sometimes I forgot that he was growing up.

"Okay," I told him. "Have them meet us at the southern edge of the village at noon. Only what they need to survive a few days."

Avid stood and walked away.

I continued working on the wood with the drawknife. What had Avid meant? These must have been physical symptoms of the Delkhi, but my eyes didn't feel any different. And I certainly didn't intend to cause that huge column of smoke to collapse. It had to have been Tella. Perhaps Avid would be a little less rattled once he set his mind to the task at hand. Either way, I wasn't going to admit to any of these strange things until I knew more for myself.

After sitting for so long with only my thoughts, I gave in to the urge to walk.

Launching forth from my fire, I strode through the early morning village, ignoring the stares of every person I passed. At first I didn't know where I was headed. As it happens, the only destination for me was Gatsi's hut.

Another problem I had to solve. Gatsi had been missing ever since my fight with Ciqala. He could be out in the grasses, or more likely along the river. Perhaps he'd gone to the Delkhi.

I think I understood that he wasn't coming back. I remembered what he said to me before the scouting trip.

"If it looks at all like death is coming...leave them."

Gatsi had always known everything. The customs of a distant people, the reasons for animal behavior, the deeper meaning behind words...he would know to leave if he needed to.

But he wouldn't leave *me*. He said that I was important. He showed me the terrifying scope of the Delkhi's vision. I knew it wasn't possible to believe these two things at the same time, but truly, all at once, I knew he was gone for good and knew he'd come back. I shook the conflict from my head.

I pushed through the entrance of his hut.

The injured scout still lay on a thick blanket on Gatsi's floor. The wounds he bore had begun to close but weren't exactly looking healthy yet. I wasn't convinced they wouldn't become infected. The woman I'd asked to watch him sat idle on a bench, and as I walked through the entrance, she glanced at me once, then pointedly avoided eye contact. She was scared of me. I swallowed my anxiousness and buried it far away.

"Has he woken at all?" I asked.

"No," she answered, shaking her head, "but he's been talking in his sleep a bit."

"Anything interesting?"

"Just nightmares, I think."

The poor man. He had escaped the coming clans with his life only to be haunted in his dreams.

"Remind me of your name."

"Onagah."

"Right," I said, nodding, "I think I knew that." In our

village, one tends to cross paths with most people at some point. "Well, I know Gatsi has some stores of feverfew in here, and you've been with him since yesterday morning. Why don't you go rest? I'll watch over him awhile."

Her eyes met mine briefly before darting away. "You're sure?"

"I'm sure," I answered.

Onagah stood to leave.

"Actually," I interjected, stopping her at the door, "I have something I need to ask you."

Her eyes wandered in my direction.

"Why are you suddenly frightened?" I asked. My tone grew fraught as I continued. "Why is my own brother apprehensive of me? Why won't you look me in the eye?"

"Last night," she sputtered out. "Last night you...you changed. You changed right in front of everyone. Your voice, your eyes...the *smoke*."

She looked up at me. Her open mouth trembled with something unspoken, but she quickly turned and stepped outside.

I found the feverfew and ground up the bits of flower and leaf in Gatsi's mortar. I would combine this with a little water to make a simple poultice that might help a man in this condition. That being said, it was dangerous to give him anything before he found a little more consciousness. I didn't want to drown him. Until he woke, I'd have to wait.

I felt my eyes grow heavy as last night's stress caught up with me.

THE MAN WITH PALE-BROWN HAIR STOOD ALONE IN HIS HUT. Someone was approaching, and he turned at the sound. A soft voice came through the entrance.

"It's Malik."

The man thought a moment before calling for her to come in. She took a seat at his invitation. The space was filled with the soft orange light of a modest fire, bouncing from her face, the walls, the man's bare chest.

"Well?" the man asked. "What did you want?"

"I'm worried, Ciqala."

"We don't know how many there are, but we'll stop them. I can keep you safe."

"You used to be clever. Before, a few years back. I think you've let that go."

Ciqala snorted like a bull. "You've come here to insult my intelligence?"

"I was too little to see it then," she continued without missing a beat. "But I see it now. You and Hashil."

His face fell slack. His jaw clenched hard a moment later to compensate. "You don't know what you're saying. What does he have to do with this?"

"You used to play fight. You'd go to the river together, you'd stalk oryx together. He was so much bigger than you, and you still fought with him."

"Courage. Taking on a bigger opponent," he complimented himself, nodding. "Your brother was my best friend, but if you think that changes how we—"

"I remember when your grandfather got angry with you for some reason. His rage was just as bad then, maybe even worse. You hid behind Hashil. He stuck up for you, tried to calm Chaska for fear of what he'd do to you."

Ciqala sat down and looked at the wall behind Malik. "Your brother and I were close—"

"I think you loved him."

With one swift motion he was back to his feet, but stopped rigid, tall and tense.

"I think," she continued, "he's the only reason you don't hate me like you hate Rennik. He's the reason you let me in to speak to you."

"This has nothing to do with the clan." He had angry tears in his eyes now, whether he was angry with himself or Malik, it was hard to tell. "You can't convince me to leave a home we've earned."

"I would've thought you'd grow up better. Who would've thought you'd grow up to be just like the man that hit Hashil like that?"

"Stop."

"You knew your grandfather was stronger than you, so you hid behind my brother. Hashil was big, but he wasn't fully grown yet. *He* was just trying to be brave. *You* were just hiding."

"Then maybe I've learned from Hashil. I'm taking a stand, Malik. He was strong and courageous. He'd have us fight."

"Your grandfather knocked my brother cold that day. Hit him hard, once, and reached for you next. You can call it courage, but if Hashil were alive today I don't think he'd make the same mistake twice. You were smarter back then, hiding behind someone. I mean it. Chaska's anger is some of the worst in the village. I'd imagine you wouldn't want to end up like him, but here we are. Death is coming any day over that ridge, and you don't have my brother to save you. You should run with us, Ciqala."

Ciqala's face changed. On the verge of fully crying, something I couldn't imagine him capable of doing, he narrowed his eyes and collected himself. "So that's what this is about. That's your plan."

Malik sat up straight, sensing an attack.

"It's Rennik," he continued. "The man was born without fire. He's passionless, guileless. He's plain as dirt but still you want him to lead."

"I want someone to show the way."

"No. You're keeping him in front of you," he continued. "I always wondered why you didn't challenge me out in the grasses. That first day, when Banar and I fought, you talked us down, but you changed after that. You kept Rennik and Ko in front of you."

"That's not true—"

"Of course it is. No one shoots better than you. You're strong enough to pick a fight with me, but you'd rather the threat come to someone else. You hid behind him just like I hid behind your brother. The difference is that I was a child, Malik."

"I fought in the grasses just like you!"

"No, no. Not like me. I fought them hand-to-hand. I looked men in the eye when I killed them. I cut them down before me. The only reason you shot at all was because Ko, Banar, and I were in the front. When we got home, it's why you told everyone Rennik would save them; you were scared. You only act from behind, and with everyone looking either to me, to Rennik, or to the horde, I bet you'll be the first to run." He was grinning now, a terrible grin, curved like a sickle.

Ciqala rolled back his strong shoulders and fell into his posture from the funeral, puffing his chest full of words and hot air.

"You thought you could use your brother against me," he continued. He pounded a fist hard upon his chest. "You wanted to soften this armor, but he's the one who gave it to me. Yes, Malik, I loved him. He was brave and strong and intelligent. He was my friend, but he was also my hero. Hashil wanted me honest, and Chaska wanted me tougher. So I've become both. I will not leave my home. I will not let harm come to those behind me. This moment is something I've seen a thousand different ways since I was a boy and I know enough now to be the one standing in front of that which needs protected."

"You need to choose your battles wisely!"

"And you'd tell me wisdom is leaving a herd of bison?" He was shouting now. "Wisdom is leaving our memories planted into this soil? Is it wise to abandon the river and let our weak, our children and our elderly go to the grasses?"

"We're built to live in the grasses. We're not meant to fight. We're not killers, Ciqala."

"Why are you still here?" He was shaking his head. "It's obvious you want to leave us, and I understand why. Hashil is dead. Your father and sister are dead. You've been alone in the village for too long. What strings hold you here?"

Malik was quiet for a moment. "And what if I don't leave? You'll push me to the ground, beat my face until you get what you want? Take an axe to my bow?"

"You've got no argument left," he said. "Go."

Malik turned toward the door, then hesitated. "South," she said to the open air, loud enough for him to hear. "We're heading south, then as far east as it takes. Just...just in case you find some sense."

She stepped into the night.

It was quiet when I opened my eyes. I must have fallen asleep waiting for Valen to show signs of consciousness. A quiet moment passed as I considered how long I'd been out.

Then, the scout woke. Normally when someone in his condition wakes, their eyes flutter open with a slow, increasing confusion. It could take hours.

That was not the case here.

He burst from his position on the floor and grabbed me by the shirt. His eyes were hard and determined, his face bloodied.

"Rennik!" he hissed through broken teeth. "They're nearly here! The armored man with golden hair — the snake — everything you saw before!"

The mortar dropped from my hand and thudded to the ground.

"Valen," I asked, grasping him by the shoulders, "Valen, what are you talking about? What have you seen?"

"Fire. Death. A sea of spears. But it isn't what I've seen, Rennik — the armored man, *he's seen us too!*"

A violent wind suddenly ripped against the walls of the hut and tore it from its mud brick foundation. Every loose item among the shelves flew off in a volley to the east, and the man before me, whose shoulders I held in my hands, began to fall apart. First, his chest loosed and turned to dust, then his head, then arms, and soon there was nothing but empty space around me, a furious and hungry void. The billowing winds grew hot as I turned to face them.

I couldn't hear my own scream as it tore from my chest.

～

THE SCOUT WAS DEAD.

I knew it as soon as I woke. Gatsi's home was usually quiet, but it was vacuous without Valen's breathing below me. The sorry bits of feverfew in the bowl would be left unused. This man would be but the first of many deaths to come in our village.

I had dreamt of Malik, of Ciqala, of a tempestuous wind. I wanted to place it on the shelf of doubt in my mind like I had tried to do with my visions before, but this time was different. I would see Malik soon, and she could confirm what had happened.

There was a sudden spurt of air from across the hut, as if it had remembered to breathe. I turned to see Avid standing near the entrance, muscles tense and jaw clenched.

"Your neck," he said, out of breath and pointing toward me. "It's got..."

I reached slowly toward my throat, and as my fingers made contact, I felt an acute pain from my skin, as though something abrasive had held it tight.

"It's like Graff's bellows," Avid continued. "Like something squeezed all the air right out of you."

"I was asleep," I choked out, voice raspy. I realized I was shivering.

"Those marks look like the ones on Gatsi's arms."

I took in the information but moved along, unsure of what to think. "Have you seen him since I've been here?"

Avid shook his head. "No, but I went through the village. People will be ready to meet you soon. You have a plan for them, right?"

I nodded.

"You're going to be able to meet them, right? Can you breathe?"

"I was about to ask you the same thing."

"Rennik," he continued. "This is just like the funeral. This...what's happening to you?"

"I don't know, Avid. But this is a time to act, not to think. Let's go."

22

MIGRATION

"It's said that an entire herd of bison represent the power in a single step of the Dalkhur's hooves."

— GATSI

The questions were nearly too much to bear. I didn't understand why I was dreaming of things I could never have seen, why the people who'd known me my whole life were suddenly looking at me as if I had nine eyes and bison horns on my head. I felt like I remembered receiving the same sort of attention after I had returned to the village alone all those years ago, when winter should have taken my life. With my new role as chieftain I had much to do, and with Gatsi gone, I had no one near me to help shoulder the mystery. As I went at it alone, I was a shell of confidence.

I left Gatsi's hut and strode through the village, past Ikoda's old home, sitting empty since she left on the trip all those days ago.

I turned the corner to see a crowd gathering along the southern reaches of the village, very close to my hut. There must have been almost a hundred of them — more than I had anticipated. Avid, my mother, and Tella stood a bit higher on what little of the ridge was present and looked down upon the villagers. As his eyes wandered, Avid's found mine, and he smiled. I nodded to affirm that he had done a good job.

My feet found little resistance in the short grass as I stepped over to him. The crowd quickly hushed themselves. I looked among them, and perhaps they felt safe in a group; whatever fear and apprehension they felt for me was not shown in any aversion to my eyes, but rather through tight, stone-faced expressions. Avid was right to have warned me this morning.

"Follow," I commanded. After a moment or two, the crowd tailed behind me as I walked away from the village, at least far enough to get out of earshot; anyone who did not need to hear our plan was simply a liability.

Though stymied by the number of people present, I smiled and addressed them. Instead of the terse tone I took with Onagah in Gatsi's hut, I tried for an optimistic one.

"As my brother has likely informed you," I began, speaking loudly, but nowhere near as aggressively as the night before, "you are to gather only light, necessary things before we move. If you have not done so already, I suggest you do it quickly. We need to reach our destination within the next few hours. Once there, you will not be able to leave."

The villagers seemed surprised, but no one spoke out.

"Eventually we will travel far and away from the coming threat, but any attempt to flee from our enemies now would surely not succeed—"

"What, then?" someone asked desperately.

"We hide," I replied quickly. I turned and pointed to the south. "There is, about two miles south of here, a plateau with which you are surely familiar, though none of you has ever climbed to its peak. We will gather at the top using a well-hidden trail along its southeastern side. You will make temporary shelters — nothing as tall as our huts here — as close to the center of the plateau as possible. Any fire pits you dig will need to make little or no smoke and should only be created if truly necessary. I estimate that we have enough dried meats and vegetables to last us a few days.

"When the horde comes to the village," I continued, "they will hopefully believe that there are fewer in here than predicted, or that we've already fled. This also greatly depends on the rest of you keeping this a secret from those of the clan who are choosing to stay."

"What about..." began a man who stepped forward, then promptly ducked his head in regret.

"Please," I comforted, "speak your mind." It was taxing to hide my frustration. I wish the people would simply trust me — was it so difficult to do?

"What about our trail? Surely our path through the grasses would be too easy to follow. Anyone who comes through here would find us!"

"A valid point, and one I've considered already. Any of you who are willing and have a horse, mount up and meet me on the northern lip of the ridge just after noon. I will join you if someone brings me a horse. Once everyone is safely at the plateau..."

I grinned shamelessly in excitement for my own idea.

"We're going to follow the biggest migration you've seen in years."

～

NO BOW IS BORN PERFECT. THEY ARE, AT FIRST, NONDESCRIPT branches among their featureless brethren growing up from the dirt of the plains. A bow must be cut off from its home and severed to size. It must be shaved down to its core, to the very material that defines its use.

Then comes the pressure. For a bow to be effective it must be put under immense amounts of pressure to push it to shape, to give it the tension in needs to strike. After these great trials of change, the bow looks nothing like it did among the comfortable branches of its home, but adopts a potential that it never once had.

After speaking to my people, I left the village early.

Striding out alone into the grasses, I journeyed to the tilling tree. This is a tree with a small metal implement bored into its trunk, which I would use to shape my newly-crafted bow over periods of time. I made this tilling tree away from the village and along the river, anticipating the fact that I might not be visiting my people's ridge ever again.

Having spread the glue over shards of oryx horn on the belly and sinew on the back, I left the new bow under tension and made to meet my riders.

WEEKS AGO, HAD I BEEN A BIRD IN THE SKY, I WOULD HAVE seen myself alone in the wilds, coursing solitarily and without a thought as to a single other person, save for Avid and my mother. The only feet on the ground would be mine, and they would be a minor intrusion at most. The path I would take would follow that of a deer or an oryx — something closer my size — so no new disturbance to the grasses would be made. If I decided to step out on my own path, which I did often and daily, it would be such a thin and miniscule line through the vegetation that the stalks would place themselves back within a day or so. It was a certain kind of peace knowing that I was alone and hard to track.

Now, I had to calculate how to walk a hundred people through the grasses with supplies in tow. True, we could walk in a slow, single-file line and hope the trail isn't too noticeable, but I wasn't confident that any path my people left could be hidden. And so I had decided that if the grasses would put our path at risk, then it was the grasses that must be dealt with.

Thirteen riders sat proudly on their horses atop the hill, most of them saddled. The horses of my village were strong and obedient — most of them trained by Ikoda, whether vicariously or first-hand — but they weren't quite like the horses our enemies rode. I wondered if Ciqala had reasoned that much when making his plans of defense.

One of the women had brought a horse for me. It was one of hers — a speckled male, ungelded and energetic. I may not have been the most experienced rider in the village, and they may do better without me, but my mother had once told me never to expect someone to do something I wouldn't do myself.

I led them north, near the river. On our way, I heard two riders behind me speak softly, as if they didn't want me to hear.

"Probably some sort of trick Gatsi taught him," said the first.

"It wasn't just a trick — it was terrifying! Would've frightened me away if he weren't speaking the truth," replied the second.

"Well, ask him about it."

"Are you serious? What if he can do other things? You *saw* that smoke last night!"

I considered slowing my horse and addressing the conversation head-on, but it was then that I saw what we had come for.

The edge of the bison herd sprawled lazily in the grasses, and its furthest members near the river drank from the waters comfortably. The creatures closest to us watched our approach and grew wary, standing up from their relaxed positions.

"This herd," I began, addressing my riders, "has sustained us for over a generation, and for the last decade has remained here, growing fat and passive."

I continued riding, leading us in a curved path toward the northern edge of the herd.

"And now," I continued, "we're going to encourage them elsewhere. The village is our first destination, then the plateau, then beyond another few miles to wherever the bison take us."

I designated a few who would ride on the western side of the herd, ensuring the path would not cut through the village. The rest of us were to ride behind the herd, shouting, charging, and slapping stragglers with the butt-ends of spears.

"Why would we do this?" a woman asked. "Are you intending to take the entire herd with us when we leave?"

"No. We aren't taking the herd with us. We want them far to the south of our hiding place. Their tracks are going to destroy any signs of passage our people have already left on their way to the plateau. It will look as though the bison migrated to avoid the coming horde."

"And that we followed them," she finished. I nodded.

"But this is dangerous," one of the men interjected. "Why are we risking any harm to the village?"

"We need to run them right over our people's tracks.

From here to the village, from the village to the plateau," I explained. "The horde, if they attempt to track us, will end up miles off target."

I raised the spear in my hand and gave a confident shout, and so began the migration.

Growing up in Kalanos, one can't help but learn to ride well. The traveling merchants used to joke that all Kalanosi children are born on horseback.

Even with horses available, traveling alone and by foot had always been preferable to me. Our horses were trained to be controlled by the slightest movements of the rider's foot and hips and could be used as cover while riding. I simply trusted my feet more than the horse's; I felt a bit trapped, and perhaps exposed, while on horseback. That being said, the fire I felt in my chest while careening through the grasses, chasing after a stampede, was nearly peerless among all the other moments in my life.

I wish I could have seen the look on Ciqala's face — or maybe Chaska's or Banar's — when we drove an entire bison herd within a quarter mile of the village. In fact, I intended to be closer to the village when we passed, but managing that many half-ton bison is a difficult task to say the least. With the combination of my horse's gallop and the shaking from the herd's stampeding I was reminded of how fragile our bodies are, that at any moment I could be pushed off of the horse and broken by the quickly passing dirt, or that I might fall at an ill-timed moment only to find myself crushed underfoot.

The huts moved by in a matter of seconds. It was a fascinating sight — all of these bison and my thirteen riders in somewhat still positions relative to my riding, while the sedentary things of the world whisked by at terrific speeds. I looked out at the bouncing images of my riders and felt a sense of pride.

We hurdled past the village and toward the plateau, nearing its sudden and steep rise.

Avid and his friends must have been in awe of the raw force exuded by the herd as they looked down from their elevated position on the plateau. Entire flocks of grass-dwelling birds were launching into the air and fleeing over the plains in terror, their swarms like a single body moving through the sky. It was a sight like no other.

Then, over the cadence of countless of hooves, I heard a panicked shout from ahead.

"Enemy scouts!"

The man's voice was punctuated by an arrow burying itself in the neck of the woman next to me. Her blood spattered against my arm.

The woman's hands dropped her spear as she clutched instinctively at her neck, blood pouring from her throat and through her twitching fingers. Her horse immediately slowed and left our charge.

I turned my shoulders and dipped low against the horse's back, maintaining its charge but searching the grasses for the source of the arrow.

It was then that I spotted all of my riders, bows and spears in hand, veering off of the path toward a group of four white-painted horses ridden by Wahto fighters. I turned my horse and followed.

As I left the herd of bison to their own trajectory, the earth-shaking sound of their stampeding lessened and was replaced by the lonely, determined gallop of my own horse.

My mount pushed forward with force enough to shake a man's teeth loose, but there was little the beast could do to catch up with so much distance between us and my allies.

Wary of what could happen, I slipped my father's thumb ring out from my pouch, grasped the old war bow in hand, and nocked an arrow.

The enemy scouts were cloaked by my own riders, and I waited anxiously for a shot.

One of my riders cut an enemy down with her spear. It stuck in the man's torso, and she was suddenly dragged to the ground with him, both of their riderless horses continuing the forward charge.

My horse leapt powerfully over them and continued forward. I heard her injured cries as we thundered past.

Another rider of mine was shot down with an arrow.

That's two.

Without their bodies to obscure the enemies ahead, I could see the Wahto clansmen and their horses.

I pulled back slightly on the string.

Normally, aiming a bow requires a steady hand. Even then, one has to know exactly when to loose the arrow, as no human body can hold weight and be perfectly still for long. This was a skill I had mastered, but shooting from the lurching rhythm of a horse's gallop was a different feat altogether. I wasn't as practiced with that kind of shot, and now the bow I held was an unfamiliar one.

I focused on the man who had killed two already, then looked to the flank of his horse. The shot was well over a hundred feet. He seemed to be the best shot among the scouting party, and he was keeping my riders from gaining much ground. As he turned from side to side, aiming his deadly shots and striking at more of my riders, I knew he must be dealt with first. A bow such as mine is traditionally drawn with an arrow on the right, but this was not the time to flirt with unfamiliar practices.

The fletching of the arrow brushed against my nose as I pulled back.

Drawing to my mouth rather than my ear might move the point of the arrow slightly to the right. Keeping this in mind, I made a miniscule adjustment and fired.

The arrow disappeared into the grasses just to the left of the enemy's horse. I had overcompensated.

Stop overthinking.

I drew again, my legs tight against the horse's sides.

The enemy turned and drew as well, but it was I who loosed the arrow first.

My arrow struck deep into the muscle and the horse's pained trumpet pierced the air. It collapsed, taking the Wahto scout down with it. We passed him quickly. One of my riders turned back around and pounded toward him, looking to finish the job.

Within seconds my remaining seven riders had stricken down the two enemies left and were circling around to reconvene.

"Where did they come from?" I demanded as my horse slowed to a halt.

"I think they were hiding," a man answered. "My guess is that they were scouting out our village and didn't expect a stampede of bison to come by. I noticed them first, and it was only when they saw us coming that they shot up from the grasses and fired. It seems they intended to be hidden, and that we caught them off-guard."

"And their horses? Surely the grasses didn't conceal them as well."

"They did, Rennik. Their horses were kneeling in the grasses to hide and took off into an immediate gallop. But the impression the horses made in the grass was large enough to be seen when we came close. I've never seen such a trick."

I looked around briefly and thought to ask my riders for advice. Was it weak for a leader to do so? Perhaps it would be better to feign confidence. I shook my head at my own stupidity and spoke.

"Do you think it unwise to split up now that we've encountered enemies so close to home?"

A scarred middle-aged woman spoke up. "I've been on several scouting trips myself. The Wahto like to send very few scouts out at a time. I think we'll be safe."

"Good," I replied, glad I had asked. I gestured to a few of them. "You three. Go gather the bodies of our fallen riders and bring their horses back to the village, and see if you can take the saddles from those scouts. The rest of you are going to come with me to continue pushing that bison herd south. We need to get that accomplished and get to the top of the plateau as soon as possible."

As we rode off into the plains, I couldn't ignore the implications of this new discovery. Our enemies may have been watching us.

And they were very close.

23

SMOKE & STONE

"It's hard to explain big concepts to children because they lack the words to understand them. Tella has both problems: big ideas and a borrowed vocabulary."

— RAISHA

On the first afternoon atop the plateau, Tella started a fire.

There was a thick black plume rising from the firepit, and I was unfortunately not the first one to reach her.

"What the hell are you doing?" cried one man, dropping to his knees and hurriedly pushing handfuls of dirt into the pit. His shouting attracted the attention of the others.

Tella looked overwhelmed — wide-eyed, drawing her hands toward to her collarbone as if to hold an invisible safety blanket, fearful of the man.

"You're going to get us all killed!" he continued.

My mother approached Tella, placing gentle hands on

her shoulders. From a distance I couldn't tell what she was saying to her.

"What do you mean it's going to be okay?" asked the man, incredulous. "She's going to give away our hiding place!"

"So are you if you don't shut your mouth!" My mother's voice whipped out of her like a snake's bite as she stood.

"We should make her leave!"

"We'll do no such thing," I asserted, finally reaching the situation at a fast pace.

The man and the others turned to look at me. He marched over to me, huffing, and shoved a hand into my chest. "I'm not going to die at the whim of an insane woman who builds a damn fire!"

"And I'm not going to die because a frightened little child won't stop shouting." The man grew red. "These people are not your enemy," I continued. "We've climbed the plateau to survive, not to fight each other. This is our clan. We are all Achare, and probably the only ones who are going to live through the week. If you can't survive with your own clan, you're welcome to strike out on your own." I pointed out toward the wilds.

"I'm not trying to be like the Sree and cast the unwanted out to die, but this is dire!" he breathed out, leaning toward me as if to push me with his presence. "I have children here! I can't fight off a horde! We can't keep everyone safe if she gives us away!"

My mother softened and stepped forward.

"Mudre," my mother said said, placing a hand on his shoulder, "I know this is difficult, but arguing among ourselves isn't the answer. Come, help me with the firepit."

The man, Mudre, seemed to size me up before conceding. "Okay," he said after a long moment. "Fine. But I don't trust that girl."

The two walked toward the pit and began mending the symptoms of Tella's meddling.

"Rennik," I heard next to me, "we're bored. Is there anything we can do?"

Avid and a few of his friends stood nearby, and having finished all there was to do with the shelters, it seemed they had idle hands.

"Go back to the village," I responded, my focus still on the situation with Tella. "Take one last look around for anything that could be useful, or anyone that wants to join us up here. Come back as soon as you can after that."

"Got it!" the boys said enthusiastically, taking to their feet like thrown stones skipping over water. They bounced away and down the plateau's trail. Avid's old rawhide pack trailed behind him in the air.

As Tella withdrew to her shelter, I heard someone speak.

"Do you think his mother is going to run the clan for him?"

I turned too late to see who had said it. The crowd around me dispersed a bit, milling around in smaller groups. I could tell, with all the dangers and worries around our situation, it was the waiting that might be the hardest for us all.

I forced a deep breath and surveyed my people.

A few of the smaller children were chasing the dog that had been following me around as of late. The dog, however, seemed more concerned with lunging out at the group of fat grouse that lived atop the plateau who were confused about their sudden visitors.

Within myself I felt the need to apologize to the creatures. I had never caused them harm before, and their sanctuary, for some inexplicable reason, felt sacred to me. And so, to quell the guilt within me while my people found safety here, I repeated a mantra over and again in my mind, something similar to what Malik said to me a few days before, something Kivik had said in our fiction.

It's us or them.

⁓

THE SUN FILTERED IN BETWEEN THE BRANCHES OF TELLA'S little shelter, speckling both our faces and the dirt below us with mismatched strips of light.

"Are you feeling okay?" I asked. Noting my mother's strategy earlier, I began the conversation with sympathy rather than command.

Tella only stared at the ground, pushing the dirt listlessly with her finger.

"I know that Mudre was angry about the smoke. I think you were trying to help, and it's frustrating when that's misconstrued. People are scared. I'm sure we're all feel better later."

"Later...smoke," she finally said.

"I'm not sure what you mean."

"Smoke..." she began, fumbling in her mind for more words. "Smoke..."

Her furrowed brows suddenly lifted high as she grabbed for a stone nearby. Pressing it into the soil, she placed two more rocks next to it in a series. She thrust her finger at them emphatically.

"*Smoke.*"

"Tella," I said softly, shaking my head, "I don't understand. Does this mean something?"

Her shoulders slumped and she exhaled in frustration, grasping out at the words she didn't have. I sighed and moved the conversation forward.

"About earlier, Tella, you really can't be making smoke up

here. We're hiding, right? We need to be subtle. We need to be unseen. The smoke is dangerous for us. So no more fires unless I say so, okay? Not just today, but in the next few days as we—"

"Today!" she squealed.

"Tella, you can't yell up here—"

"*Today!*" she whispered loudly, pointing again at the rocks. She was gesturing at the stone in the middle of the other two. Her fingers dug into a pocket, produced a pinch of sage, and placed it upon the rock. She thought for a moment and continued. "Next days." She mimicked my voice. Her fingers found a long hair on her head, plucked it from her scalp, and lay it upon the rock on the right.

Her finger pushed the stone a bit. She seemed a bit overzealous in her explanation.

"*Smoke.*"

I studied the stones. I was, of course, at a complete loss. Then I thought back to the fires she had started in the village.

"Tella," I began, "You said before that—"

"Before!" she exclaimed, putting a hand on the stone to the left. She reached into a pouch and produced what I quickly recognized as a small, disjointed bird skeleton.

"Do you..." I started. "Do you just carry *bones* around?"

Tella grinned like a child. There had been bones in the remains of her hut...

"Okay, but you said before that there are words in the smoke. Are you trying to say that the smoke connects the days? Do the words say things about other days? What is to come?"

Tella nodded eagerly, smiling at the rare success of communication.

"What is to come," she said slowly and with exaggerated lips, trying out the words as if she was savoring a new taste.

Most people feel some sort of anxiousness when others around them know something they don't. It's natural to want to collect information, like a squirrel stows food away for winter. But here, looking at the simple diagram in the dirt at my feet, my anxiousness grew as her meaning unfurled before me.

"Did Gatsi show you these...stones? The words?"

She nodded hesitantly, as if to say "yes, but..."

"Is this..." I began, treading carefully for fear of upsetting her. "Is this why you set your own home on fire?"

She hung her head sadly, like a child acknowledging something they've done wrong.

"No more fires," she said. Whose words she was repeating I did not know.

"What did the smoke tell you that day?"

Without lifting her head, she pointed to the west.

"I don't understand. Did it want you to go west?"

She shook her head.

"Who is speaking to you? How..." I struggled to phrase it. "How does the smoke know what to say?"

She moved her hand to point upwards, jostling the roof of the low shelter.

"I've got nothing," I told her.

She stepped out of the shelter, made her face an angry one, and made a windy sound before pounding her fists into the top of the roof.

"You're talking about your hut, aren't you?"

Tella puffed out her chest and dropped her voice low. "We will learn to take our breath from the distant breezes!"

It was strange to hear her say so much. I stayed silent.

"We will nourish ourselves on the bounty of the passing lands!"

I listened.

"We will live in spite of those who want us dead!" Her voice switched to mimic a small child's. "*Mother, what is that?*"

It suddenly dawned on me that she was repeating my words from the funeral, though I didn't remember hearing that last phrase. Tella drew her hands up slowly like a child about to pounce on a small animal.

"We will leave with the rising sun so as to see it time and time again!"

Tella made a harsh "whooshing" sound and pounded her hands down flat against the dirt and stones, sending little tufts of dust in every direction. An uninhibited, toothy grin spread across her face. She looked at me again.

"*Beckoned them.*"

AFTER THE CONVERSATION HAD REACHED A CERTAIN POINT, Tella had retreated both into her shelter and into her mind. I found my mother and Mudre elsewhere, portioning some vegetables for a meal. It occurred to me that my need to always be busying myself with hands-on work likely came from my mother.

"I was wondering if we could talk," I said to my mother, approaching with a nod to Mudre.

Mudre looked to me warily before walking away.

"I'm not sure how you do that," I began. I sat in the dirt across from her and helped with the food.

"What do you mean?" my mother responded.

"An hour ago you were arguing with him. Now you're portioning vegetables and acting like nothing happened."

"I was angry, at first," she explained, "and that's typically my first reaction. But once you entered the conversation with even more tension, I thought it'd be better to calm everyone down."

"That's why you lowered your voice," I added.

"We aren't dogs, Rennik. People need to be treated like people, and you can't always bark orders at them when they don't do what you want. People get angry when they feel they've lost control. So if others see *you* get angry..."

"It looks like I've lost control."

"It makes you look a bit like...well, you know," she said, gesturing with her head in the direction of the village.

"What?"

She dropped her hands to the ground and thought for a moment, smiling nervously. "It makes you look a bit like *him*."

"I am nothing like Ciqala," I said sternly.

"Bark all you want. It doesn't change what people have already seen."

I felt the first taste of anger on my tongue. "I don't want you to undermine me."

My mother looked appalled. "I'm sorry?"

"I'm glad Mudre is calmed down, but when he walked away away, one of the villagers' comments implied that you made me look weak. You had the right answer, and I didn't."

"Being wrong doesn't mean you're weak. Failing to admit to it just makes you arrogant."

"I need to be strong if they're going to trust me!"

"You need to be *human* if they're going to trust you!" She gestured dramatically with a carrot in her hand.

I raised my voice, probably too loud. The people nearby

started to look our way. "If they need to see me being human, why can't they see me fail? You should have let me handle Mudre."

"This isn't the time to fail."

"Can't you let me make my own mistakes?"

"Not when they can get us killed!" she shouted.

I held back an impulsive comment. I knew this should've been a private conversation, but my mistake had been made, and it was too late to stop it.

"Rennik, I'm trying to help you. I'm your mother!"

"And I am your son, but I'm not a child! I'm a chieftain!"

"Rennik!" a hushed and panicked cry failed to pierce our argument.

"*You* are a chieftain, but *we* are a clan!" my mother continued, volume teasing at the precipice of a shout. "You can't pretend to be something more than the rest of us!"

"*Rennik!*" came the voice again.

"I'm not tryi—"

Malik grabbed me by the shoulders. "*Would you shut up?*"

I was suddenly aware that all of the villagers had quickly clustered together, away from the edge of the plateau. Terrified chatter sewed them together with the needle of fear, ashen faces looking to my mother, Malik, and I.

The dog dropped its ears and whined, pressing itself against my leg.

Looking once at my mother, we rose to our feet and ran to the edge.

A massive wall of black smoke eclipsed the horizon to the west. At its feet, the grasses parted for what must have been hundreds of horses and men combing through the stalks like cutters on a calm sea.

"They're here," I heard myself mutter. My mouth moved without my knowledge, adrenaline rising, flooding to the surface of my being, drowning my heart with the unchallenged horror of a nightmare turned real. "Get back!" I whispered, turning to my people, waving them away and keeping my voice low, as if my enemies could hear it. "Lay flat on the ground and keep quiet!"

I turned back to the view, my mother's hand on my shoulder, her other hand tracing her heart.

The grasses near my home were pouring forward weakly as the brunt of the Kalanosi horde made its approach. The smell of fire and dirt hit the plateau.

There were countless mounted horses, painted in whites and reds. Something metallic reflected sunlight and caught my eye.

Armor.

The image of the pale man speaking to the other clans reappeared in my mind.

Forcing myself to look back again, I took stock of all that we had. The shelters were built low and were plentiful. The firepits were unlit. The food was enough. The people...

Avid.

I stepped toward them, my eyes frantic.

"Where's Avid?" I asked the villagers before me.

They stared back in horrified stupor.

"*Where is he*?!"

The blood drained from my face, weighted like a stone disappearing into the depths of a dark lake.

I looked down upon the doomed and half-deserted village, and without a single comforting doubt in my mind, I knew exactly where my brother was.

THE PROMISE OF FIRE

"Dremma's strength, Drakka's speed."

— AN ACHARE GOODBYE

Never before had I covered the distance to my village so quickly. The smoke to the west rose dominantly in my vision, and though the horde was approaching, the only sound in my ears was my own heavy breathing and the hiss of the stalks passing by. The grasses bit at my arms like berry bugs as I rushed through them, and I tried not to choke on the grains and seeds tumbling around me.

I told myself that he might have made it out. I envisioned Avid and his friends hiding in their mulberry tree a mile from the village, or crossing the river safely to the other side, but I knew it wasn't possible.

My mother had broken down, collapsed to her knees when I took to my heels to descend on the plateau's trail. I was bleeding again. Sliding down the rocky trail too quickly had opened old wounds, as well as a few new ones. The dog had followed me down the plateau but ran off in a different direction as soon as we were down.

Soon, the seeds in the air were replaced by falling ash.

I pushed my way up the ridge and threw myself prone on the ground in an effort to remain unseen.

Get him, get out.

The horde clutched at the west side of the village, crowning most of the ridge. The deep smoke that trailed behind them was the only indicator of a hidden inferno, a fire that should have reached the village by now. It had seemed close enough from the top of the plateau.

The Achare who'd chosen to stay stood in a semicircle in the center of the village, near the chieftain's hut. There was a breathless tension surrounding a conversation that became clearer as I approached.

"You must understand the guilt into which you plunge. We need not harm the others among you. We come seeking only the one. By feigning ignorance, you select for your death." I recognized the voice immediately. It sounded strangely like the hiss of a hognose snake. With no sign of Avid, I crept toward the crowd.

"How did you know?" It was Ciqala, asking as if he'd repeated himself. "How did you know our chieftain would be dead?"

I stood a safe distance away, searching the crowd for any sign of Avid.

Get him, get out.

It was then that one of the villagers saw me. I made eye contact, and he stepped solemnly to the side, drawing back the curtain of the crowd. And it was then that I saw my brother.

What was left of the Achare here ensconced a wide swath

of space where stood Ciqala and a sun-darkened Kazel man, facing each other at a distance of thirty feet. Quivering before the Kazel man was Avid, kept still by a heavy hand resting upon his shoulder. He was staring at the dirt, breathing shakily, the weight of terror pressing him into place.

I stepped into the open space and all eyes turned to me.

"Rennik!" Avid whispered.

The Kazel man looked in my direction with steel in his eyes. "A brother, no doubt," he deliberated after sizing me up. "Perhaps you'll be of greater help to me."

I stood frozen to the spot, bow already in my hand, meeting with a wall of unfamiliar challenges. Ash fell silently upon my village. An army of lightless vultures on horseback sat upon the ridge, their backs to the sun, hungry and waiting.

"My name is Zamri Malnostos. I am a diplomat of sorts, yet it seems I can find no one here proficient in the magic of reason. And so my task is made difficult. Tell me," the snake named Malnostos continued to say, his hand tightening on Avid's shoulder. "We look for the man who should have succeeded your chieftain after his death. *This* dolt is not he whom we seek." His eyes gestured quickly to Ciqala. "Where is the one named Gatsi?"

I shared a confused look with Ciqala. "We don't know where the old man's gone," he said.

After a moment, I'd found my voice. My words had fire in them. "Let my brother go. Now."

The Kazel man exhaled, the entire encounter clearly an inconvenience. He wore a sword and several daggers on his belt. Against his hip was tied a small wicker box. "I am proposing a trade, Rennik. Your brother for a few words. A worthy deal, I assume. Now tell me where he's gone."

"How did you know he would be dead?" Ciqala demanded, punching into the attention of Malnostos again.

"Because, you fool, *I am the one who killed him.*" His hiss had risen to an abrasive scrape. "We were also sure to kill Satra with her party in the grasses."

Ciqala recoiled and looked to me. His face was one of revelation.

"Gatsi disappeared days ago," I said. "He's left us."

"And you must understand, boy, that each clan we've come across has told us the same thing. The one they hide has conveniently disappeared, but the truth is often found on the tongues of the tortured. We are not in the habit of leaving without our quarry."

I fought back an assault of worries, worries that my mother would be found atop the plateau, worries that the hand of Malnostos would leave Avid's shoulder and return with a dagger, worries that I knew where Gatsi was, but couldn't fish the information from this deep well of fear.

Zamri Malnostos' scraping shout was now aimed at all who watched. "There is a man among you who communes with a greater creature nearby. He will have told you things he could not know. He will have given you knowledge you would not otherwise have. This man is the only one we seek, and should any of you give him to me now, you will be spared."

He paused for an answer, but the crowd only looked within itself, desperate for a solution.

"The Achare are not a fighting people," he continued. "You need not meet your deaths today."

There was, sitting atop the scene, a tacit understanding of consequence. If someone were to strike at this man, not only would Avid be killed, but the vultures on the ridge would begin their charge. He stood before us with the greatest shield one could wear.

And he began to walk backward toward his vultures.

Avid's eyes widened, became wet, flooded with the fear of death. "No," he managed, weakly. His hands clawed helplessly at the hand of Malnostos, who now clutched at Avid's hair, dragging him back.

I nocked an arrow stepped in time with the Kazel man.

All movement stopped. Malnostos eyed me. He moved a hand patiently from the box at his hip, and from it produced a small, striped snake. Its head was pointed toward Avid's neck.

"I don't know why you've come for Gatsi. I don't know who you are, or who the pale man with you is." His eyes grew wide. "I am not here to save these people. I have no quarrel with you."

"I'm no stranger to the threat of a talented Achare hunter," he replied. "I know many Kalanosi who don't often miss, but consider the seconds after. The only thing keeping this snake from killing your brother is the grip in my hand. Should it go slack, your brother dies."

I pulled my fingers into the weight of the bowstring, just an inch. The vicious wheel of cause-and-effect played through my mind's eye: I loose the arrow, the snake bites Avid, the vultures descend, spears through my chest.

"We've come for Gatsi because of his unique nature. He communes with greater creatures that lend him farsight. He could see distant things, and in the seeing becomes an enemy of this 'pale man' you speak of." The snake's head was allowed to reach to Avid's neck a fraction more. "And if you know of our leader yourself, *Rennik*, it means we have come for you as well."

His voice rose again, his eyes whetted on a clever stone. "I offer a new trade, men and women of the Achare. You kill the one named Rennik, and you earn a second chance."

Now there were vultures on all sides. They'd spent their lives dismissing me. The image of the last mammoth pierced my heart like a spearhead. There was the sound of white knuckles tightening on weapons behind me, a sound that rode on a wind shifting directions.

"You're a fool," spoke Ciqala from his chest, not just to Malnostos, but to everyone, "to think we'd give you any one of our own. This is our home, and—"

It was a practiced motion. The feathers brushed my hand. The string came back. In a fleeting moment the arrow sung through the air, splitting through the head of the snake, piercing the Kazel man's hand, and punching into his ribs. The shock of the arrow pushed Zamri Malnostos away from Avid and down to the earth, kneeling, staring at the bloodied hand sewn against his body.

Avid's eyes met mine for a second before the thunder began. The vultures on the ridge pounded their horses into the village. Ciqala began yelling commands. Avid ran past me, but I wasn't finished yet. I felt the flood of anger like I had in the grasses, before I'd struck Ciqala. The Kazel man looked toward me again, swearing a silent vengeance as the storm of his horde raged behind him.

And then his eye was a bouquet of bloody plumage. The deer whose bones lent form to the arrowhead slammed through his skull, and Zamri Malnostos was dead before he hit the earth.

I turned my back to death and ran.

Please, I asked the Delkhi, thinking toward the river. *Please, do something.*

Villagers began loosing arrows, and arrows were returned, pounding into the earth like hail. I threw myself against the mud bricks of Gatsi's hut and tried to make myself small, my chest convulsing, lungs grabbing at whatever they could.

No, no, no!

Horses ripped through the huts like knives through hide, leveling the homes that had stood for a decade. Blood spilled against their walls, red paint on untouched canvas, stains that would never cease to be.

"Find him!" I heard someone shout over the sounds of battle. "Kill each one of them!"

I saw Avid crouching in the short grasses at the edge of the village.

One often hears about heroism in stories, and how in moments of valor, physical pain seems to disappear. Adrenaline quells the body's unease so that injured mothers can frighten off predators who hunt their children, or the mighty hunter can venture miles with broken bones to make it home with dinner.

I felt no such relief as I ran through the storm around me. Neither warrior's spirit nor hero's valor lessened the pain in my ribs as I sprinted, ducked under spears, and halted at the paths of charging horses. It would make for a better story to say that my focus, like the eyes of a hawk, scoped-in on my frightened brother, and everything else in the world faded to nothingness.

But in that moment I felt every ounce of my pain, and the fatigue my body felt screamed for me to stop, to simply hold still and breathe while I still could. Clods of dirt and arrows alike were thudding to the ground as the horses swept through.

People were dying quickly. Our warriors lunged forth with spears, lacerating the flesh of man and horse as they finished running through and traced the perimeter of the village, firing arrows quickly. They were a flock of ravenous crows surrounding a hunter, picking at him bit by bit until he collapsed.

As we watched in horror, crouched in the grass, an arrow buried itself into the throat of a charging Wahto just a dozen feet away. He fell sideways from his horse and landed dead on the upturned earth. The horse slowed down and stopped near us.

I leapt on its back.

"Come on!" I yelled, extending my hand to Avid.

He took my hand and I hurled him up to the horse to sit behind me. Climbing higher up may have been foolish, but getting Avid away from that killing field was my only goal. We settled swiftly onto the horse, and in mere seconds we were careening into the grasses, leaning low against the horse's back. It rode well, accepting us with no protest.

The grasses poured like splashing water from either side of the horse as it pushed powerfully into the fields, the seeds at their tops hissing through the air like a thousand swarming insects.

A quick glance over my shoulder revealed two mounted Sree riding in our direction, erupting from the village and coming over the ridge with the impetus of charging mammoths. One drew back an arrow and aimed.

"Duck!" I yelled.

Avid and I threw ourselves as low as possible just as the whistle of the arrow sounded inches above my head. I immediately checked to see if the horse had been hit. Fortunately, it hadn't; the horse pounded forward, further from the village.

"Where do we go?" shouted Avid, his voice panicked.

I surveyed the bouncing hills with one sweep, and the plains of my home revealed the solution.

Turning my hips, the horse understood my body language and altered its path. I looked behind to see the red-painted Sree still following, failing to close the distance we kept but still well within firing range.

Avid screamed in pain.

From the corner of my eye, I could see him grasping at his thigh where a long laceration appeared. An arrow had sliced through the side of his leg. Blood gushed out from between his fingers. It didn't look to have cut an artery, but running away on foot was no longer an option.

I reached my target and turned quickly to the right, perpendicular to the path of the oncoming Sree.

"What are you doing?" wailed Avid. "They're going to catch us!"

"Lean forward!"

We put all of our pressure forward on the horse and dipped slightly to the left of his back, providing a small amount of cover from arrow fire. The deadly shots whistled over our backs, over the spine of the horse as the Sree came closer. They shifted direction and aimed to catch us where our paths would intersect.

"We need to turn and run!" yelled Avid, clutching his wounded leg.

Almost there, I thought.

I turned to look at the enemy. One reached for another arrow at his hip. The other was already drawing to his cheek. I closed my eyes, wondering if it would be the last thing I ever saw.

Just then, the painful squeal of a Sree horse filled the air as its legs were taken out from under it. The rider was thrown over its head as it dropped, and he fell full-force into the four-foot patch of ripgut below.

He had no time to scream.

The second rider had only a moment to slow his horse before it too was taken from the blade-like grasses slicing at its legs.

The brief shaking of the razor-sharp stalks told me they were dead.

And suddenly, we were alone. A half-mile away were the cries and smoke of our village.

"We have to help!" shouted Avid. My brother cradled his head, listening to the slaughter through mulberry-and-bloodstained hands.

I dismounted the horse and studied his wound, and suddenly, my feet were leashed to the earth, tangled in the grasses. I tried to step away from the knotting, but I fell backward, and my hands became knotted as well. The grasses gripped at me like living fingers. I felt myself pulled against the dirt.

"Rennik!" Avid cried, looking down from the horse. His face was one of terror. "What's–"

The grass reached over my face. Dirt spilled in over me.

Sight and sound were stripped from me, and sleep swept in on choking roots.

25

THE MAMMOTH PRICE

"Time will shift the sand, and sand swallows mountains."

— KAZEL PROVERB

In the belief of my people, the world is perfect. The tribulations testing the survival of each species have come and gone after eliminating those unfit to exist. At the end of that long proving period, Dremma knew that the work was done, and that the world would be perfectly and naturally balanced from that point on. The terrors of extinction themselves were meant to have died off.

This sacred balance was interrupted once when the mammoth population was destroyed in Kalanos. Already they had been weakened by the harsh weather of the time, but man took no heed. He hunted them to extinction, forever disrupting the balance of our world.

Without the mammoth, the animal predators that feasted on them had a suddenly lacking food source. When they started to die off from starvation, other prey animals blossomed in population, as there were fewer threats in the grasses. Then, suddenly, the predators found that their dwindling food was plentiful, but not before they had adapted to hunting other creatures as well.

This swinging imbalance eventually corrected itself, but the grasses were forever changed. The mammoth's old predators had been forced to become more adventurous in their hunting and found that man himself was an ample meal if one could catch him alone. It was as if Dremma had personally rendered a punishment for our actions. We were reckless, and now our home was more dangerous than ever.

I never knew how such an eradication was possible, but here I stood amidst the ashes of my people. People I'd known my whole life, whose smiles I had memorized, were burnt to bone and scattered upon the scorched earth that once held homes and happy children.

The sun beat down on one of the hottest days of the year so far, made hotter by what remained of flame beneath my feet. With every step, cinders and coals reignited in small bursts. I don't remember feeling the pain under my toes, though I knew it was there. A strong wind blew the dust into the eastern horizon in a pattern of waning and waxing. My people were swept away.

I inhaled and began to choke. The ash burned in my throat. A blackened bone stood in the dirt, but I saw it as I saw the remnants of Tella's fire days before. The oppressive, charcoal smells of ruin swarmed upon me.

"Today," Tella spoke from my memory, pointing to the herb.

"Before!" she squeaked in my ears with bones upon the earth.

"What is to come," she said solemnly, with human hair to burn.

"Smoke."

The panicked rhythm of my breathing ushered in smoke, ushered in the secrets it held, and like my night at the roots of that horrid creature, I began to see distant things.

~

"THOUGH IT WILL NOT CHANGE THE OUTCOME OF OUR meeting," the pale man said, "I wish to make you understand. I wish, if only for the moments you have left to hear, that you know why I must do this."

A woman dressed waist-down in a patchwork skirt stood with the dominating Inkwood at her back. She was Yohri, and likely their leader. "I cannot stop you from speaking," she said stubbornly. "So speak."

The pale man nodded, his disposition a patient one. "Perhaps some will be spared. My journey through Kalanos is young still, and I require soldiers. May your strongest survive at my side."

It was as if he meant it to be some sort of blessing. She only returned his stare in silence, and he continued.

"There are those of us gifted with a talent for knowing impossible things. There is knowledge I must find, and it is as infinite as the void of the night, boundless and long passed from observation. You know, of course, that there are ways of divining things that cannot be seen. With bone, one may see things hidden to time. But I speak not of the small auguries you and other of our kind perform. I speak of grand movements, worlds of knowledge conjured like a flood in the lungs and the mind. This grand collection demands a higher sacrifice, chieftain. It will not answer to the burning of a bird, to a single charred creature."

It was as though he'd wrought tears from a stone. The woman, rigid and courageous in her posture, could not stop them. She feared for her people. She feared for her life. But above all, there was the slow domination of understanding — understanding that this man, this terrible, pallid stranger was a force of nature, as flame to the grass of life.

"Your people," he continued. "Your men, your women, your children. They are the door through which I welcome my knowledge, chieftain. I wish you to know that your death has meaning. Your people are a currency. For your own sake…"

He stood, raising a hand to his deadly riders behind him.

"…I wish you to accept this."

Blackness came with her death.

"I know of a Turin woman." Gatsi's voice echoed from a great distance.

The plains spun; grasses wove themselves into solid branches.

Then came my own voice, as if spoken by a stranger.

"Bring the boy."

The Delkhi dominated all with its endless roots and its spidering branches.

"Bring the boy."

My throat burned. The smoke billowed from my mouth, and I saw my village once again.

I FELL TO THE EARTH AND COUGHED.

Of course the visions were from the Delkhi — its presence had become unmistakable — but Gatsi, Tella…had they used the smoke before as a way to commune with the creature? Just as the Delkhi could reach to me, perhaps this smoke, this dust rendered from death was a way to reach to it in turn.

My mind was empty of thought, and in the emptiness the words spoken in my visions rambled back and forth in an overwhelming cacophony.

I wish to make you understand.

I know of a Turin woman.

Bring the boy.

As the pounding in my ears receded, they directed me to a soft, shivering whimper. I made my way to its source.

It's a strange thing when a man dies of his burns. Those educated in medicine will tell you it's not far from freezing to death, from the perspective of the one dying. After it's burned away, the skin has no power to keep in warmth. The body begins to crave the very heat that killed it. At some point, dying of extreme burns is not without the helpless cold of hypothermia.

And so I watched Ciqala, a man whose skin was cut and burned and blistered and red, shiver his life away in the heat of the noonday sun. He lay curled in a ball in the center of what used to be the chieftain's hut. His eyes were open, though he didn't appear to see through them. I knew he was too far gone to consider any longer. He must have sought shelter here and been caught in the inferno. Over his head had collapsed the tall and ancient mammoth tusks, now leaning against each other, a massive, skeletal hand clutching the dying man in its grasp.

There were no signs of anyone, save for the dying man under the tusks.

How long have I been out?

I had first woken up spitting dirt from my mouth. My

fingers had clawed up at the grass as if to come back from a grave, to pull me up from wherever I had been.

I went back to where I had fallen during the assault. There was no sign of any earthly disturbance where I had lain, but I'd swear on all of my reason that I'd been buried or had fallen into some sort of pit.

I looked for signs of Avid next. He was not next to me, as he had been. The horse was not behind me — there were no horses anywhere. The village, or rather, what had *been* the village, was a smoldering scar of black. It looked nearly like the ashen plain we'd found on our scouting trip. Similarly, the fire had, for some inexplicable reason, immolated the space of the village and had gone no further than that.

I looked to where Avid had been standing, and I saw a haphazardly-trodden trail leading east, toward the river. This sort of ungainly trail spoke of injury. Dried blood traced the grasses, marking the way.

I found him next to the river. He was sucking at the surface of the water, white with blood loss.

"Avid!" I collapsed next to him. His forehead was hot with fever.

"Rennik," he croaked. His voice was weak and sounded like sand. "They found them. They found the plateau. I don't know if anyone got away."

"No, Avid," I replied softly, shaking my head as if I could reject his words. "No, they didn't find them. Everyone is going to be safe."

"But they burnt it." He coughed. "They burned everything up there. They went to the plateau like they knew exactly where they were going."

Warm tears dropped from my face. They hit the mud and disappeared.

"I don't feel good," he pittered out, voice heightened with a half-quelled panic.

"I know, Avid." His pants were stained black with dried and dead blood, and I remembered the arrow that had cut him. I felt again the strong heat of his head when I pressed my hand against the wound. "I need to look at your leg."

"I can't move it."

"I know."

I took out my hunting knife and carefully pushed its point into his pant leg. Once it was punctured, the blade cut through the material easily. Avid winced.

A horrible stench swept up from the skin. It was the tremendous miasma of a bad infection, a choking, strangling smell.

Gatsi had warned me that one must be distant and dispassionate when healing wounds. He had told me so much, but I couldn't recall a time when even he could heal an infection such as the one now rooted blackly into my brother's leg. The heat radiating from his thigh was as torrid and angry as the fever in his head. The leg was inflamed — red, fat, and puffy against a jagged wound that seeped yellow. It took little to see that the infection had already spread.

"Mud brick."

"What?" I managed to ask.

"Gatsi's mud brick was the only thing that didn't burn. We can..." he stopped to cough. "We can make the next village out of mud brick so it doesn't burn. Seal them like those Rucosti wagons, to keep the damp out. We can..."

His eyes were focused out above the water, fixed on some point that only he could see.

"What did you do?" he asked.

"What?" I asked again, staring dumbly at the dead limb.

"He said Gatsi saw things. Said you saw things, too. Then

his eye, and you fell, and I couldn't see you anywhere. Once they were gone, I crawled. You were gone for so long...What..." his voice trailed off and his eyes lost focus for a moment. "What did you do?"

"I don't know, Avid." My voice was trembling now. I knew what he saw was right, that I had been saved somehow by the Delkhi.

He's going to die.

I shook my head as if to loose this harsh reality from it. The horror came out in indiscernible syllables; there were no words I knew to save him.

Bring the boy.

"It's..." he began.

My eyes were drawn upriver, toward the only hope I had left.

~

THE SHALLOW RIVERBED SWALLOWED AT MY FEET, THE STONES too wet to walk upon. Avid's added weight made the crossing difficult as he hung loosely from my arms, draped over them like a corpse.

Bring the boy.

"Please," I begged aloud.

There were no creatures, no bison, no mountain lion, no rabbit flesh at the roots. No life played among the branches as I approached.

"Please."

The massive tree stood tall and indifferent. Its branches spidered out in each direction, thick like twisting columns of weathered granite.

I set Avid at the roots of the Delkhi.

"Please," I repeated. I don't know what I expected to

happen, or if it could hear my desperate cries at all. The Delkhi was motionless.

Something yellow drew my eyes to the shore of the Delkhi's little island.

Feverfew.

It was futile, like gluing my split bow together, but it was the only action to be taken. With a moment's exploration I had found what was necessary for a simple treating of the infection.

I thought of my mother's hands, busy with needle and hide, and began to treat my brother's leg.

26

NEW GROWTH COMING

"Sometimes the worry is worse than the wound."

— RAISHA

I wanted to see.

My mother, I thought. I stood on the ash my home, dreading the truth. *Show me my mother.*

And so the smoke rose, and so the Delkhi granted me sight.

MY MOTHER WAS SCREAMING.

From her mouth came a visceral appeal to all that be, to the light and the shadows, to the earth and the skies, to the stones and waters of the world. It began with our names, with pleas for her children, then faltered into wordless shouts too full of meaning to take shape. She saw nothing upon that scorched earth, and so nothing we became in her mind. Eighteen years she'd raised me. Eleven years with Avid. Our two fires were brought to ash before her.

The hands of other survivors held her shoulders as she melted upon the dirt, the last of her energy descending into chokes and sobs. She lay on the ground, silent, destroyed, alive.

A group of women stood at the foot of the plateau. The fires of the village were still burning, the horde rampant on the horizon.

"We need to move *now*." It was Malik who spoke.

"She's in no state," replied one woman.

"Then join the rest of them," Malik said bitterly, gesturing to the burning village. She was already stepping south into the plains. "I snuck the five of you down here, but I won't stay with you. I'm leaving. If you want to stay here and die too, fine."

"Come, Raisha," the woman said to my mother. "The horde is still nearby. We need to leave." Another of them approached, and together they brought my mother to her feet.

Days went by. He had begun to look around, to move his head, to mumble a bit. The swelling was nearly gone. The searing fire in his leg and head had cooled away, and it was clear he was recovering.

I looked with doubt at the pitiful poultice I'd made, looked knowingly up at the Delkhi. It stood resolute, unmarred, unfound, untargeted by the horde.

"Southwest," he replied weakly, when his words returned.

"Yes," I told him. "That's where we'll find mother. And Malik, and a few others, I think." Avid sipped at a bit of fresh water I'd brought to him. "Knowing Malik, the trail will be hard to follow. But it's the only direction we have right now."

"Will you lead them again?"

"No," I said with certainty. "I made a mess of things. I can't talk to people like I need to, my plan failed for the most part, I almost lost you...no, Avid. I won't be leading anyone anymore. Malik is better suited for that."

"But you were like a hero in a story," he said. "You gave that speech at the funeral, you disappeared in the battle, you saved my life, you met a Shiver and lived..." his voice trailed off, and the rising tides of sleep embraced him.

I'd done none of those things. In each of those memories, the ridges of the Delkhi's fingerprints had shut me in, had given me just one path to follow. But more than that, something my brother said sunk into my heart.

I had never told him about the Shiver.

THE DOG FOUND ME. AT THE TIME I DIDN'T STOP TO THINK that it was unfair that it lived, and so many others hadn't. Animals have a tendency to leave when danger approaches. It's a simple sort of life-saving instinct. The creature fell in step with me on my way south, along the river. I didn't know then how comforting it was to walk with a living thing, but in hindsight, that dog may have saved me in one way or another.

Grief had not yet hit, not truly. It must have been some form of shock that kept me moving at first, or perhaps the strength of my denial.

I told myself, in the shallows of my mind, that I had saved him. That the fever was milder than I'd thought, actionable like all the others.

The deeper waters within me held the truth, difficult to reach in dark and icy depths. In those unexplored crevices I knew that I had never seen someone recover from such a fever. Avid had help.

I knew that few on top of that plateau could possibly have found a hiding place, and that the thick, overpowering stench of burn and ash and finality that hung heavily from its height was as telltale a sign as any.

The simplest truths...

Looking out at the grasslands that now held no points of reference for me, I should have been lost. There was never anywhere else to go besides home, and now that it was gone...

And yet a strange sort of knowing crept up from my chest, snuck slowly and confidently into my being. It was the Delkhi again, the part of my home that was still speaking, and it brought the flash of a memory to the front of my mind.

"*I know of a Turin woman.*" It would not leave me. Gatsi had spoken of someone who was like me, had I interpreted his half-answer correctly.

There were destinations to be determined. Malik had my mother in tow; we'd need to find her. Then, if a woman in the Turin lands was like me, it was possible she'd have some answers.

Gatsi would know. He would know what happened, who the pale man was, what the strange and smokey visions were, and why I'd become a target as well. But I felt at this point that I had less a chance of finding him than I did of finding this Turin woman.

I had to walk southwest and leave the corpse of my world behind me.

When Avid was ready, we traveled a long circle around our dead home so as not to see it.

My new bow was at the tilling tree, along with an adze, a drawknife, several arrows, and the beaver pelts I'd gathered before. Taking the bow from the tree, I let it from the tension and wrapped it in the pelts. Ideally it would be kept under tension for a longer amount of time, but I didn't plan on staying on the site of my people's slaughter. The only thing to do was leave, and the best I could do for the bow was to keep it dry.

I scanned the skies, worrying at the imminence of the rainy season. It was late this year and would soon claim dominance over sky and earth.

When we had last traveled as a people, I was very young, and my mother had carried me the entire way. Never had I taken a step, not a single push of the foot in a direction without knowing where I'd end up. The destination was always, inevitably and comfortingly, there and back home again.

I let myself, my home, and all things I'd yet to know go to the grasses, and with the dog's push against my hand and the string of the bow pawing at my shoulder, Avid and I took our next steps together.

SNEAK PEEK: WHERE THE RIVER GOES

Before me were three women of stone.

The first took her hue from the mountains. They were great, god-like mountains, sanguine with the presence of iron. Her height, well over fifteen feet, would have dwarfed me were she not flanked by peaks that pierced the sky. Her expression was stern: furrowed brows gathered above severe cheekbones and a farsighted stare. She was vigilant. She was commanding. She was the first of the Turin to call the mountains their home.

The second had no head. Her likeness was defaced, quite literally, after she led the losing side of a small civil war. Water had thus collected in the crags of her jagged neck and dwelt deep in her chest. One exceptionally cold winter was all it took to turn her heart to ice, to expand within the white marble from which she was hewn, and split her bosom like the schism of her people. Her name was Grim, and her history was likewise.

The third woman was grown of flesh and bone, though her voice suggested a stony core. Our first meeting began with her passionless and slate-like gaze poring over my painted body. She and her companions carried with them the scents of their home — grass, wildflowers, and earth smells, though I wondered if all Turin smelled of raw iron like her. She bore with her a patient disposition as she studied every inch of me. In the rainy season, there is always a storm coming, either on the horizon or more distant in the plains, and these storms were hers as the patience was hers. Something in her words and movements spoke of a lightning that reveled in the silence just before it struck.

RENNIK'S STORY WILL CONTINUE IN WHERE THE RIVER GOES...

ABOUT THE AUTHOR

I was lucky to have parents that fed me books. I'm pretty sure there were chicken strips, too, but my childhood was defined by the stories I read and the worlds I constructed with building blocks. Writing a book seemed like a natural outlet for that unending urge to build something.

Where the Valley Meets the Sky takes place in my childhood back yard. The pine trees near my old home formed the mountains of the Turin. The pasture to the north became the plains of Kalanos. Rennik's plateau is my grandfather's tree stand, and the creek to the east is — you guessed it — the river to the east.

I earned my BA in English from University of Iowa and teach various high school courses in my home state. When I'm not teaching or writing, I'm playing music with my band, working in the woodshop, or spending time with my wife and dog.

Check out my website at benwritesbooks.com for expanded lore!

You can find me on Twitter! @BenLikesBooks

CPSIA information can be obtained
at www.ICGtesting.com
Printed in the USA
BVHW071048010621
608543BV00003B/551

9 781737 122616